VIP

What Reviewers Say About Jackie D's Work

Spellbound—*Co-authored with Jean Copeland*

"The story is a mixture of history and present day, fantasy and real life, and is really well done. I especially liked the biting humor that pops up occasionally. The characters are vibrant and likable (except the bad guys who are really nasty). There is a good deal of angst with both romances, but a lot of 'aww' moments as well."
—*Rainbow Reflections*

"*Spellbound* is a very exciting read, fast-paced, thrilling, funny too. …The authors mix politics and the fight against patriarchy with time travel and witch fights with brilliant results."—*Jude in the Stars*

"[T]he themes and contextual events in this book were very poignant in relation to the current political climate in the United States. The fashion in which existing prejudices related to race, socioeconomic status, and gender were manipulated to cause discord were staggering, but also a reflection of the current state of things here in the USA. I really enjoyed this aspect of the book and I am so glad that I read it when I did."—*Mermaid Reviews*

The Rise of the Resistance

"I was really impressed by Jackie D's story and felt it had a truth and reality to it. She brought to life an America where things had gone badly wrong, but she gave me hope that all was not lost. The world she has imagined was compelling and the characters were so well developed."—*Kitty Kat's Book Review Blog*

"Jackie D explores how racist, homophobic, xenophobic leaders manage to seize, manipulate, and maintain power."—*Celestial Books*

"The best thing about the writing is the seamless blending of two very different genres. First we have the uber action packed main plot, but it is blended artfully with the second romantic plot so that the two never feel tacked on. More often than not, I prefer my dystopian novels to be lighter on the romance and my romance to be light on the action, but I really enjoyed seeing them play out alongside one another in this book."—*Lesbian Review*

Infiltration—*Lambda Literary Award Finalist*

"Quick question, where has this author been my entire life? …If you are looking for a romantic book that has mystery and thriller qualities then this is your book."—*Fantastic Book Reviews*

"This book is an action-packed romance, filled with cool characters and a few totally uncool bad guys. The book is well written, the story is engaging, and Jackie D did a great job of reeling the reader in and holding your attention to the very end."—*Romantic Reader Blog*

Lands End

"This is a great summer holiday read—likeable characters, great chemistry between the leads, interesting and unusual premise, well written dialogue, an excellent romance without any unnecessary angst. I really connected with both leads, and enjoyed the secondary characters. The attraction between Amy and Lena was palpable and the romantic storyline was paced really well."—Melina Bickard, Librarian, Waterloo Library (London)

Lucy's Chance

"Add a bit of conflict, add a bit of angst, a deranged killer, and you have a really good read. What this book is is a great escape. You have a few hours to decompress from real-life's craziness, and enjoy a quality story with interesting characters. Well, minus the psychopath murderer, but you know what I mean."—*Romantic Reader Blog*

Pursuit

"This book is a dynamic fast-moving adventure that keeps you on the edge of your seat the whole time. ...Enough romance for you to swoon and enough action to keep you fully engaged. Great read, you don't want to miss this one."—*Romantic Reader Blog*

Visit us at www.boldstrokesbooks.com

By the Author

After Dark Series:

Infiltration

Pursuit

Elimination

Lands End

Lucy's Chance

Rise of the Resistance: Phoenix One

VIP

Co-authored:

Spellbound (with Jean Copeland)

Swift Vengeance (with Jean Copeland and Erin Zak)

VIP

by
Jackie D

2021

VIP

ISBN 13: 978-1-63555-908-8

This Trade Paperback Original Is Published By
Bold Strokes Books, Inc.
P.O. Box 249
Valley Falls, NY 12185

First Edition: July 2021

Credits
Editors: Victoria Villasenor and Cindy Cresap
Production Design: Susan Ramundo
Cover Design By Tammy Seidick

Acknowledgments

Thank you, Vic Villasenor and Cindy Cresap, for taking this journey nine times with me—even when I'm sure you wanted to bop me on the head. Thank you, Bold Strokes Books, for always embracing my genre-hopping whims. Standing ovation for my mom, who reads every single word before it's published with a loving and diligent eye. Thank you to my wife and son for being insanely patient while I toil away at the keyboard. Last but not least, all my incredible friends: Stacy, Stacey, Erin, and Jean. Your laughter and encouragement are priceless.

Dedication

For my grandmothers:
one was ahead of her time, one was effortlessly brave,
one was brilliant. All of you still live in me.

Chapter One

The thumping started in her chest and worked its way through her body to the tips of her fingers. She did her best to control her breathing, so she didn't pass out from exertion. She pulled her firearm from its holster. The sweat accumulating on her back caused her shirt to cling to her.

"Ready, Callan?" James nodded to the door, ten feet away.

She took a deep breath and gave him a silent nod. She put one hand on top of the decimated cement wall and hurled her body over, never letting go of her gun.

"And cut!" The director pushed out of his chair and raised his hands. "That's a wrap, everyone. Great work." He walked over and put his arms around her. "It's been an absolute pleasure, Audrey."

She handed the gun to the prop master. "The pleasure was all mine. I hope we can work together again in the future."

She accepted the towel handed to her and dabbed her face. What she really wanted was to strip out of her sweaty clothes and take a hot shower. But that would be rude. It was customary to stay and congratulate the crew for a successful project.

She made her way through the handshakes and smiles. She reiterated her thanks to everyone, from the grips to the camera operators to the producers. She smiled, blushed when appropriate, and pretended she had no idea how good this film was going to be. People didn't like it when you knew how good you were, and she didn't want anyone thinking she took her life for granted.

"Ms. Knox, you have to leave now to make your dinner reservation," her assistant, Kylie, said.

Audrey slipped her arm around Kylie's shoulder. "How many times do I have to remind you to call me Audrey?"

Kylie pulled her tablet closer to her chest. "It's more professional if I say it that way. I don't want anyone to think I got this job because we're friends."

Friendship was the last reason Kylie was her assistant. Kylie was smart, articulate, organized, and one of the few people Audrey trusted. She'd taken over when Audrey discovered her last assistant was selling stories to a gossip rag. It was never meant to be a permanent fix, but Kylie had finally given in after weeks of Audrey begging, and now it looked like she'd be by her side for as long as Audrey could keep her.

"Whatever you're comfortable with, Ms. Shielding." Audrey walked past her, and she could almost hear Kylie rolling her eyes. "I need to shower."

Kylie caught up to her to inform her that she did not, in fact, have time to shower. Audrey already had her rebuttal ready when she ran directly into her intended dinner date.

"Oh, hey, I'm glad I caught you." Tia Perkins's voice was unmistakable. It was crisp and refreshing. The way words rolled off Tia's tongue made you want to listen to her for hours.

"Hey, you." Audrey kissed her cheek and ran her hands up Tia's arms. "I missed you." Audrey saw a flash of annoyance in Tia's eyes and wanted to make it go away as quickly as it appeared. "We're all wrapped. You have me for the next few weeks." Audrey kissed her cheek again.

Tia pushed her backward. "That's what I wanted to talk to you about." Tia crossed her arms and glanced at the people passing. Some waved, and she smiled politely.

"What's up? Do you want to go to my dressing room?" Audrey tried to lead her in that direction, but Tia seemed rooted in her spot. "Is everything okay?"

Tia ran her hand through her lengthy black hair. The annoyance was back. "I can't do this anymore." The words had fallen from her lips in a rush like she was compelled to say them, a necessity born of indifference.

Audrey felt her cheeks burn. Tia must be talking about dinner. She must be talking about her newfound love of vegan food—not their relationship.

"You can't do what?"

Tia pointed between them. "This. Us. I just can't."

There were words, even entire sentences, bouncing around in Audrey's brain, but she couldn't catch one. And she desperately wanted to catch one. She tried to say something. But she couldn't. All she could do was stare blankly at Tia. Tia, who was breaking up with her in front of everyone. Tia, who'd clearly had time to process this, a luxury she wasn't going to afford Audrey.

"Are you going to say anything?" There was that annoyance again.

Audrey felt the shiver of rejection climb its way down her spine, invisible needles pricking their way along her nerve endings. The sweat that had dried now caked to her skin, leaving her feeling scaly.

"Why? Why are you doing this?" Audrey felt her voice crack at her words.

"I just don't love you anymore. I'm not sure I ever did."

Breathe. Audrey felt as though she might fall over. *Breathe.* The bile started to rise in the back of her throat. Everything was spinning. She desperately needed to ground herself to something. She needed to sit down. She needed to run. She needed…

"Audrey, I have your agent on the phone. She needs to speak with you about your schedule." Kylie gently pulled her toward a car.

Audrey let herself be led toward the waiting vehicle. She held out her hand for the phone. She didn't want to talk to her agent, but it was an involuntary reflex.

Kylie leaned into her and pulled Audrey's head onto her shoulder. "There's no phone call, sweetie. Let's get you home."

Audrey felt her body revolt, but instead of vomiting, it came out as a sob. She was hurt and confused. Tia had been on the winning side of their relationship from the beginning. She'd been a struggling actress when they'd first started dating and had landed much more significant roles since. Audrey knew their relationship had increased her exposure, and she was okay with that. She was happy to see her succeed. Now Tia had the audacity to humiliate her in front of a room of colleagues. Audrey wasn't one to keep score, but if she were, she'd be on the losing end of this situation for sure.

CHAPTER TWO

Harlow Thorne dropped the headset onto the table in front of her and pulled the guitar strap from over her head. "Did you get everything you needed?"

Casper pushed the button from behind the glass. "That was fantastic, Low. You really nailed the hook on that take."

She stepped out of the booth and pulled her hair into a bun. "What do you think, one more day?"

Casper got out of his chair and came into the studio. He leaned against the edge of the piano. "Two at the most." He seemed unable to control his excitement and picked her up in a giant hug while spinning her around in a circle. "This album is fantastic. It's your best—no question."

When he finally set her down after she swatted at him, she took off the yoga pants she'd been in all day, and pulled on a pair of jeans. "You say that with every album release."

"You get better with each one." He clapped his hands and rested them against his mouth. "You're so goddamn talented."

She took off her sweatshirt and replaced it with a tight black tank top. "You got all the talent in the family, little brother. You make me sound good."

He hugged her again. "We both know that's not true."

It was stupid, really. She consistently sought the approval and praise of her brother. It didn't matter how many albums she sold, how many awards she won, or who was climbing at her heels. She needed to hear it from him. Maybe it was because their father drank himself into an early grave while cutting her down every chance he got. It could've been because they hadn't seen their mother in over fifteen years, who only called when she needed money. *Daddy and mommy issues, to say the least.* It was no doubt all those things, but mostly, it was because she valued Casper above anyone else. His opinion, his insight, his love—they were vital to her existence. She cherished him, their relationship, and everything they'd built together over the last thirteen years.

"Where are you going, by the way? Do you need me to call you a car?" He pulled his phone from his pocket.

She grabbed a fluorescent pink wig from her bag and moved it around on her head, checking her appearance in the mirror. "I'm going to the Rainbow. And no, I'll walk."

"We've had this conversation. You can't just walk the streets. You're one of the most recognized faces in the world."

She pointed to the wig. "I'm undercover."

He stood behind her in the mirror and straightened the wig. "You take too many risks."

She turned and kissed his cheek. "You worry too much. I just need a little release. You know, blow off a little steam."

"Is Megan still the flavor of the week?" He sounded annoyed, but she could tell by his eyes that wasn't the case.

"Megan who?" She winked and headed for the door.

"This will all catch up with you someday."

She was out the door before he could say anything else.

Despite all her bravado with Casper, she did her best to stay in the shadows while she walked the few blocks to the Rainbow. It wasn't the easiest task on Sunset Strip, but keeping her head down, her arms crossed, and wearing a pink wig was a surprisingly effective technique.

The Rainbow was a restaurant, but like a person, it was so much more. The second floor was home to one of the most exclusive clubs in Los Angeles. Exclusivity meant anonymity. It meant she could be herself for a few short hours without worrying about paparazzi and without someone watching her every move. It meant freedom, and that wasn't luxury anyone could put a price tag on in her position.

"Hey, Jimmy." She pulled her wig off and let her hair down.

Never one for small talk, he pushed the door open after witnessing her transformation. "Have a good night, Ms. Thorne."

The room was poorly lit, which always added to the appeal. Sparse decorations and leather benches made up the seating area. There was a small stage, a full bar, and a few tables if you wanted to be closer to the music. She didn't. Harlow weaved between people until she found a seat on an empty leather bench. Other patrons spared her a few glances, but no one approached her. She loved it here for just that reason. The type of people who enjoyed the Rainbow were like her; they needed anonymity, space, and privacy.

A server appeared before she had a chance to get situated. She handed her a lowball glass filled halfway with whiskey and two ice cubes. "Your usual, Ms. Thorne."

Harlow took the glass and handed her a hundred-dollar bill. "Thanks."

The server walked back to the bar without looking back. Harlow leaned on the table and gazed around the room. Bodies pressed into each other, and glasses tipped toward waiting mouths. The music thrummed through her body, and it felt as if her pulse was following the bass. She loved it. She made eye contact with a tall redhead a few feet away, knowing it wouldn't take long before the woman came over. She sipped her whiskey and waited for the inevitable.

The redhead sat down next to her. "Want some company?"

Harlow swallowed the rest of her whiskey in one smooth gulp and set the glass down. "I like making new friends."

The redhead smiled and leaned back closer to her. "You're in luck then, I'm very friendly."

Harlow watched the redhead's lips move, knowing for certain she'd have them on her skin in a few short hours. She never had trouble attracting attention from both men and women. It had taken her years to learn how to harness her power of seduction, but she was an expert now. A few hours spent in the bed of a stranger was how she managed to keep the demons at bay. Demons she'd spent a lifetime running from, and always would.

CHAPTER THREE

I'm not going." Audrey pulled the blanket over her head.

"You are going." Kylie removed the blanket and pushed Audrey's legs off the side of the bed. "It's been two months, and you committed to this party six months ago. You can't sulk here forever."

"Tia will be there." She hadn't meant to whisper, but the dread choked her words, lodging them in her throat.

"I know." Kylie sounded remorseful.

"So, you understand why I can't."

Kylie sighed and tapped the space between her eyes. "It's part of the promo for the movie. You're contractually obligated."

Audrey pushed herself up and ran her hands over her face. "What does some album release have to do with the movie?"

It was a rhetorical question. She knew two songs from the album were featured in the movie. She understood how the business worked, but it didn't mean she had to like it.

Kylie pushed her toward the shower. "The real question is, how did Tia get invited? She must've pulled some strings."

Audrey turned the shower on, giving in to her fate. "To torment me." She pulled off her clothes. "You've heard everything she's been saying about me. I still don't understand why. She's acting like I wronged her. She left me."

She could hear Kylie talking but couldn't make out the words under the spray of the water. It didn't really matter. Not only did Tia embarrass her by breaking up with her at work, but she also continued to embarrass her by talking about their relationship to anyone who would listen. Tia called her any number of things: prude, clingy, whiney, controlling. All of it was news to Audrey. During the year they'd spent together, Tia never mentioned being miserable or disliking so many things about her. Audrey had breakups before, but none of them had attacked her from all sides like this.

Audrey stepped out of the shower, wishing the pain could be scrubbed away with the rest of the grime. She pulled her robe tightly around her body and stared in the mirror. *It's just a party. You can do this. You will not let her see you cry.* Nonsense, all of it. She wasn't sure if she could do this, and she certainly wasn't sure if she could see Tia without crying.

"I'll be with you the entire time." Kylie was leaning against the bathroom door.

"Thank you. I can't tell you how much I appreciate everything you've done." Audrey let her wet hair fall around her shoulders. "I guess there's no getting out of this."

Kylie walked up beside her and handed her a small black cocktail dress. "You should wear this. Of everything you own, nothing looks better on you than this."

Audrey took the dress and held it in front of her, admiring it. "You're right about that."

"I'm right about a lot of things." Kylie stood behind her and straightened Audrey's shoulders. "Like when I say that you can do this. I'm not just saying it—I mean it. You're stronger than you think and more beautiful than Tia ever deserved."

Audrey closed her eyes. "I don't know about that. Have you seen some of the women she's been running around with? They're flawless."

Kylie kissed her cheek. "I wasn't talking about physical beauty. Although, you have that in spades." She rested her chin on Audrey's shoulder. "I meant you're too beautiful on the inside for someone like Tia. She's shown her true colors, and she doesn't deserve you. She never did."

Audrey nodded because she was afraid that if she spoke, the tears would begin to fall again.

Kylie pulled the chair from under the vanity and forced her onto it. "Now, sit. Hair and makeup are here."

❖

Harlow closed her eyes as her fingers glided along the piano keys. People moved around her—faces she wouldn't remember tomorrow. Carts full of dinner and glassware clanged together as they passed by. Voices of men and women shouted out orders over noisy employees who prepared for the coming event. Harlow didn't hear any of it. All she could hear was the melody that had started to take shape in her mind. She wasn't sure what it would transform into, but she loved it already. That's how it usually happened. A thought would become a lyric. A sound would become a beat, and inspiration would become a tone. It would usually occur when she least expected it, and because of that, she never turned it off. Music was as much a part of her as her eye color. It coursed through her veins and hid in every strand of DNA.

Casper sat down next to her. "New song?"

"Hmmm." She let her head sway. "The beginning of one."

She opened her eyes and looked at him. Casper looked handsome in his suit jacket and white V-neck shirt. His blond, messy hair was intentionally casual. His blue eyes sparkled with excitement, and she couldn't help but put her head on his shoulder.

"You look very dashing tonight." She elbowed him in the side.

He squeezed her. "You can't be the only heartbreaker in the family." He leaned back, his expression serious. "Have you decided on a second night in Dallas? I sent you over the information three days ago."

"Casper, you know I don't care. Just tell me where to show up, and I'll be there." Harlow put her fingers back on the piano keys.

"Okay, I'll get it all worked out."

"I know." She smiled.

Casper handled the details, and he always had. It would be too much to manage on her own, and he was the only person she trusted. He knew her likes and dislikes. He knew how much she could handle regarding turnaround times, and he was cognizant of making sure she had ample rest. Hell, sometimes she wondered if he knew her better than she knew herself. It was entirely possible.

He glanced at his watch. "The party starts in an hour. I need you to do some press before."

Harlow tilted her head, trying to decide if G-flat or G-sharp worked better. "I'll be there. Five more minutes."

Casper walked away without argument because he knew she wouldn't be late. She might be unpredictable at times, but she was always a professional. She hit the keys a few more times and smiled. G-sharp.

Press questions were always the same. Harlow spent an hour rambling off the same answers in one hundred different ways. Yes, she was thrilled about the album. Yes, the tour was going to feature her new and old songs. No, she wasn't dating anyone. Yes, having her songs in a summer blockbuster was thrilling. Although, to be fair, this was the first time her songs had ever graced the silver screen. So she let the annoyance over that one slide.

She was on the verge of losing her mind when Casper thanked the press and promised them more soon. "Time for pictures with the cast."

"Took you long enough." She elbowed him on the way down from the small press stage.

"You know I like watching your eyes glaze over with boredom."

She was in the process of formulating a response when she caught a glimpse of Audrey Knox entering the room. Audrey wasn't just beautiful. No, that word wouldn't do her justice. She was elegant, poised, and had an aura about her that made her seem just out of Harlow's grasp. When people in the industry talked about someone having the "it factor," they meant Audrey Knox.

"Don't even think about it," Casper whispered against her ear.

Think about it? Hell, she'd been dreaming about it since she was sixteen years old. Harlow wasn't one for crushes. That wasn't her style. But she'd always made an exception for Audrey Knox.

"Relax, Casper. You're always telling me I need friends." She gave him a wicked smile.

"Friends, yes. People to watch movies with. People to drink cosmos with and laugh at failed relationships. People who—"

"Could literally stop traffic in that dress. She could probably do it in jeans, too." She tried to say it in a joking tone, but Casper knew her better than that.

Casper sighed, but she stopped listening to anything he had to say. She couldn't take her eyes off Audrey, who moved from person to person, kissing their cheeks, hugging them hello. When she spoke to them, she seemed solely focused. It appeared she possessed that rare quality of making people feel like they were the only ones in her orbit for that passing moment.

Audrey stepped in front of her and put her hand out. "I'm Audrey Knox, It's a pleasure to finally meet you."

Harlow may have been in a daze of lust, but she was far too smooth to let it show. "Harlow Thorne, and I assure you, the pleasure is entirely mine."

Audrey tilted her head slightly to the side. She seemed as though she were making her mind up about something, and Harlow wished she possessed the power of telepathy. "I loved the songs you made for the movie. You seemed to have really connected with the characters."

"I truly enjoyed doing it." Harlow took a step closer. "If you'd like, we can get together later, and I can show you which songs didn't make it to the final cut."

Audrey stared at her with so much intensity it could only mean she'd take her up on her offer—or place her on a mental list of absolute fucking weirdos. Audrey parted her lips to answer, and Harlow felt her pulse quicken. She was close enough to smell the light perfume Audrey wore. Her golden hair sat on her shoulders as if it knew the exact part it needed to play to accentuate her features. Audrey's eyes left hers for the first time since they started speaking. The flecks of gold seemed more pronounced against the blue once she shifted her head.

"I have to go. I'm sorry," Audrey said as she turned and headed the other direction.

Harlow looked around, wondering what could have possibly caused the sudden shift, but nothing seemed out of place. She looked back, trying to see where Audrey had gone, but she'd already disappeared into the sea of people.

"Shit," she mumbled under her breath.

A music producer grabbed her arm and flung Harlow back into an evening of small talk and fake smiles. Harlow tried to force herself to listen to what he was saying. Granted, it was nothing of consequence. Even in the best of circumstances, this type of conversation would send her screaming for the hills. But she couldn't shake the feeling she had when Audrey made eye contact. The slight glimmer in her eyes had given away an inkling of interest. Harlow was well aware of when people found her attractive, and she'd seen it when Audrey looked at her. Even if it had only been for a split second, it was there.

❖

"Hello, Tia," Audrey said as she waited for her ex-girlfriend to introduce the woman who stood next to her.

"Audrey, I wasn't sure if you'd be here." Tia slipped her arm around the short brunette.

Kylie had positioned herself between Audrey and Tia. "Why are *you* here? That's the real question. You're not a big enough name to have gotten an invite."

It wasn't like Kylie to direct that much bite toward anyone, but she'd apparently made an exception for Tia. Audrey sent her a mental *thank you* and tried to compose herself again.

"I know Casper Thorne. Not that it's any of your business." Tia squinted, a sign Kylie had gotten to her.

Audrey wanted out of the situation as quickly as possible, but running full speed to the closest exit wasn't in the cards. "It was really nice running into you, Tia. I'm afraid I have to go, you know, press and all that."

Tia grunted and rolled her eyes. "You never did have time for me."

Audrey wanted to point out how unequivocally false that statement was. She wanted to remind her how she rearranged every shooting schedule she'd had to accommodate Tia. She wanted to remind her of all the places she'd flown her so they could spend a few days together. She wanted to remind her of the hours spent on video chat, of the flowers and cards she sent for no reason. She wanted to remind her that despite all of that—it was Tia who had ended things while dozens of eyes watched. But she said nothing and walked away, praying she could find a place where prying eyes wouldn't find her.

"You okay?" Kylie hugged her after they ducked into the nearest restroom.

Audrey stared at herself in the mirror. "I don't remember her being so cruel." She patted away the tears that had started to well in her eyes. The last thing she needed was for her waterproof mascara to fail.

Kylie snorted. "Believe it or not, this isn't a new thing."

Audrey didn't respond. She knew how Kylie felt about Tia, and the only thing her lamenting seemed to do was annoy Kylie.

Kylie put her hand on her hip. She was determined to change the subject. "What was going on with you and Harlow Thorne, by the way?" She fanned herself. "I could feel the heat from ten feet away."

Harlow Thorne. Audrey had always heard she was magnetic, but it didn't really make sense until she was standing in close proximity to her. Harlow wore a black Gucci jumpsuit, with black fern lace covering her arms and cleavage. She had heels on, which made her already tall frame seem that much more alluring. She'd worn her long blond hair down, and it had framed her face perfectly. She'd always thought Harlow was gorgeous, but being near her had elicited a whole different set of reactions. She'd been compelled to touch her, and Audrey had never had that kind of reaction to anyone she'd just met. Harlow was more than she'd expected.

"There was nothing to see." Audrey pulled her lipstick from her purse and reapplied it. "She invited me to listen to some of the songs she wrote that didn't make it into the movie."

"You said yes, right?" Kylie's eyes grew larger with excitement.

"No."

"No?"

Audrey dabbed her lips with a tissue. "I didn't say anything. I saw Tia and walked away before I had a chance to answer."

"Are you fucking with me?" Kylie was practically on top of her now. "You should absolutely take her up on her offer."

"No, I shouldn't." Audrey turned and leaned against the sink. "She's too…I don't know…smooth."

Kylie groaned. "What does that even mean?"

"It means she thinks I'm going to take advantage of her," a voice on the other side of the bathroom stall said before a toilet flushed.

Audrey was sure she was going to have a heart attack right then and there. She shot Kylie the *oh my God* look, turned back to the mirror, and tried to make herself look busy.

Harlow walked to the sink and washed her hands. "You know, even smooth people need friends." She reached past Audrey for a towel. "Excuse me."

"I didn't mean to offend you or imply—" Audrey leaned out of the way.

"That I was trying to get in your pants?" Harlow's smirk was one of victory.

"I'm sorry?" Audrey couldn't tell if her voice reflected her confusion or annoyance. She wasn't sure which she preferred.

"You can make it up to me with dinner." Harlow placed the towel in the basket.

"Dinner?" Audrey fidgeted with her lipstick.

"You know, sustenance. You do eat, right?"

"Yes, I eat." Audrey zipped her purse. "I can't have dinner with you."

"Why?" Kylie asked at the same time as Harlow. She scrolled through her tablet. "You're free Wednesday at seven. I'll send Audrey's address over to Casper. She's a great cook, by the way."

"I'll see you then." Harlow winked as she walked out the door.

"I hate you," Audrey said to Kylie, who seemed all too pleased with herself.

"No, you don't."

"Yes. I do."

"No. You don't. You need me to push you sometimes." Kylie motioned to the door. "Let's get you back out there."

Kylie was right, she did need to be pushed sometimes, but she didn't want to be pushed into the arms of some pop star goddess. She didn't want to be pushed when her last failed relationship had just started to be forgotten by hungry paparazzi. She didn't want to be pushed when she didn't feel like she had anything left to give.

Chapter Four

Harlow rechecked her cell phone. Ten minutes to seven. She was sitting two blocks from Audrey's house but didn't want to seem too eager by showing up early. She tapped her hands on the steering wheel, still playing with the melody she'd been working on last week. She checked her reflection in the mirror again and looked down at her clothes. It would be hard to convince anyone she'd changed her outfit a dozen times, trying to find the perfect combination of casual and sexy. *What is wrong with you? She's just a woman. This is your thing. Pull it together.*

When she finally arrived at Audrey's house, one minute before seven, she gave herself a moment to examine the outside. The old Tudor style home had vines growing up the front, adding to its charm. The massive windows gave off a warm glow, making her feel welcome. The staircase that led to the front door was cobblestone and absolutely charming. It reminded her of Audrey, and she decided it was a perfect fit.

Audrey opened the front door before she had a chance to knock. She was wearing jeans and a green, silk, V-neck shirt. Her hair was pulled back, and she was wiping her hands on a towel. For a split second, Harlow wondered what it would be like to come home to this every night.

"Hi. I wasn't standing at the window waiting for you. I was walking through the living room and saw your headlights," Audrey said nervously.

Harlow smiled. Audrey was adorable. "Don't worry. I didn't think you were anxiously awaiting my arrival."

Audrey stuck her hand out to shake and seemed to change her mind, leaning in for an awkward hug instead. "Come on in."

"Smells great," Harlow said honestly.

"Thank you." Audrey blushed and led her toward the kitchen. "Would you like a glass of wine? I have red, white, rosé, and I think there's some champagne here somewhere."

Harlow sat at the expansive kitchen island. "Whatever you're drinking is fine."

Audrey poured her a glass of red and raised her own. "To new friends."

Harlow tapped the offered glass. "What made you change your mind?" She inhaled the red deeply before taking a sip. "You didn't seem all that interested last time I saw you."

Audrey opened the oven door. "You're very blunt." She shrugged. "I haven't been myself lately. It's not like me to blow people off without giving them a chance. I shouldn't have done that to you."

Harlow wasn't sure what to say. She used bluntness to catch people off guard. It helped her to get a glimpse of their true selves. Reactions usually said far more than words. Audrey responded with vulnerability and honesty, and that had never happened before.

"It's okay. We all have off days."

"More like off months." Audrey pulled the tray from the oven. "Oh God, I never even asked. Do you eat chicken?"

"I do. Is there anything I can do to help?" Harlow took off her leather jacket and draped it over one of the bar stools.

Audrey brought the plates over to the table. "No. Please, just sit."

"Do you mind me asking why you've had a bad few months?" Harlow took a bite of the chicken and almost proposed to Audrey on the spot. "This is fantastic."

"Thank you," Audrey said as she wiped her mouth. "I don't mind you asking. It's splashed all over every gossip magazine anyway. I just went through a pretty public breakup."

Harlow hadn't heard anything. She never picked up any of those magazines, terrified she'd find pictures of herself in a compromising position. She left that stuff up to Casper.

"Were you together for a long time?"

Audrey pushed the chicken around on her plate, seeming to let the food distract her from her thoughts. "A little over a year."

"That's about a year longer than any of my relationships." Harlow laughed at her statement. It wasn't because she believed her stunted relationships were funny, but to try to lighten the mood. She didn't want Audrey to feel uncomfortable, and it seemed the perfect time to throw in some light self-deprecation.

It worked, and Audrey smiled. "I've heard that about you." She pointed her fork across the table.

"Everything you've heard is only half true."

"Which half?" Audrey sipped her wine, and damn it, if she wasn't the most beautiful woman Harlow had ever seen.

"Which half are you hoping for?" Flirting with Audrey came naturally.

Audrey took another bite of chicken and continued to study her, but a smile pulled at the corner of her mouth. "I see everything I heard regarding your cocky nature is true."

Harlow dabbed her mouth. "So you've been inquiring about me."

"It's hard to miss you. You're on damn near every cover of every magazine."

"Hmm. You know better than most that you can't believe everything you read."

Audrey leaned forward, and the glimmer of interest Harlow had seen the previous week was apparent in her eyes. "What do you want me to believe?"

There were so many things she could say to play into the flirtatious banter they'd started. Her clever retort was sitting behind her teeth, waiting for deployment. But for some reason, she didn't want to play the usual games she played. Not with Audrey.

Harlow placed the napkin on the plate. "That was truly wonderful, thank you."

Audrey watched her closely. She was used to people staring at her. It had stopped making her uncomfortable a long time ago. But staring wasn't what Audrey was doing; rather, she seemed as though she were analyzing. The heat from Audrey's gaze was like a blanket on a fall evening. Harlow wanted to wrap herself in it, in Audrey, and stay there.

"Do you want to sit out back with me for a bit?" Audrey picked up their wine glasses and headed toward the back porch before Harlow answered.

The truth was, Harlow couldn't think of anything else she'd rather do, and that was an entirely new feeling.

Audrey hadn't planned on enjoying dinner as much as she had. She hadn't thought she'd invite Harlow to stay after, and she absolutely didn't think she'd be looking at Harlow's calloused fingers, wondering what they'd feel like on her skin. Harlow was sexy as hell. She knew it, hell, everyone knew it. Harlow's skinny jeans, sheer white shirt, tanned skin, and ice blue eyes were enough to make anyone trip over themselves. Surprisingly, that wasn't the most attractive thing about her. The tenderness behind her bravado was what intrigued Audrey. Beautiful women were a dime a dozen here in LA. Genuine people were as rare as rain. She wanted more of Harlow. She wanted a glimpse behind the proverbial curtain.

Harlow laid back on the lounge chair next to her. "Thank you for inviting me tonight."

Audrey rolled her head on the back of the lounge chair to look at her. "Technically, I didn't invite you."

Harlow smiled into her wine glass. "True, but you didn't uninvite me either."

"Sometimes I need to be pushed."

"I'll remember that."

Audrey finished the last of her wine and poured more into her glass. "Are you looking forward to your tour?"

Harlow held her glass out for more. "Casper is, and I like making Casper happy."

"You don't like to tour?"

"It's not that. I don't mind touring. I enjoy meeting fans and traveling."

"Then what is it?" Audrey was surprised by how genuinely curious she was. She wasn't just making small talk. She wanted to know what made Harlow tick.

"I've stood on hundreds of stages. I've heard millions of fans scream for me for hours at a time. I've seen young girls burst into tears when I say hello."

Audrey raised her eyebrows. "Seems like a pretty good gig."

Harlow stared up at the sky. She seemed to consider if she was going to continue her thought. "It's a great gig. But every time I'm up there, every single stage I step on to—I wonder if that will be the last one. I wonder if they'll get tired of me. I wonder if my next album just won't be enough. I wonder if I made the most of it."

Audrey reached over and touched her arm "I think you have a long time before you need to worry about that. Your albums just keep getting better. I think you're going to be around for quite some time, Ms. Thorne."

"You listened to my new album?" Harlow seemed genuinely surprised.

"Full disclosure." Audrey leaned back in her chair again. "I have listened to and own every one of your albums."

Harlow looked over at her and then back up to the sky. "I've seen every one of your movies." She took another sip of wine. "Several times."

This pleased Audrey far more than she anticipated. She liked the idea of Harlow watching her.

"I read you were discovered by chance, is that right?"

Audrey looked up, remembering that night. "I was lucky. I've managed to be in the right places at the right times, meeting the right people. I'm not under any illusions. There are hundreds of other actresses out there, and most are probably better than me. But they weren't as lucky." She turned to look at Harlow. "My first big break came when I was sixteen years old. My family had taken a trip to see a Broadway production of *Phantom of the Opera*, and a man approached my parents and me in the lobby when the show was over. He told me he was working on a project and that he'd been shocked to gaze across the audience and see the face he'd been searching for." She shook her head, remembering the whirlwind that had changed her life. "A few months later, I was on the set of my first movie. The film was brilliant, and I was fortunate enough to play the tortured teenage daughter of one of Hollywood's biggest stars. The awards poured in, and my life would never be the same. That was fifteen years ago, and sometimes I still can't believe it's real."

"I remember that movie. I loved you in it. But for the record, it wasn't just dumb luck that got you here. Maybe it played into getting you noticed, but everything since is because of your talent."

"I appreciate that. Thank you," Audrey said. She hoped the darkness hid her blush.

"Do you want to go to a party with me next Friday?" Harlow blurted out after a few seconds of comfortable silence. "Not a big deal, or anything, just something I promised a friend I'd pop into."

She seemed nervous, which Audrey found endearing. "I'd love to, thank you."

The Audrey from three hours ago would have delivered a resounding "no" to such an invitation. But Audrey from three hours ago hadn't been the object of Harlow's full attention for an extended period of time. Now, she wanted more of whatever was happening between them. The newness, the excitement, the understated flirting felt good.

"I should get going. It's getting late. I have to meet my trainer at five in the morning." Harlow's tone held a tinge of apology.

Audrey felt a pang of disappointment that started in her throat and slid down to her stomach. "Okay, I'll walk you out. I meet my trainer at seven. It would be impossible for me to get up before then."

Harlow pulled her jacket on at the door. "Thank you for such a lovely evening. I had a great time."

Harlow took her hand and pulled her into a hug. She smelled like late summer nights and sunshine all mixed together. Audrey let her cheek rest against Harlow's. Her brain was screaming for her to stop. She shouldn't be thinking about anyone like this right now. She wasn't in the right headspace. That's what her brain was saying, but her body wanted nothing more than to run her hands up Harlow's back and through her hair. She wanted to pull her closer. She wanted to put her mouth on her neck. She wanted her.

Harlow kissed her cheek. "Good night, Audrey."

"Good night," Audrey whispered.

Audrey stood in her entryway, unable to move. Her body was humming, and her mind was racing. She had no idea what she was getting herself into and wasn't sure if she wanted to find out.

Chapter Five

If we don't give her the money, she'll just show up here. Neither of us wants that, so just wire it to her and be done with it." Harlow watched Casper in the bathroom mirror as she applied her mascara.

"You've given her close to a million dollars over the last six years. It's ludicrous. She doesn't deserve it." Casper, who was typically enraged by this kind of information, seemed remorseful as he pinched the bridge of his nose and shook his head.

"I'd pay her ten million to get her out of our lives for good."

He sat on the bed, seeming defeated. "Why couldn't she be different?" It was a rhetorical question that he verbalized frequently.

She sat next to him, determined to answer this time. "If Mom were different, we wouldn't be who we are. We turned out okay despite our parents."

"Sure. We aren't damaged at all. We both have crippling commitment issues, sleep with as many women as possible, and our only friends are each other. We're a picture of mental health."

"Well, when you put it like that." She laughed and rubbed his back. "Everyone is a little damaged. Especially in this town."

He put his head in his hands and sighed. "Where are you running off to tonight, anyway?"

She didn't want to tell him that she was going out with Audrey, but she never lied to her brother. "To a party."

"What party?"

"Dominic's." She walked back over to the mirror and continued to put on her makeup.

"I'll go with you. I know you hate going to those things alone."

"That's okay. I'm going with a friend." She hoped her voice sounded as nonchalant as she intended, but she was sure it wouldn't deter him from further inquisition.

"I thought we just covered that we don't have any friends." He was directly behind her now, probably to gauge her response.

"*You* don't have any friends." She turned and poked him in the chest. "I have friends."

He raised one eyebrow. "No, you don't." He was doing mental calculations, an obvious thing whenever he started chewing on his bottom lip. "Wait. Are you going out with Audrey?"

"It's not like that. We're friends." She shrugged and checked herself in the mirror one last time before heading for the door. "But yes, I'm going to pick her up now."

"I'm coming."

"No, you're not."

"Yes, I am. If you're just friends, it shouldn't matter." He waved his finger in her face.

She gave in because further protest would make him even more adamant. "Fine. But don't be weird."

"When am I weird?"

"Every day I've known you."

The car ride to Audrey's was filled with the usual chitchat she and Casper always shared. Casper talked about the upcoming tour, and Harlow added her input when necessary. They'd spent the last several months planning out every detail, but these final stages, when it was on the brink of coming to fruition, were her favorite part. It reminded her of when they were kids, lying in the grass of their backyard talking about all the places they'd go as soon as they could get out of their small town. She never pictured a future without Casper. It was always them together, until the end.

Harlow hopped out of the car when they arrived at Audrey's. "I'm going to go get her."

"What? Why? Just text her."

"That's rude. I'm going to the door. Get in the back."

"I thought this wasn't a date." He raised his eyebrows as he unbuckled his seat belt.

Audrey opened the door, and Harlow's mouth went dry. She looked stunning in her white shimmering flare skirt and red halter top. The look accentuated Audrey's long legs, and Harlow had to force herself not to stare.

Harlow wanted to tell her how beautiful she looked, but couldn't find the words to do her justice, so she flailed. "My brother, Casper, is coming with us. I hope you don't mind."

Audrey's back stiffened slightly, and Harlow wished she'd told him no. "The more, the merrier." Her words were cordial, but her eyes didn't reflect the sentiment.

The initial awkwardness drifted away as they occupied themselves with discussions of mundane things like the ever-present brutal LA traffic and impeccable weather.

"Dominic Ramos is a friend of yours?" Audrey stared at the famed house on Mulholland Drive as they approached.

Harlow smiled, thinking of her friend and unsurprised that Audrey recognized his house. "Dominic took me under his wing for a few years when I first came on the scene. He became something of a mentor and a really good friend. I'd do damn near anything for him." Dominic had been in the music industry since the 1970s. He was a legendary guitarist and lyricist with the rare ability to tweak a few elements in a song and make it a number one hit instead of DJ filler. So, when he was adamant about her attending this party, she agreed without thinking twice.

There had been documentaries made about the party culture surrounding Dominic. He hadn't slowed down any since his early days, and he proved that every weekend. Flashing lights penetrated every window of the house and poured onto the sidewalk below. The music pumping through the grounds could probably be heard for miles around, and the shouts from the people inside were deafening.

Harlow had asked Audrey to come because she wanted to see her again, but now she wasn't sure it was the right call. She wasn't sure how Audrey would feel about being with throngs of people she didn't know. She'd never brought someone to one of these things before and had no idea what the protocol was. "We don't have to stay long."

Audrey smiled. "I won't break, Harlow. I wouldn't have agreed to come otherwise. This will be fun."

Casper put his arm around Audrey. "I knew you'd be fun."

Audrey laughed at his comment, which stopped Harlow from smacking him. The music started to fade, and the screaming grew even louder.

"Let's get inside before the next band comes out, so I can find Dominic," Harlow said.

Harlow weaved through the gaggles of people. Audrey grabbed the back of her waistband to stay close, and Harlow was surprised by how much she enjoyed the small gesture. Several people took pictures as they passed, and a few said hello to Audrey like she was an old friend, but no one stopped them. She waved to a few people, who pointed toward the backyard. She continued to scan the party guests until she spotted Dominic.

When they finally made it to him, he grabbed her, wrapping her in a bear hug. He reached over and grabbed Casper, pulling him in as well. He led them to a small area behind the somewhat large stage before he spoke.

"I can't believe you came. You haven't been to one of my parties in years." Dominic kissed both her cheeks and held her out to take her in completely. "You're beautiful as ever." He turned his attention to Casper next. "Casper, my God, do you ever age?"

Casper laughed. "I try not to, my friend."

Dominic's gaze fell on Audrey. "Audrey fucking Knox. You've got to be kidding me." He grabbed her hand and shook it. "Dominic Ramos, and it's an absolute pleasure to meet you. I loved you in *Midnight Promises.* You were fucking brilliant."

Audrey put her hand over his. "Thank you for having me. You have a beautiful house."

Dominic poured whiskey into four glasses from the table next to him and handed them each one. "You should see it without all these damn people. It's magnificent."

"I thought you liked having parties? I came to one a few years ago, but we didn't get to meet." Audrey took a sip of the whiskey.

Dominic downed the contents of his glass. "I do it to showcase talent." He poured himself another four fingers and turned his attention to Harlow. "I appreciate you coming. I have a favor to ask. I have a new kid looking for her big break. Her agent is shit, and she's not signed. But she's the real deal."

"What do you need from me?" Harlow knew the answer before she asked.

"Let her open for you." Dominic was serious now. His face took on a certain sternness when he talked business.

Harlow could feel Casper's eyes on her. But this was Dominic, and she hated disappointing him.

"Okay, let's see what she's got." Harlow purposely kept her eyes on Dominic, never looking at Casper. The thought of an additional opening act to the tour would send his stress level through the roof.

Dominic pointed to the stage. "She's getting ready to go on now. Get up there with her and see how it feels."

Audrey grabbed her hand and pulled her close. Harlow could smell the whiskey on her breath. The liquor had given her cheeks a bit of a blush, and Harlow pushed down the urge to kiss her.

"Good luck up there," Audrey whispered against her ear.

Harlow tilted her head slightly so she could feel Audrey's skin against her own. "Thank you."

Harlow climbed the small set of stairs attached to the stage. She could hear everyone start to cheer, but all she could think about was Audrey standing ten feet away.

Audrey wasn't sure what had come over her. She wasn't one to grab women and pull them to her. But she also wasn't one for parties like these. Harlow had a strange effect on her, and she hadn't figured out if she liked it or not—although she was leaning toward the liking. She'd been a ball of nerves all day waiting for Harlow to arrive. She'd continuously reminded herself that it wasn't a date, which had been confirmed when Harlow arrived with Casper in tow. Even after she convinced herself they were friends and nothing more, it didn't stop her body from reacting to Harlow once she laid eyes on her.

Harlow, with her effortless swagger. She had so much confidence—it seemed to seep from her pores. Every piece of clothing Harlow owned looked as if it had been made with her specifically in mind. The simple leather bracelets around her wrists forced her eyes to trace the lines of strong defined arms, which were made more pronounced by her tight white tank top. The lengthy silver chains that hung around her neck were ideally situated to draw attention to her long elegant curves and cleavage. Her ocean-blue eyes reminded Audrey of a lazy weekend at the beach, when the sun kissed her skin, and the sand massaged her feet.

She hadn't realized she'd been daydreaming and biting her lip until Casper bumped her with his shoulder. "Sorry I crashed your date."

Audrey wasn't sure if he was seeking information or being sincere. "It's not a date."

"Sure, it's not." He sipped his whiskey and grinned into the glass.

His eyes were the same intoxicating color as Harlow's. In fact, the longer she looked at him, the more similar they seemed.

"Who's older, you or Harlow?"

"Harlow, by three minutes." Casper's smile suggested this was something he was rather proud to pronounce.

So they were twins. Audrey wanted to know more, but before she had the chance to ask, the music started. Audrey had listened to Harlow for years but had never managed to see her in concert. She knew this setup was nothing compared to the shows she usually put on, but it didn't matter. Harlow, on stage, was magic. The audience drank her in like they'd been starved for water in the desert. The screams were almost loud enough to drown out the words. Harlow moved with purpose and elegance, which wasn't an easy balance to maintain. She held the microphone as if it was an extension of her body—which in a way it was.

The young woman singing next to her had introduced herself as Shauna Greer, and Audrey could see she was just as enamored as everyone else. Shauna had a great voice, and there was no doubt she could move, but she had nothing on Harlow.

"She was born to do this," Casper said.

Audrey nodded her agreement. "They love her."

"You should come to one of her shows and get the full effect."

The slight irritation Audrey had felt toward Casper for crashing her non-date melted away. She slipped her arm through his. "That would be amazing." She didn't care if she sounded as enamored as she felt.

Harlow finished up the third song, thanked Shauna, and came down the stairs. She grabbed the bottle of water Casper offered her and finished it in its entirety. Audrey almost reached out to wipe the hair stuck to Harlow's face but stopped herself. Harlow made her act strangely, and she needed to get it under control.

Dominic smacked her back. "What did you think?"

"I thought she was great, but it's up to him." Harlow gestured to Casper.

Casper rubbed his chin. "Have her come by the office first thing Monday morning. We can talk about it, but I'm not making any promises. I'd like to hear her whole set. Tell her to bring me some headshots too, whatever she has." He pointed to Dominic. "No promises."

Dominic put his hands up in surrender. "I get it, man. She'll be there at nine in the morning."

Harlow hugged Dominic. "Thanks for having us, but we have to get going. I have an early morning."

He kissed both her cheeks and said good-bye to Audrey and Casper. It took a little more effort to get out than it did to get in. This time people did stop them to ask for pictures and to have a chat. This aspect of the job never bothered Audrey. She didn't mind taking selfies or signing autographs. She understood that the few seconds she'd spend with someone would be a story they'd tell for years, and she always kept that in the back of her mind during the interactions. It was also nice to catch up with a few people she hadn't seen in a while, and it amused her the way Harlow seemed surprised when she stopped to talk to someone they both knew. Harlow seemed eager to leave though, so she kept the conversations short, with promises to talk again soon. When they made it outside, Audrey felt a pang of disappointment. She wanted to spend more time with Harlow.

"Thanks for coming. Sorry we had to leave so quickly, but that's just not my scene." Harlow sounded apologetic.

"You're more of a Rainbow chick now." Casper buckled his seat belt and rolled down the window.

Audrey had heard of the Rainbow—everyone in celebrity circles had, but she'd never been. She decided not to ask any more questions based on Harlow's eye roll. It was clearly something she didn't want to discuss. Audrey followed Casper's lead and opened her window. It was a beautiful Los Angeles evening. The air was hovering right at the place where it wasn't warm, but it wasn't quite cool. The wind on her face felt wonderful. She glanced over at Harlow and caught her looking at her out of the corner of her eye.

"You were incredible up there tonight," Audrey said.

"Thanks. Dominic loves to put me on the spot."

"I'm glad he did."

Casper leaned forward so he was between them. "Can you drop me at the Viper Room? I need to meet up with Tony."

"Sure, no problem." Harlow turned on her blinker, and Audrey thought she looked as if she was suppressing a smile.

Audrey felt a sudden rush of adrenaline flood her system. She'd wanted alone time with Harlow all night, and now she was going to get her chance. She was both supremely excited and equally terrified. She forced an expression of indifference. She didn't want to give away how she was feeling to Harlow yet, much less Casper. It had been a long time since being near someone initiated a wave of pure excitement. She was slightly undone by Harlow's presence, and it was a feeling she wanted to explore further. *Looks like you're going to get your chance.*

CHAPTER SIX

Harlow pulled the car to a stop in front of Audrey's house. "Here we are, safe and sound."

Audrey looked up at the house and turned her attention back to Harlow. "Want to come inside and have a drink?"

There was nothing Harlow wanted more. Well, that wasn't entirely true. There were lots of things she wanted at that moment—a lot of things her body wanted. She mentally weighed the right move. She genuinely liked Audrey, and she didn't want to ruin whatever was happening by moving too fast.

"I start shooting my new film tomorrow, so I'm pretty tied up for the next few months." Audrey's voice held an apology. "It would be fun to hang out for a bit, you know, before reality sets in."

It didn't matter what the right answer was anymore. Harlow wanted to do what Audrey wanted, whatever that entailed, especially if their opportunities to hang out would be cut short.

"Do you have any whiskey?" Harlow posed the question but was already opening the car door.

"I think my dad has a bottle tucked away somewhere in the cupboard," Audrey said as she hurried up the walk to open the door.

Harlow watched as Audrey opened cupboard after cupboard until she found what she was looking for. "Is Whistle Pig any good?" Audrey pulled it down and pulled off the cap. "Sounds terrible."

Harlow held out the glass Audrey had placed in front of her. "Better than good. Your dad has excellent taste." She followed Audrey out to the lounge chairs by her pool. "Tell me about your parents."

Audrey sipped her wine and was quiet for a moment. "They've been married for thirty years. My dad is a day trader, and my mom is a retired nurse. My dad thinks he's the funniest man who has ever lived, and my mom is the smartest person I've ever known." She took another sip of wine. "People have been hoping there was some weird story for years, but they're very normal. I often disappoint people with how ordinary my childhood was and how close I am to my parents." She shrugged. "I'm fortunate. I didn't come to LA to escape anything or anyone. I came because I was given an opportunity to do so."

Harlow swirled the whiskey in her glass and inhaled it deeply. Her family life had been a train wreck. She didn't want to scare her off by delving into the details, so she did what she always did when a question about her family was looming; she changed the subject.

"You excited about starting the new movie tomorrow?"

Audrey set her glass down and put her hands behind her head. "Do you really think you can change the subject so you don't have to answer the same questions? I know this game, remember?" She looked over at her, amusement on her lips. "Are you close to your parents?"

Harlow listened to the ice clink against the glass as she twirled it. "No. I'm not." She wanted to tell her more, but there was no right place to start. She wasn't about to ruin a perfectly good night by lamenting about her childhood.

"Who was the last person you dated?"

Audrey seemed determined to peel back her layers and was letting her off the hook when it came to her parents. Still, she was rubbing up against another controversial aspect of Harlow's life. "Dated is a strong word." Harlow smiled at her, hoping to lighten the mood.

"Do you date women? I've noticed that you never answer the question outright and the photos of you with women aren't conclusive." Audrey sounded serious now as if she'd wanted to ask that specific question for quite some time.

"Tell you what," Harlow said as she finished the whiskey in her glass and noticed the play of the light on the pool beside them. "You can ask me whatever you want, and if I don't want to answer, I'll take off a piece of clothing. If I do answer, you have to take off something you're wearing. And vice versa, of course." So much for taking things slow so she didn't screw it up. She couldn't seem to help herself.

Audrey raised an eyebrow. "Seriously?"

"Was that one of your questions?"

Audrey sat up in her seat. "No. That's not fair." She swallowed what was left in her wine glass. "Let me think."

Harlow tapped her wrist. "You only get twenty seconds."

"Who was your first crush?" Audrey winced, seemingly disappointed with her question.

"Jane Fonda." Harlow pointed at Audrey. "You should start with the shoes."

Audrey sighed but took off one of her high heels. "Jane Fonda? I wouldn't have thought that."

Harlow tapped her finger against her lips. "Where was your first kiss, and who was it with?"

"Brian Decker during recess in the fifth grade." Audrey waved her finger. "That was two questions. You owe me two shoes."

Harlow pulled off her boots and placed them next to the deck chair.

Audrey poured more wine into her glass. "What age did you start singing?"

Harlow downed another finger of whiskey. "Since before I can remember. You owe me another shoe."

Audrey pulled it off and twirled it around her finger before putting it next to her. "Why won't you talk about your parents?"

Harlow pulled at the hem of her shirt and lifted it over her head. The air was cool, and her skin prickled. She could feel Audrey's eyes on her, and for a second, it felt like she was being touched. There were dozens of questions bouncing around in her mind. She wanted to know everything about Audrey, but there was time for all that. One question pushed its way to the front based solely on the way Audrey's eyes traced the outline of her body.

Harlow pulled her hair down and let it fall to her shoulders. "Do you want to touch me?"

Audrey's skin flushed slightly. "Yes." She licked her bottom lip, and Harlow had to concentrate on not reaching out and running her thumb across it.

Harlow stood, unbuttoned her jeans, and slid them off. She kept her eyes on Audrey as she tossed them over the chair. She still had on her bra and panties, but she was delightfully exposed in a way that made her skin tingle with desire. She'd been with countless women, but no one had ever looked at her the way Audrey was now. It was both disconcerting and exciting. Audrey looked at her like she wanted to really know her. Harlow had never wanted that from another person until now. In an attempt to push away the frisson of fear that caused, she jumped up, grinned at Audrey, and leaped into the pool.

Audrey wasn't sure where this conversation or evening was headed. She'd watched Harlow with painful anticipation as she'd taken off her clothes. If Harlow hadn't jumped into the pool, she wasn't sure if she would've been able to stop herself from reaching out and touching her.

Audrey had never been in her pool with anything besides a swimsuit on, and certainly not with a woman who looked at her the way Harlow had been all evening. There was a hunger in her eyes that Audrey couldn't quite identify. It seemed almost primal.

"Are you going to get in, or are you going to let me swim alone?" Harlow ran her fingers through her wet hair.

Audrey unzipped her skirt, keenly aware of Harlow watching her every move. She pulled off her shirt and tossed it next to the other abandoned garments. She walked to the pool edge, trying to decipher the look on Harlow's face as she lowered herself in. The cool pool water should've extinguished the heat she felt building, but it didn't.

Harlow put her arm up on the pool edge and grabbed Audrey's hand, pulling her close. Her mascara created a slight darkening under her eyes, and there were droplets of water sliding down her exquisite features. Audrey's heart was pounding, and she was grateful the water would hide her slightly trembling hands. What was it about this woman that had her so off-kilter?

"I do date women. I don't make public comments on my private life to the press, because I like my private life to stay that way, as much as it can in this business. The information is there for people to see if they want. I just don't make a big deal out of it," Harlow said as she moved even closer.

Their bodies were touching, and Audrey found it difficult to form coherent sentences. There were just words bouncing around inside her head that didn't add up to anything of substance. She couldn't take her eyes off the way Harlow's lips moved when she spoke and how they always seemed right on the verge of a smile.

Audrey ran her thumb across Harlow's bottom lip before she could talk herself out of it. "You have perfect lips."

Harlow turned her head to Audrey's hand and kissed her palm. "I'd really like to kiss you."

"I've been waiting for you to all night," Audrey said.

Audrey tried to keep her breathing even, a fight she was rapidly losing. Her body seemed to want nothing more than to inhale her. Harlow, with her perfect cheekbones and lazy smile. She always seemed so confident, but Audrey could sense a deep cave of secrets and pain. There was so much more hidden right behind the self-assurance. She was like a priceless piece of art, and Audrey wanted desperately to study and learn every inch and every stroke.

"Honey, are you back here?" her mother called from the patio.

Audrey's thrumming arousal rapidly morphed into mortification. "Mom? What are you doing here?"

"I told you I'd meet you here as soon as your father and I got back into town. You wanted me to look at some of the script changes." Her mother was walking closer. "Who's in the pool with you? I don't have my glasses."

Harlow grinned and raised her eyebrow. "Guess it's time to meet your mom."

Mortification and annoyance at her mother's timing eclipsed anything she'd been feeling moments before. She made a somewhat serious mental note to change the locks to her house.

"I'm so sorry." Audrey squeezed her hand before climbing out of the pool.

Her mom handed Audrey and Harlow both a towel. "I feel like I interrupted something. Did I interrupt something?"

Harlow wrapped the towel around herself. "Not at all. We were just going for a swim." She stuck out her hand. "I'm Harlow Thorne. It's a pleasure to meet you. Audrey's said so many lovely things about you."

"I'm Kathy Knox. It's very nice to meet you too." At least her mom had the decency to look guilty. She turned her attention to Audrey. "I tried to call, but you weren't picking up." She looked at

Harlow again. "Which I see now, should've been an indication not to come over. Oh, honey, I'm so sorry."

Harlow walked to the lounge chair and grabbed her clothes, looking for all the world like she walked around in front of strangers in her wet underwear all the time. "I should get going anyway. It's getting late. I have an early day."

Audrey didn't want Harlow to leave, but there was no way to get her to stay without embarrassing herself further.

"Harlow, let me grab you some sweats to drive home in. I'm sure Audrey has something for you to wear." Her mom hurried into the house.

Her mother was in mom mode now, and there would be no deterring her. It was better to let her run free and do as she felt compelled.

Audrey sighed as she watched her mother go inside. "I'm really sorry about that. I thought they were coming home tomorrow."

Harlow wrapped her towel around them both and kissed the side of her head. "There's nothing to apologize for, honestly. Your mom seems really sweet."

Audrey chuckled into Harlow's shoulder. She enjoyed the easiness she felt around her. "She is many things, and you're right, sweet is one of them."

The mortification that had initially gripped Audrey upon her mother's abrupt arrival had melted away. Harlow didn't seem at all bothered by the intrusion, and that made her like her even more. Often, people in this business were tightly wound and overwhelmingly entitled. Harlow didn't appear to encompass either of those things. She took the interruption in stride, and Audrey appreciated that immensely.

"What's your shooting schedule like?" Harlow had taken a step back and was drying her hair with the towel.

"Sixteen-hour days for the next six weeks." Audrey tried to sound upbeat, but she knew her schedule was brutal and no one wanted any part of that.

"Any days off?"

"Yeah, actually. I have a four-day stretch in three weeks." Audrey tried not to sound too hopeful.

Harlow walked toward the door where her mother was just emerging. "Perfect. Save them for me?"

"All four?"

Harlow turned, walking backward, and shrugged. "Unless you get a better offer."

A better offer? Was she serious? She hurried to catch up to her.

Harlow took the clothes from her mom without elaborating. "Is it okay if I use the pool house to change? I don't want to track water into the house."

Audrey nodded, still slightly dumbstruck at the thought that Harlow wanted to spend more time with her. "Yeah, of course. It's open." She pulled on the clothes her mother gave her. "Thanks."

"Honey, I'm sorry I interrupted. But I'm glad to see you getting back out there."

Audrey ran the towel over her hair. "We aren't—it wasn't—"

"Okay, I just think it's nice." She pushed her glasses up her nose while staring at the pool house. "She's gorgeous. Do you know her from work?"

"No, she's a singer."

Her mom thought for a second, and then her mouth fell open. "Oh, my goodness. When she said her name, I didn't even put it together. I didn't recognize her because she was all wet. But, honey, that's Harlow Thorne."

Audrey sighed and headed for her kitchen. "I know, Mom."

Her mom was hot on her heels. "Were you two on a date?"

Audrey pulled a water bottle from the fridge. "No. Well, I don't think so." She took a long sip. "I honestly don't know, and you showed up before I could find out for sure."

"I really like her music," she said as she continued to stare at the pool house.

"Mom, you don't listen to Harlow."

Her mom waved her hand, dismissing her. "I most certainly do listen to her. You aren't with me every second of every day." She started singing Harlow's newest release.

Panic and embarrassment engulfed Audrey. "Mom, stop. Seriously, if she walks in while you're doing that, I'll never talk to you again."

"Doing what?" Harlow asked from the door.

Harlow looked impossibly sexy in Audrey's sweats and T-shirt. She wasn't wearing a bra, and Audrey could make out the gentle swell of her breasts against the fabric.

"I was singing your latest ditty." Her mom beamed.

Ditty? Oh, for fuck's sake.

Harlow smiled widely. "Are you any good? I need a new backup singer for the tour."

Her mom blushed. "You think you're being nice, but I'll end up following you onto that bus." Her mom waved her hand as if she was dismissing her, but Audrey knew she was enjoying every second.

Audrey needed this to stop. She pointed to the door. "Mom, Harlow has an early day. I'll walk her out."

"It was nice meeting you, Harlow," her mom called after them, still waving like an excited kid.

"You too," Harlow called back. "She's great." She stuck her thumb toward the kitchen.

"Yeah, she's one of a kind."

"I had fun tonight." Harlow stepped closer. "Thanks for hanging out with me."

The butterflies Harlow incited trumped Audrey's annoyance with her mother. "I had a great time." She kissed Harlow on the cheek. "See you soon."

"I hope so."

Audrey closed the door and felt a strange sensation of missing her. She didn't understand why she was feeling that for someone she'd just met. It made even less sense because it wasn't all that long ago that she was moping around the house feeling heartbroken. *Is Harlow some kind of rebound?* She didn't think rebounds incited these feelings. It felt like all the other beginnings. It felt like this had the potential to be something more.

CHAPTER SEVEN

I don't pay you to kill me." Harlow gasped between words.
Tony, her trainer looked over the top of the treadmill and hit the incline button again. "No, you pay me to keep you in shape and ready for the tour."

Casper put down the weights he'd been lifting. "You have to be able to sing your entire set list while on the treadmill. It's the only way you'll be able to keep up with all the dancing and feel good about whatever you're wearing."

She tossed her towel at him. "I know the drill. This isn't my first rodeo."

Casper dodged the towel and squirted water into her mouth. "I met with Shauna and Dominic. I think we should let her open for you."

She gave him a thumbs-up, and tried not to look at the remaining time. "Sounds good."

He laid back down on the weight bench. He trained with her for fun and because he liked the stress relief. "Rehearsals start in a few weeks."

Her trainer finally slowed the spinning wheel of death, and she closed her eyes as she slowed to a walking speed. "Anything else I need to know? It seems like you have something else you need to say."

Casper wasn't telling her anything they hadn't already discussed a million times before. There was something going on, and she'd preferred he just spit it out instead of playing the long game.

His weights clanked. "Why would you say that?"

She put her hands on her hips, still trying to catch her breath. "None of this information is earth-shattering. You usually don't come to my training sessions unless you have something vital to tell me."

Her trainer grabbed his bag. "Sorry I have to bail early, but I promised my wife I'd make it to our OB appointment. We get to hear the baby's heartbeat today." He headed for the door. "You know the rest of the drill. Stretch for fifteen minutes, and tomorrow is back and shoulder day."

"Can't wait," she said flatly. Tony had been with her for almost five years and was used to her attitude regarding arms and shoulders. "Tell your wife I said hi."

"Will do," Tony said as the door closed behind him.

"Mom is here." He let the weight drop onto the bar, the clang echoing through the small workout space.

Mom is here. He didn't say she was coming. He didn't say she was making plans. *She's here.* Harlow hadn't seen her mother in over a decade. She hadn't bothered looking for them until Harlow's first album had been released. Casper had told her of the phone calls and letters asking for money, but never anything more. Harlow wasn't sure what her mother had to say. She'd let Casper handle all of it. She couldn't manage the emotions that went along with managing her mother, and now was no different.

"What does she want?" Harlow braced herself on the treadmill, waiting for the answer.

"I don't know." Casper was typing on his phone.

He was so calm. Casper had the ability to shoulder difficult information with an ease she never possessed. He could handle any situation. Nothing ever rocked his boat or threw him off-kilter. She'd always admired that about him. He'd always been her lighthouse in the storm. She could always find the horizon because of Casper.

"I can't deal with her and get ready for the tour." She rubbed her arms because she needed something to do with her hands that didn't involve throwing inanimate objects.

"I know. I'll find out what she wants and handle it." He came over and rested his hands on her shoulders. "I'll take care of it."

The relief at his words was overwhelming. She hugged him and closed her eyes. Her mother wasn't a door she wanted to open. Not now, not ever. That door led to nothing but sad memories and lost innocence. Casper had been her buffer, keeping her safe and letting her focus on the now. She didn't understand how he was able to compartmentalize that part of their lives, but she was grateful he did it for her. The less she had to deal with it, the better. In the beginning, she'd wondered if that was fair, but over time, it became a habit. Neither of them seemed in a hurry to shake up practiced patterns.

There had been times over the years where she'd considered reaching out to her. Granted, those times had usually followed a night of heavy drinking and other poor decisions, but she had considered it, if for no other reason than to understand what they'd done to provoke such a break in their familial ties. But those brief lapses in judgment were just that—brief. She didn't owe her mother anything, especially the real estate in her mind.

The best course of action was the same one they'd been taking— pay her when she popped up like some deranged Whac-A-Mole, and continue on with their lives.

Audrey's trailers had improved over the years, but this was the best yet. It came with a shower, full vanity, couch, bed, refrigerator, and a television. The more famous she'd become, the more luxurious her accommodations, but right now, she didn't care. She'd showered and fallen onto the bed after a sixteen-hour day of shooting. She was debating whether to go home or stay here for the night. She was exhausted, and her brain was fried.

"Knock, knock," Kylie said as she opened the door to her trailer.

Audrey grunted, words eluding her.

"I have the script changes for tomorrow." She set the stapled packet on her back. "Do you want me to email them to you too?"

"How many changes?" Audrey barely lifted her head from the pillow.

"Only four."

"I'll look at them tomorrow." Audrey stared at her bag next to the door, still weighing her options. "I'm so damn tired. I'm thinking about just sleeping here."

"Don't do that. Go home. Get a good night's sleep and leave work at work." Kylie picked up her bag. "Seriously."

Kylie was right. She didn't want to sleep in her trailer, no matter how nice it was. She wanted her bed, her pillows, her coffee.

Audrey forced herself up and grabbed her bag. "Come on. I'll drive you home."

"Actually, I meant to ask you, is it okay if I stay with you tonight?" Kylie looked embarrassed. "Luke has a bunch of friends over, and I just can't deal."

Audrey hated that Kylie even had to ask. Their friendship was vital to her. They'd been friends since high school. They'd had countless sleepovers, vacationed together, and had keys to each other's houses. Working together had slightly shifted their dynamic, but it didn't erase their history.

"Of course, you can. You don't even have to ask, and you know that."

Kylie shrugged. "I didn't want to assume. This shooting schedule is rough."

Audrey tossed her bag in the trunk of her car. "Is everything okay with you and Luke? I thought you liked his friends?"

"Yeah, we're fine. Everything is fine. It's completely normal to date for seven years and not be engaged. People do that all the time."

Even if Audrey hadn't known Kylie for over half her life, she would've picked up on the sarcasm. Kylie wanted to be married, and she wanted kids. Neither of which seemed included in Luke's long-term plan.

"I mean, we're thirty. It's normal to stay up drinking with your buddies four nights a week. It's normal to go eight months without a job. It's normal to still say comic books are your favorite literary works. Everything is good." Kylie looked like she was going to start crying.

Audrey hadn't realized she was so unhappy, and she hated herself for not paying attention. Kylie noticed everything. Kylie scheduled her dental cleanings, made sure her dry cleaning was picked up, she even reminded her to eat. Audrey had been so caught up in her own world, she hadn't been what Kylie so clearly needed—a friend.

"You know you can stay with me if you need a break. Seriously, as long as you want."

Kylie stared out the window. "Maybe." She rested her head against the pane. "Seven years, and I may have nothing to show for it."

Audrey pulled into her driveway. "That's not true. You finished school. You started a career. You've bought your parents a new car. You've made a name for yourself."

"All thanks to you," Kylie whispered.

Audrey rubbed her shoulder. "We both know that isn't true. You made all of it come true. Besides, if the roles were reversed, you would've done the same for me."

Audrey wanted nothing more than to crawl into her bed, but Kylie was pulling a wine glass down from the cabinet. She could spare one more hour.

"You don't have to stay up with me," Kylie said as she headed out the back door.

"It's a beautiful night, may as well enjoy it."

"What am I supposed to do now?" Kylie looked toward the sky, seeking answers from whatever spiritual being would answer.

"You don't have to have it all figured out now. Take your time and decide what you really want. Plus, you're almost done with that screenplay you've been working on for a year. It's a hit, I know it."

"Thanks, it's one of the few things I'm proud of right now." Kylie sighed. "I want to be with someone who shares the same dreams as me. Someone who cares about how I feel. I want someone who cares, period. That's not Luke. It hasn't been for a long time." She sipped her wine. "He hasn't even texted me to see when I'm coming home."

"Then you stay here until you figure it out, no rush."

"I'm going to ask him to move out."

That sounded like the best idea, but Audrey didn't want to push her in any direction. "I'm here to support you no matter what you decide. I hope you know that."

"I know." Kylie's grin was faint, but it was there.

Sharing silence was one of the unspoken gems of true friendship. She loved that they were able to share space without having to fill it with words and noise. Audrey had always appreciated that about Kylie. They could sit together and share moments of quiet.

Audrey's phone buzzed next to her, and she smiled when she saw the text from Harlow.

I know it's late. I just wanted you to know I was thinking about you. Sleep well, and good luck on set tomorrow.

Audrey stared at her phone and tried to tamp down the smile she could feel forming on her face. *I saw your billboard on Sunset when I drove to work today. It made me miss you. Have a good night.*

"Why do you look like a girl who was just asked to prom?" Kylie teased her.

"I didn't even go to prom." Audrey leaned back in her chair. She didn't want to look at Kylie and give her feelings away.

"Was that Harlow?" Kylie positioned herself on the edge of her chair.

"Tonight is about you. I want to talk about what you're going through."

"Psht! I don't. Let me live vicariously through you. Please, I need this."

Audrey searched Kylie's face and saw she was telling the truth. "It was Harlow, but she was just saying hello."

"Do you blush like that when I text you hello?"

Audrey laughed. "You never text me hello. You text me instructions. Sometimes you text me reminders, and occasionally you throw in a few threats. But it's never just hello."

Kylie ignored her comment and pressed forward with her inquisition. "Is she as charming after three hours as she is after three minutes?"

Audrey finished her wine. "Even more so." Audrey didn't add that it was the ease of Harlow's charm that had her a bit uneasy.

Kylie fell back on her chair. "I need a Harlow."

"You need a woman with a reputation for hot flings and never settling down? I'm not sure that's good for anyone." Audrey said good night and climbed the stairs to her room. She had to get up in four hours, and it was going to come much faster than she wanted. She reread her text messages and thought again about what Kylie had said. Was that what Audrey had been missing? Did she need a Harlow too? Or was it that she needed a reminder of what it felt like to have someone's complete attention? Harlow was easy to be around, and she looked forward to spending time with her, but was Harlow capable of anything more than a few fun nights? She'd said it herself. Her longest relationship hadn't broken the barrier of a few months. Audrey wasn't wired for flings.

But what she'd done in the past hadn't worked. Maybe it was time to try something different. Perhaps she could see how things progressed without getting attached. Maybe she could trick herself into believing that would be enough.

Chapter Eight

Harlow stared at the dozens of costume designs on the wall. They were stunning. She hadn't thought it possible to top her last tour, and yet, these undoubtedly would. People had no idea of the intricacies that went into planning such a large-scale production. Even the sequins were strategic. Each detail would highlight another. The lighting, stage design, costumes, intensity of the bass—everything was intentional. It wasn't just some person on stage singing; it was a show meant to bring an audience to its feet.

She pulled one of the designs off the wall and ran her fingers over the swatch of fabric. "I'll open in this one."

Jasmine, her costume designer, jotted down her selection. "That's what I'd hoped."

"You outdid yourself once again." Harlow pulled another down and handed it to Jasmine. "You're brilliant."

Jasmine beamed. "I wanted you to pick your opening and closing outfits. I can fill in the rest if you want."

Harlow nodded. "They're all exceptional. I'll be happy with whatever order you decide." She glanced at Jasmine's tablet. "Do you have the set list?"

"Harlow, Audrey Knox is here," Rebecca said through the speakerphone that sat in the middle of the desk.

Harlow looked down, aware that she was still in her sports bra and running pants from her workout. *Audrey? Jesus, do I smell?* She tried to smell her armpit subtly. *Nothing too pungent.* She quickly let her hair down and pulled it back up, desperately wanting to look more presentable.

Jasmine laughed. "Harlow, I'm not sure what you're trying to do, but if you're worried about how you look—don't. You're gorgeous."

"You have to say that. You make me gorgeous for a living."

Jasmine raised her left eyebrow. "Yeah, I'm the only one that thinks that. As if there aren't ten million people fantasizing about you on the daily." She shook her head.

Harlow felt herself blush and hoped Jasmine didn't notice. "I'll be back."

Audrey was sitting at the kitchen table when Harlow came around the corner. She looked nervous and was rubbing the top of her hand like she was trying to make a decision.

"Hi." Harlow's stomach filled with a warm sensation when Audrey turned her head and smiled.

"I'm sorry to just drop by your house like this. Kylie and Casper had exchanged our information before we had dinner that first night, in true super-assistant style." She handed her an iced coffee. "Your house is exactly how I pictured it. It's all modern and sleek. Not necessarily my taste." She put her hand over her mouth and looked embarrassed. "I didn't mean that how it sounded. It's beautiful. It suits you." She took a deep breath. "I had a three-hour break, and I—" She put her hand on her forehead and shook her head. "I guess I just wanted to see you. Now I realize you're probably insanely busy, and I definitely should've called first. I know better. How totally rude. I'm so sorry."

Harlow tried not to smile when she looked at the way Audrey's leg was bouncing. "I'm glad you did." She pointed to her casual clothing. "I apologize. I have to work out three times a day right now, so I stay in these all day. I was going over costume designs when you got here."

Audrey stood, her face flushing. "I'm sorry, I should leave you to it."

Harlow grabbed her hand and pulled her back down. "Please stay. I've been thinking about you."

"Did you know there's a billboard of you right next to the lot I'm shooting on right now?" Audrey took a deep breath. "I find it slightly distracting."

Harlow thought about the different marketing campaigns she had going at the moment. "Is it the one where I'm wearing a white dress and sunglasses?"

Audrey nodded. "Short hair, red lipstick, sleeveless white dress."

Harlow felt her stomach flutter again. "Very specific." She clenched her hands in her lap, trying not to touch Audrey. "I'd say I'm sorry, but I'm not."

Audrey cocked her head. "There's that thing you do again. The blatant truth."

Harlow wanted to explain that she wasn't telling the whole truth. A million emotions were swirling through her right now, and all of them could be sourced to Audrey. She wanted to let her in, and she didn't understand why. She barely knew Audrey. She had no reason to feel anything she was feeling, but there was the truth of it. She wanted to know if she cracked the door open, would it be safe?

Audrey wasn't sure what Harlow was thinking. She was breathing a little more rapidly, and she'd slightly flushed. She had this overwhelming urge to put her at ease. She slid her hand across the wooden tabletop and intertwined her fingers with Harlow's. The sensation of excitement was immediate. Whenever they touched, Audrey felt it in every part of her body. It was exhilarating and terrifying.

"I'm not sorry, either. I like thinking about you," Audrey said before she had the chance to talk herself out of it.

Harlow picked up their entwined hands and kissed Audrey's knuckle. "I think about you all day."

Audrey was transfixed by Harlow's lips against her hand. She imagined them against her neck, against her ear, and traveling down her collarbone.

"You should probably get that."

"What?" Audrey had been lost in her thoughts, and she had no idea what they were talking about.

Harlow pointed to Audrey's phone buzzing on the table. Audrey grabbed it, still a little fuzzy after her quick rendezvous into dreamland.

"They need you back on set," Kylie said before Audrey had a chance to say anything. "They're going to reshoot the sixth scene, and it has to be done before we can move on because of lighting."

Two women had entered the room while she was on the phone and were already hovering over Harlow, showing her different drawings.

"I'll be right there. Give me thirty minutes." Audrey ended the call. "I have to get going."

"I'll walk you to your car."

When they arrived at her car, Audrey leaned against her door. She didn't know when they'd get another uninterrupted minute together, and she wanted to take her in completely. Harlow looked incredibly sexy in her workout clothes and hair pulled back. Her confident smile accentuated her beautiful features, but nothing was more intoxicating than her eyes. Impulsively, Audrey reached forward and pulled Harlow against her.

Harlow wrapped her arms around her and pressed her lips against her ear. "Go, be brilliant."

Audrey pulled her head back so she could see her. "I'm not sure how you do that."

"Do what?"

"Make my whole body tingle with just a few words," Audrey whispered.

Harlow stared at her lips. "Everything in me is saying to kiss you." Her words were clipped, and her voice a little hoarse.

Audrey's breathe caught. "Don't. I don't want our first kiss to mean good-bye."

An emotion flashed across Harlow's face that Audrey couldn't place. It looked like a mixture of regret and desire. Audrey wanted nothing more than to touch the skin on her cheek. She wanted to take the time to discover how her body reacted to Harlow's lips on her skin. She wanted to know if she'd been right or if it was all in her head.

"I'm sorry, it's just that I—"

"Why do you do that?" Harlow asked.

"Do what?"

"Apologize for things you want. You don't owe me or anyone else an apology for doing what is best for you." Harlow was adamant and sure. "Don't ever apologize for being you."

"I'm not sure how else to be," Audrey said because it was the truth.

"Be you. Be all the wonderful things you are. Be your worst, your best, rational, emotional, lost, found. Be whatever you are, because it's good enough. *You* are good enough."

Audrey had always been the good girl. She never upset people intentionally. She never did what she wanted if it meant upsetting someone else. She never wanted anyone to be mad at her. She wanted people to like her. She wanted people to believe she was sweet and kind. She wanted all those things, even if it meant feeling herself breaking apart on the inside.

She'd never thought there was another option. It wasn't until Harlow pointed out the alternative that she considered doing anything else. Harlow hadn't been the first one to notice the issues, but she was the first person who'd gotten through to her.

Harlow stepped back, and Audrey missed the weight against her. "Until next time, Ms. Knox. Thank you for the coffee."

Audrey opened her door and got inside before she threw her entire career away and dragged Harlow upstairs. "Any time."

Audrey's body was still on fire as she drove toward the studio. She'd never met anyone quite like Harlow. She'd never been so drawn to or entranced by another person. She needed to keep her wits about her. She'd heard about this kind of thing. The warning of becoming so wholly engulfed in someone that you lost yourself completely. She'd never thought she'd be in danger of something like that happening. Her relationship with Tia had been toxic on many levels, but she'd never felt in danger of losing herself. She remembered the way Harlow had felt pressed against her. The way the words against her ear had almost made her knees buckle. She thought about the way her skin burned every time they touched. If anyone was going to take her down, it could very well be Harlow Thorne.

CHAPTER NINE

Audrey put the cold rag Kylie handed her around her neck and sat on the curb. She'd just finished the seventeenth take of one of the most challenging action scenes she'd ever done. These days, car explosions were done with CGI, but not with this director. He liked the authentic look of real metal burning. That meant lots of takes from a lot of angles. She was hungry, tired, and in desperate need of a cold shower. The last two weeks of filming had been brutal, and she couldn't wait to finish this film.

"You killed that last take." Kylie handed her a bottle of water as the hair and makeup artists tried to fix the effects of the hot sun and burning metal.

"Thanks." She wiped the towel down her arms to remove the dirt and sweat. "Any messages?"

Kylie grinned. "I heard some of the crew talking. Apparently, Harlow Thorne is shooting her new music video on the lot. There was a last-minute change because of a double-booking, and they're here today instead of Sunday."

Cathy continued to brush out Audrey's hair. "I'm going to try to sneak over and watch after this. Harlow Thorne is perfection in heels. I love her music."

"I heard she's dating the lead singer from that one boy band. You know who I'm talking about." Megan leaned her head back to think. "Nick Day. I knew I'd think of it." She blended the foundation under Audrey's eye.

Cathy shrugged. "I didn't think she was dating anyone. Isn't she into girls?"

Megan leaned back to assess her work. "I don't think so." She put a light layer of lip gloss on Audrey's lips. "Are you friends with her?"

"We've met." Audrey wasn't mentally prepared to deal with any of this information. She tried to keep her face as neutral as possible and reminded herself she was allowed to have friends. "She did a few songs for my last movie. We went to a party together." *Why did you add that, Audrey? They don't need to know that. Stop talking.* Audrey stood. "I may go over and say hi." *Cool. Cool, cool.*

Kylie raised her eyebrows and stared at her. She seemed just as surprised as Audrey felt. "Thanks, ladies, she's all set." Cathy and Megan moved on to the next actor. "Are you okay?"

Audrey put her hands up. "No, clearly, I'm not." She shifted her hands to her hips. What she really wanted was to pace, but that would draw attention. "I haven't seen or heard from her in almost two weeks. And now she's here, and I had no idea she would be. Maybe she isn't interested anymore. It was just a…a…flirtation."

Kylie handed Audrey her phone. "I found out she was shooting here because she texted you to let you know." She nodded toward Cathy and Megan. "I didn't think you'd want me to say that in front of them."

Audrey opened her text messages. *Hey! There was a double-booking, and now we're shooting on your lot. Come say hi when you're wrapped. I miss you.*

Audrey handed the phone back to Kylie, relief flooding her. "It's possible I'm losing my mind."

Kylie nodded slowly. "Entirely possible. Or, and hear me out, you're reacting like someone who really likes another person but doesn't know where it's going."

Audrey took a step closer. "Keep talking."

Kylie led her a few feet in the other direction. "You two have only gotten to see each other a few times. Everything else has been texts and phone calls, and you've both been too busy for even that over the last few weeks. You've built it up in your head because your four-day break is coming up, the break you're going to spend with her. You're worried it's not going to meet your expectations."

Audrey nodded. "Or, I'm terrified it's going to exceed all my expectations, and I don't know what to do with that."

Kylie chuckled. "Doesn't seem like a bad spot to find yourself in." She put her hands on Audrey's shoulders and shook her slightly. "It is impossible not to love you, Audrey. Jesus, it's not like you're some hag that has nothing going for her. You're one of the most sought-after actresses in Hollywood. You're also kind, smart, and gorgeous. Give yourself some credit."

Audrey ran her hand through her hair. "I'm sorry. I don't mean to make you stroke my ego. I'm not sure why I get all twisted up when it comes to Harlow."

"Because you like her. Like I said."

"Want to come with me when this is over?" Audrey asked when she heard the director call for them to reposition.

"Obviously."

Audrey walked back over to her mark while she tried to push the thought of seeing Harlow out of her mind. She needed to concentrate. Josh Branch, the male lead, wrapped his arms around her as they took their positions. He was a nice enough guy. He was easy to work with, pleasant, and professional. Josh's arms were strong, his jaw was prominent, and he was very handsome. She reminded herself that she was playing a woman who was hopelessly in love with the man in front of her.

"You okay?" Josh whispered while the final boom arrangements were made.

"Yeah, sorry. My head was somewhere else for a minute."

"Hot date later?" He flashed the smile that made women all over the world swoon.

"Not sure yet."

The director yelled from the other side of the camera. "Action."

Audrey let herself be pulled into the scene. She focused on her male counterpart and did her best to play the lovestruck woman she had been written to play. A part of her, no matter how much she focused, was fixated on what was waiting at the end of her day. *Harlow.* She smiled up at Josh and thought this may be the most convincing she'd ever been in a film.

Harlow checked her phone for the twentieth time. She hadn't heard from Casper, and it wasn't like him to miss a video shoot. She was starting to get worried.

"You ready to go again?"

Harlow nodded, adjusting her black wig. "Yes."

"For what it's worth, this is a great look on you." She pointed to Harlow's dark locks.

"Thanks." Harlow checked herself in the mirror and caught a glimpse of Audrey coming through the hanger doors.

Her heart rate increased at Audrey's presence. Her hair was still damp from a shower, and her sheer white shirt gave the slightest hint of the black bra she was wearing underneath. Jeans and a T-shirt had never made Harlow's throat go completely dry, but here she was. Audrey did that to her. Without even trying, she could shift Harlow's internal chemistry.

Harlow knew she'd missed her but hadn't realized quite how much until she walked through the doors. She could feel Audrey's eyes on her, entirely focused. She loved the sensation. It felt like Audrey was touching her, even from twenty feet away.

She took her position on stage. The wind machines started, and her song "Wildest Imagination" started playing through every speaker on the set. She'd written this song about a woman. Not a specific woman, but one she hoped for in the future. Most people speculated it was about a man, but people heard what they wanted to. That was the great thing about music.

The dancers moved around her, and she let the music flow through her. She tried to focus on what she'd felt when she'd written the song. She'd envisioned a love so strong that you'd feel it for the rest of your life. A love that you may not be able to keep, but one that burned so fiercely that it branded your soul.

Harlow hopped off the stage as soon as the director indicated the shot was complete. She hurried over to Audrey before anyone had the chance to stop her.

"You always amaze me," Audrey said. She reached up and touched Harlow's wig. "I love this, too, by the way."

Harlow knew she was staring, but the look in Audrey's eyes spoke of desire and passion. Harlow had seen the look a million times from a million different people. This was different. It was like Audrey wanted to see all of her. Her body reacted to Audrey the way it always did, as if there was an invisible force leading her toward her. Her hands ached with the need to touch her. They hadn't spent nearly enough time together in the last few weeks, and the anticipation had been building. She could hardly wait for their four uninterrupted days together and all the possibilities that held.

"Hi. Not sure if you remember me. I'm Kylie." She gave a small wave.

"Of course, I remember you. You talked Audrey into having dinner with me," Harlow said. "It's so nice to see you again. How are you?"

"I'm well, thank you for asking. Thanks for letting us watch that." She pointed to the set. "It was incredible."

"I'm glad you both could make it. How was shooting today?"

Audrey held up her arm to show a bruise that stretched from her wrist to her elbow. "Took a pretty nasty hit from one of the prop guns, but other than that, it went great."

"Oh, my God." Harlow touched the bruise carefully but felt her face flush when she saw the goose bumps appear in the wake of her fingers. "Are you sure you didn't break anything?"

"Uh-huh," Audrey said. "Just a bruise."

There was no reason for Harlow to continue to hang on to her, especially with a million eyes on them, so she regretfully released her arm. "I'm really looking forward to next Thursday. Do you have any objections to taking a road trip to Monterey with me?"

Audrey took a deep breath, and her cheeks turned a slight shade of red. "No, that sounds great."

"I guess our invitations got lost in the mail," Casper said as he walked up and pointed to Kylie and then himself. "That's fine."

Harlow rolled her eyes. "I always go up there before I go on tour. Nothing new."

Casper crossed his arms. "True. But you usually go alone."

"Do you two want to come?" Harlow's attempt at nonchalance was a poor one by the expression on Casper's face.

He rolled his shoulders, probably to irritate her and make it seem as if he was thinking about it. "No, I have other things to do here." He put his arm around Harlow and squeezed her waist. "I appreciate the genuine invite, though." He dipped his head slightly. "Can I talk to you for a minute?"

She'd been looking forward to talking to Audrey since it seemed like forever since she'd seen her, but the look on Casper's face told her it was serious. She glanced over at Audrey and noticed the disappointed look in her eyes. She'd intended to pull her into a corner and spend as much time as either of them could spare together. She'd imagined asking about her day and hearing all the little details she missed out on consistently. She wanted to spend every bit of the ten minutes she had before the director had her back up on stage. But none of that was possible at the moment.

Harlow reached over and squeezed Audrey's hand. "Can I call you later?"

Audrey smiled and nodded, but it didn't reach her eyes. "Sure, no problem."

It hurt to let go of Audrey's fingers, but she did. She waited until Audrey and Kylie had walked away, and she turned her attention to Casper. "What's up?"

"Mom says she'll leave, but she wants a hundred thousand. Normally, I would push back, but with the tour coming up—"

"Just give her the money." Harlow pulled her blouse from the restraints of her waistband. "I don't want to deal with her."

"Are you sure? This may never end."

"Did you see her?" Harlow wasn't sure where the question came from. She usually didn't want to know the whereabouts of their mother.

Casper sighed. "Yes, I just came back from seeing her."

"How did she seem? Do you think she's on something?"

Casper looked surprised. "I don't think so. That's not how she seemed to me, anyway."

Harlow nodded. "She's just needed more money than normal lately. I was just curious about what the hell she's spending it on." She wrapped her arm around Casper's waist. "I trust you. Do what you need to do to keep her away from the press." She let go of him and headed toward her dressing room.

"Harlow, I—"

She turned and looked at him. "Yeah?"

His hands were on his hips, and he was looking at the ground. "Nothing. Forget it."

She was going to push but decided against it. Casper would tell her whatever was bothering him in his own time. He always did. What she wanted to focus on now was getting through the next few days. The thought of spending four days with Audrey had been helping her through the lengthy tediousness of preparing for the tour, and now that it was almost here, she could barely think of anything else.

CHAPTER TEN

Audrey held the chilled glass in her hand and tried to focus on the man in front of her. This would usually be an easy task, but tonight she was falling short. He was an up-and-coming director, and Audrey was bored with the repetitiveness of the story. It was nauseating. Men in this town were given opportunities like people handed stickers to toddlers. He thought he landed the new film because of his talent. She knew better. He may very well be talented, but he also shared the last name of one of the most famous studio executives Hollywood had ever seen.

"I think you'd be perfect for the part," he said.

Audrey nodded and put on her best smile. "Please, send the script over to my agent, and I'll take a look."

"You could do a private reading for me now if you have time." One of his manicured eyebrows rose at his innuendo, and Audrey had to keep herself from tossing her drink in his face.

Audrey had starred in twelve major pictures, and this man insinuating that she should do a *private* reading was not only unprofessional, it was also ludicrous.

"Shane? It is Shane, right?" She didn't give him a chance to answer. "I'm not sure what you heard, but that's not how I operate. If you'd like me to read for a part, you'll need to go through the proper channels. I will not read for you in private or play a role in whatever little fantasy you've concocted in your head. You better hope that I find myself in a better mood at the end of the night than I am right now, or I'll make sure to pass a message along to every actor and actress I've ever worked with. This isn't Weinstein's Hollywood anymore."

He blew air out through his nostrils and took a step closer. "You dumb, dyke bitch. Do you know who I am?"

"I know exactly who you are," she whispered. "You've made the mistake of not knowing who I am."

He took a step back and studied her. "You're too old for the part anyway."

She raised her glass in acknowledgment and watched him walk away.

Kylie leaned into her. "Who was that guy?"

Audrey rolled her eyes. "He was no one."

Kylie stepped in front of her and was staring at someone behind her. "Well, I hate to do this to you, but Tia is here."

Audrey sighed. "For fuck's sake."

"Yeah, and she's coming this way."

"Perfect." Her nerves were frayed, and she was exhausted. The shooting schedule had been one of the most intense she'd ever experienced, and it was taking everything she had to keep herself upright. The last thing she wanted to do was suffer through a painful and pointless conversation with her estranged ex. She wasn't sure she had the mental bandwidth to endure her passive-aggressive comments, but there wasn't another way out at this point without drawing attention.

Audrey felt a tap on her shoulder, and she reluctantly turned around to face the inevitable. "Tia, hi. I didn't expect to see you here."

Tia crossed her arms. "Because I'm not as famous as you?"

"No." Audrey paused. She wasn't sure where that came from. She'd never made Tia feel like that. "Because you hate industry parties."

Tia shrugged with her left shoulder, seeming to try to ignore the truth of that statement. "It was hard going to them with you. I don't have anything against them for myself."

Audrey wanted this conversation to be over. She didn't need to hear for the millionth time how Tia felt about their careers in comparison.

"Is there something I can do for you, Tia?" She gave her best fake smile.

"I'm going to be on the set of your movie tomorrow, and I didn't want it to be awkward."

"It won't be. We don't have any scenes together. We don't even have to talk," Audrey said. She still wasn't sure of the point of the conversation. Tia knew she was a professional. She gave herself credit for not pointing out that Tia's part only consisted of four lines in two scenes. She was a secondary, and forgettable, character.

Tia looked unsure of herself, which wasn't like her. "Can I get you a drink?"

Audrey looked at the glass in her hand and then back at Tia. "I already have one."

Tia scrunched her nose. "There's something different about you."

Audrey sighed. "I'm exactly who I've always been. But you've never really known me, have you?" She hadn't considered it until it came out of her mouth, but it was true, and it felt good to acknowledge it.

"I don't recognize this version of you. Bitter isn't a good look."

Audrey almost spit out her drink. "I'm not bitter, Tia. I'm just not here to stroke your ego anymore. You're used to me bending to your every need and whim. You'll need to look somewhere else if you want that. I'm not interested."

"Is there someone new?" Tia didn't seem deterred.

"Yes, there is. Me. I'm watching out for myself now. That's what's new."

Audrey turned to leave, but Tia grabbed her arm. "I like the new you. It's hot."

How many times had those words stopped Audrey in her tracks? How many times did she give in during an argument because Tia had ended it with sex? How many times had Audrey put herself last to put Tia first?

Tia smiled. "What are you thinking?"

Audrey pulled her arm away. "That I can't believe I ever fell for any of that. You never cared about what I thought or what I wanted. You never considered me. You shut down every thought or feeling I ever had. You used sex to put a Band-Aid on everything, and I let you." She handed Tia her empty glass. "Good night, Tia. Good luck tomorrow, and with finding someone else to put up with your shit from now on."

Kylie caught up with her after a few steps. "Wow! Where did that come from?"

Audrey thought back to the conversation she'd had with Harlow while pushed up against her car. "Inspiration from a friend."

Kylie bumped her. "I like it."

"Me too." Audrey looked down at her dress. She was uncomfortable, and her heels were killing her. "Let's get out of here."

Kylie smiled so brightly her eyes sparkled. "I love that idea."

❖

Harlow looked over to see Shauna lose her footing and hit the ground. "Are you okay?"

Shauna rubbed her ankle. "I think I'm just tired."

The choreographer stopped the music. "We need to do it again."

Everyone was exhausted. The dancers looked defeated, and it was almost one in the morning. The tour was going to be a long one, and they needed practice. But Harlow had been doing this long enough to know that they were past the point of learning anything.

"I think we should call it a night," she said when she walked over to him.

"Your tour starts in two weeks, and there are five weeks' worth of work to do."

"We aren't getting anywhere else tonight. We'll be back first thing in the morning."

He threw his hands up in defeat. "Don't say I didn't warn you when it all falls apart on stage."

"Noted."

He turned and faced the room. "Be back here at seven."

Some of the dancers had moved Shauna over to a bench by the time Harlow got to her. "You okay?"

"I'll be fine." She winced when she tried to move her ankle in a circle.

Harlow handed her a bottle of water and sat down next to her. "You remind me of me at your age."

Shauna gulped down the water. "You'd already had three albums out at my age," she said breathlessly.

Harlow laughed. "I was also relentlessly determined and underestimated."

Shauna blushed and put her head down. "Thank you for saying that. Sometimes it all feels so daunting, and then it's thrilling, and then something happens, and it feels daunting all over again."

Harlow patted her on the back and stood. "Can you make it to your car?"

Shauna tried to stand and then fell back onto the bench. "I'm not sure."

Harlow helped her up and put her arm around her waist. "Do you live close enough to get ice on it soon?"

Shauna nodded. "I'm only about ten minutes from here."

Harlow led her out of the studio and down toward the parking lot. She opened the driver's door and helped her into her seat. Fortunately, the ankle she injured was her left and wouldn't hinder her from driving.

Harlow shut the door and leaned her forearms in the open window. "Text me when you get home, so I don't have to worry about you."

Shauna pulled her seat belt over her shoulder and buckled it. "You aren't what I thought you'd be."

"What did you think I'd be?"

Shauna shrugged and smiled, her face blushing. "More of a diva, I guess."

"Sorry to disappoint you."

Shauna was staring at her intently. "It was definitely a pleasant surprise. I've heard so many things about you, and I've never been sure which are true." She leaned forward and kissed her.

Harlow pulled back and stared, partly in shock and partly confused. "Shauna, I'm sorry, but I don't feel like that about you."

Shauna turned an even darker shade of red and put the keys in the ignition. "I don't know what came over me. I'm so sorry. I'd heard that you were—"

Harlow put her hand over Shauna's on the steering wheel. "It's okay. Please don't be embarrassed."

Shauna stared at Harlow's hand. "Am I just not your type?"

Harlow heard the clicks of the cameras before she saw anyone. Then came the incessant shouting of questions.

"Harlow, are you dating Shauna?"

"Harlow, is that your girlfriend?"

She squeezed Shauna's hand. "Get out of here. You don't need this."

Shauna looked mortified. "I'm so sorry." She started her car and drove away.

Harlow walked to her car, ignoring the questions from the paparazzi who followed closely behind. She was accustomed to this kind of scrutiny and used to avoiding the questions she didn't want to answer, but Shauna wasn't. She didn't want her budding career eclipsed by an alleged relationship with her. She needed to get away.

She got in her car and called Casper, but there was no answer. She tried several more times with the same result. *Fuck.* She pulled out of the parking lot and onto the street. Luckily, no one followed her. But she knew within a matter of minutes, there would be people waiting outside the gate to her house. She wasn't sure what to do, so she did the only thing that felt right. She headed to Audrey's.

CHAPTER ELEVEN

Audrey was curled up on her couch with Kylie, trying to find something to watch on Netflix. The next three days would consist of all-night shooting, and she was trying to adjust her internal clock accordingly.

"Please don't make me watch another serial killer documentary. I'm begging you." Kylie flung her head back for dramatic effect.

"I'm pretty sure I could get away with murder now." Audrey shook her finger at Kylie. "We'll have to warn your next boyfriend."

"I'll mention it on the first date." Kylie stuffed her mouth with a handful of popcorn. "Thanks again for letting me stay here. I didn't want to stay in the apartment after Luke and I officially ended things. I want a fresh start."

"You're welcome to stay for as long as you need. It's nice having someone here with me." Audrey's phone buzzed, and she practically flew out of her chair. "My security cameras just turned on. Someone is here." She squinted at her phone screen. "Okay, not just someone. Harlow."

"It's two in the morning. Did you have a booty call arranged and not tell me?"

Audrey looked down at her flannel cat pajamas. "Yeah, you caught me. That's why I put on my lingerie." She groaned. "I look ridiculous."

Kylie munched on her popcorn. "It's interesting that you're more worried about how you look than you are alarmed as to why she's here at this hour."

Audrey walked to the door, partially to meet Harlow and partly so she didn't have to comment on Kylie's observation. She opened it before Harlow had a chance to knock. She looked upset.

"I'm sorry. Jesus, I didn't realize how late it was. It's just that I—can I come in?"

Audrey stepped aside. "Of course. Is everything okay?"

Harlow was wearing spandex pants and a sports bra, with no jacket. Either something was really wrong, or she had a minimal wardrobe. Audrey figured it was the former.

Harlow stepped into the living room. "I'm ruining your evening." She waved to Kylie. "I didn't know what else to do or where to go."

Audrey sat her down on the couch. "Just start from the beginning."

Audrey listened as Harlow relived her evening. She was surprised by the fierce jolt of jealousy that shot through her at the mention of Shauna kissing her. She did her best to stay focused and not reveal her discomfort. Harlow was clearly upset, and she wanted to do whatever she could to help.

Kylie grabbed her laptop from the coffee table. "Let me shake some branches and see what falls loose."

Audrey rubbed Harlow's leg. "Are you upset they saw you kissing someone, or is it something else?"

Harlow ran her hands over her face. "I've done my best to keep my private life out of the public eye simply because that's who I am, but it's not that. Shauna is so new to this world. She's right on the brink of making a name for herself. Not to mention, she's about to go on a year-long tour with me. If this becomes the story, it will never be about her talent. They'll say she slept her way to the top, or whatever contrarian bullshit they decide to spin. She'll have to beat back those stories along with her budding career. Combine that with my reputation, and it won't be good for her."

Audrey chose her next words carefully, unsure where things stood. It wasn't like they were exclusive in any way. Hell, they weren't *anything*, yet. "Well, if you two really care about each other, maybe it's a challenge she's willing to take on."

Harlow looked dumbfounded. "I don't care about Shauna. I mean, I care about her, but not like that. I wanted to help her. I wanted her to get her name out there. I don't want to *date* her. Christ, she's *way* too young for me."

"I'm sorry," Audrey said. "I guess my feelings are a little all over the place right now, which isn't fair. This isn't about me at all. I shouldn't have said anything."

Harlow took her hand and kissed it. "What have I told you about apologizing for your feelings?" She smiled.

Audrey watched Harlow's facial expression to confirm her sincerity. Harlow was so different. She continuously proved that she wanted the best for the people in her life, which was a rare quality to come by.

Kylie closed her laptop and picked up her phone. "Okay, who normally handles these things for you?"

"Casper."

Kylie nodded. "I have the numbers of all the media that was there tonight. Do you want to try to get a hold of him, or do you want me to squash this story?"

Harlow looked down at her phone. "He still hasn't called."

"So, squash it? It may be expensive," Kylie said in her business tone.

Harlow nodded. "Thanks, Kylie. I'd really appreciate it."

Kylie stood and walked out of the room to make the calls.

Harlow nodded in her direction. "She's awfully handy."

"She's the best."

Harlow pushed a strand of hair out of Audrey's eyes. It felt so natural, like something she'd done a million times before. Audrey's heart was hammering so hard she could feel it in her head. With the simplest of touches, Harlow could undo her. She could so easily fall into those ocean blue eyes. She could so easily lose herself in Harlow's smile. She was trying to remember all the reasons she needed to take things slow. Harlow wasn't exactly known for being emotionally available. She didn't have a track record in longevity of any kind. And yet, she didn't give off any alarming signals to keep her distance. Harlow seemed to welcome their connection.

"Do you like serial killers?" Audrey blurted out without thinking.

Harlow smiled and leaned back against the couch. She kicked off her shoes and tucked her legs under her. "I do." She put her arm around Audrey's shoulder and pulled her close.

Audrey allowed herself to take in this breath of contentment. All the trepidation and questions were products of her imagination.

She wanted to just exist with Harlow at this moment. She could hear Harlow's heart pounding against her chest. The noise was strong and sure. It was Audrey's new favorite sound.

❖

Harlow hadn't been sure what to expect when she impulsively drove to Audrey's. She just knew she needed to be with her. Audrey understood the pressures of the public and the effect a single photograph could elicit. As she sat in the dark, on her couch, with Audrey curled up against her side, she knew she'd made the right choice. She found peace whenever she was with Audrey. She wasn't sure how she'd screw it up, but she knew she would.

Kylie came back into the room and was smiling triumphantly. "I got all the pictures. They were crap anyway. I mean, you can tell it's you two, but you can't tell for sure that you're kissing. It would definitely raise some eyebrows, but it's nothing definitive. They're going to cost you fifteen thousand, though. Unfortunately, there were three photographers."

"Thank you for taking care of that for me."

She would've paid double that amount to avoid the shit storm something like this would bring on not only herself, but on Shauna and the tour.

Kylie waved her off. "No problem at all."

Audrey pushed herself off the couch. "I'm going to make more popcorn."

Kylie watched Audrey retreat into the kitchen and then turned her attention back to Harlow. She looked like she wanted to say something.

"Was there another issue?"

Kylie chewed on her thumb and peered into the kitchen. "The whole good-girl thing isn't an act. She's exactly who she seems to be. She trusts you. Please try to remember that." There was no malice in her voice. The words were clearly just a statement, not an accusation.

"She's lucky to have a friend like you." Harlow hoped she picked up on her sincerity.

Neither Harlow nor Audrey had discussed what their evolving relationship and feelings would mean. Harlow hadn't cared about anyone enough to give it careful introspection. She'd always assumed she'd be alone, except for Casper. Her baggage was heavy and could fill a closet. She never wanted to burden anyone else with it. Hell, she didn't *want* to burden Audrey with it, but she was drawn to her. The normal excuses she made didn't hold up next to Audrey, and she wasn't sure what that meant.

"We watch out for each other. We always have." Kylie smiled. "And we could both get away with murder if needed."

"What?"

"You heard me." Kylie winked.

Audrey flopped back down on the couch with the biggest bowl of popcorn Harlow had ever seen. "What did I miss?"

Kylie stretched. "Nothing. I'm going to bed." She walked up the stairs. "Stay out of trouble, you two."

Audrey held out the bowl to Harlow. "You're not leaving me too, right?" Her question held a sad undertone that was unmistakable.

Harlow grabbed a few pieces of popcorn. "I'm not going anywhere."

"Good," Audrey said as she snuggled back into her side.

Harlow watched the documentary but couldn't pay attention. The way Audrey felt next to her was distracting. She tried to pinpoint another time where she'd felt so content just existing in a room with another person. There wasn't one. Of all the places she'd been, all the people she'd met, everything she'd seen, nothing had ever felt so right.

Contentment gave way to drowsiness. A combination of extinguished adrenaline, long hours, and happiness lulled her to sleep.

CHAPTER TWELVE

A few hours later, the sun coming in through the large front window roused her. Audrey was draped across her lap, and the half-eaten bowl of popcorn sat at her feet. She carefully maneuvered out from under her and kissed the top of her head. She checked her phone, and there were four missed calls from Casper. *Dick.* Where had he been when she'd needed him?

She quietly went into the kitchen to leave a note for Audrey. *When did you become so romantic?* She shook her head at her absurdness. Spending the whole night with a woman wasn't anything she ever did, much less leaving her a handwritten note. Especially when they hadn't even had sex. She jotted down a few words and ducked out the front door without making a sound. She would've liked to have stayed and had breakfast, but she was already going to be fifteen minutes late for rehearsal.

She wasn't surprised to see Casper leaning against his car when she pulled in. She grabbed the gym bag from her back seat and groaned at the fact that she hadn't managed to shower. She was tired and had a long day ahead of her. The last thing she wanted to do was fight with her brother.

"Hey, I got your messages." He followed closely behind her to the studio. "I tried calling."

"I took care of it." She opened the door and didn't bother holding it for him.

"You did? How?" He seemed undeterred by her rudeness.

"Audrey's friend, Kylie."

"I'm sorry, Harlow. I didn't get reception where I was. It's not like I knew you'd be caught up in another scandal."

She turned on him. "It wasn't a scandal. Nothing happened between Shauna and me. It was an opportunistic shot."

He held his hands up defensively. "Okay, I'm sorry."

She changed her shoes and started to stretch. "Where were you, anyway?"

"I was with some friends."

"What friends?"

"Just some of the guys," he said and shoved his hands in his pockets.

Harlow didn't want to fight. He was entitled to a life outside of taking care of her, although it was weird he wasn't sharing any details. They hardly ever kept anything from one another, and if they did, it wasn't for long. She was being unreasonable because her feelings were hurt. She rolled her shoulders and tried to get her emotions under control.

"If she's not here, can you drive over to Shauna's and check on her? She got hurt last night before everything happened. I'm sure she's a little freaked out, and I doubt she'll be here today."

He clapped his hands together. "You got it. I'll bring you iced coffee when I come back."

"Make it a triple," she yelled after him.

The music started, and she checked her phone, smiling when she saw a text from Audrey. *Thanks for the sleepover. See you soon. Xoxoxoxo*

She smiled and felt her stomach tighten. It was still hard to believe she was going to be spending four entire days with Audrey Knox. She just needed to get through the next seventy-eight hours. *Talk about incentive.*

She popped up and jogged to the center of the mirrored room. "All right! Let's do this."

Audrey took the bottle of water her agent offered her. It had already been a long day of shooting, and the night was just beginning. Her legs ached from her partial stunt work. She knew the shots would be worth it, but her body would be screaming for the next several days.

"Thanks, Jane." She walked toward wardrobe, needing to change for the next scene. "What's up? You normally just call."

Jane slid her phone into her pocket. She only put it away if she had something important to say. "People's Choice Awards."

"Yes, I know what they are." Audrey pulled on the leather jacket that was handed to her.

"Who are you taking? And please wow me with your answer."

"My mom."

Jane's mouth dropped open, and her head fell back. "No. Do better."

Audrey checked herself in the mirror. "I'm sorry to disappoint you, but that's who I'm taking."

Jane grabbed her shoulders. "You've been single forever. You need to be seen with someone."

"I've been single for six months. That's hardly a reason to start worrying about my spinster status." Audrey started walking back toward the set.

"You know what, I'll set you up with someone great."

"Don't. Seriously. I'm taking my mom. She's so excited." Audrey finished the water and handed Jane the empty bottle.

"If you're taking your mom to this one, you have to take a date to the American Music Awards. A real date. Not your mom—and don't you dare say you're taking your dad."

"What's wrong with my dad?"

Jane ignored her. "You have a few days off coming up, right? What are your plans? Can you manage some press junkets?"

Audrey didn't want to tell Jane where she was going. She wanted to keep whatever was happening between her and Harlow to herself until she could figure out what it was. But that wasn't how this town worked. Her agent would need to know in case someone saw them. Blind-siding your agent was never a good idea.

"I'm going to Monterey."

Jane waved her hand in a rolling motion. "For what? With who?"

She sighed and closed her eyes. So be it. "For a break. And I'm going with Harlow Thorne."

Jane's eyes became large, and a huge smile split her face. "Are you now?" She clapped her hands together. "This is excellent news.

She has such a bad girl thing going for her." She put her hand on her chin. "I'd heard she was into women."

"We're friends. Don't make this into something it's not." Audrey crossed her arms, feeling defensive. "And she's not a bad girl. She's kind and funny and smart."

Jane laughed. "And gorgeous, successful, and driven. I like this pairing." She shook her finger at her.

Audrey made direct eye contact. She wanted to make sure she really heard her. "Harlow and I are *friends*. We've never slept together, we've never kissed, we're friends."

Jane grabbed her bag from the table. "Let's check in when you get back and see if that's still true."

Audrey grabbed her arm. "Do not make this a thing. Please."

"Audrey, I'd never do anything that wasn't good for your career. I like teasing you, but I wouldn't do anything to hurt you." She kissed her cheek. "Give me a call if there's anything I need to know."

Four scenes, forty-seven takes, and one hot shower later, Audrey was sitting at her dining room table. Her mother was watching her twirl the stem of a wine glass between her fingers. Audrey knew she wanted to ask her what she was thinking, but that wasn't her style. She'd always been grateful to her mom for giving her the space she needed.

"Are you hungry?" Her mom walked over to the fridge and pulled the doors open. "I could make us some salad and pasta. How does that sound?"

"I'll just have a salad." Audrey sipped her wine.

Her mom lobbed a head of lettuce into the sink. "Nope. That's your second glass of wine. You'll have pasta too."

Audrey didn't protest. She loved the way her mom still looked after her. She'd always appreciated that about their relationship. She knew of dozens of parental relationships that had taken a much different turn after their children headed for fame and success. But not Kathy Knox. Her mother never stopped playing that critical role in her life, and she was thankful. Audrey wouldn't have stayed on track without that kind of stability.

"Mom?"

"Yes, honey?" Her mother put the pot on the stove.

"Should I go to Monterey with Harlow?"

Her mom came and sat down beside her. She put a hand on her leg and squeezed her knee. "I think I could answer your question better if I knew why you *wouldn't* want to go with her."

Audrey continued to twirl the stem between her fingers. "I might be getting in over my head. I'm not sure I'm ready for a Harlow Thorne."

Her mom smiled and sighed. "Oh, honey, none of us are ever ready for a Harlow Thorne." She rubbed Audrey's leg. "Would you regret not going?"

Audrey nodded because she didn't trust her voice.

"Then what's the real issue?"

"Because I think if this one blows up in my face, it will hurt more than the others." She closed her eyes so she didn't have to look at the expression on her mom's face. She just wanted to say it. "I'm afraid I'll be more invested than she is. I already feel this comfort around her that I've never felt before, and I'm worried it will end up being one-sided. I'm scared that I'll be another footnote on her long list of conquests."

"I can see why that would be scary." Her mom grabbed her hands. "But, honey, it sounds like you're making assumptions about her without giving her the chance to be anything else. I'd hate to think someone would do the same to you."

Audrey nodded. "So, go?"

Her mom kissed her cheek. "You wouldn't be where you are without taking a leap. Sometimes to get the biggest rewards, you need to take the biggest risks."

Her mom was right. Harlow's reputation was a product of her past. She was getting to know the person she was, and so far, she liked everything she saw. Making decisions based on what could go wrong wasn't how she lived her life, and she wasn't going to start now.

Chapter Thirteen

Audrey watched as Harlow jogged up to her front door. She looked incredible in her jeans, tank top, and leather jacket. Audrey's throat was dry, and her heart was hammering like it always did when Harlow was near. She pulled the door open just as Harlow raised her hand to knock.

"Hi."

Harlow slid her hands into her back pockets and smiled. "Hi." She leaned down and grabbed Audrey's bag from the doorway. "Is this all you're bringing?"

Audrey was suddenly very nervous. "Do you think I under packed?"

"No. I just wanted to make sure there wasn't another one hiding behind you." Harlow smiled, and Audrey felt more at ease.

Audrey was surprised by the classic car in the driveway. It was dazzling, with flawless sleek lines, a gorgeous black shine, and perfect chrome fenders. The door squeaked when she opened it, and Audrey loved it. It was an ideal fit for Harlow's personality. Slick, cool, and classy.

"This car is incredible," Audrey said when Harlow got into the driver's seat.

Harlow turned the key, and the engine growled to life. "It's a 1968 Mustang GT California Special. There were only four thousand one hundred and eighteen ever produced. My father talked about this car with so much reverence when I was growing up. It was all he ever really wanted to own. So, when I signed with my first label, it was the first thing I bought."

"That's really sweet."

Harlow put the car in gear and started driving. "I didn't buy it for nostalgia. I bought it because he never could. It was my way of saying 'fuck you.'"

That was a tidbit of information Audrey hadn't heard before, and she filed it away. "Well, I love it. You should drive it all the time."

"I only ever drive it to Monterey. So, welcome to one of my favorite traditions, and thank you for agreeing to come."

"I wouldn't have missed it," Audrey said before her brain had a chance to catch up with the feeling in her chest.

Being near Harlow felt like the sun was shining just for her. There was no other way to describe it. Her magnetism wasn't just filler for magazine articles. Audrey was sure she'd never experienced anything like it. She knew more famous people than non-famous, and still, none of them had anything on Harlow. The energy she exuded was like a drug. *Relax. It's been ten minutes.*

"You ever drive up PCH?"

Audrey slid her sunglasses on and leaned back in the seat. "Nope, I've always just flown up north, but I have a feeling that's about to change."

Harlow slipped off her jacket and tossed it in the back seat. "It's one of the best parts of the trip. You'll love it."

"I have no doubt," Audrey said and knew it was the absolute truth.

Audrey had a terrible voice—like, screeching cats bad. Harlow was sure she'd never heard anyone with worse pitch, and it was adorable. Audrey butchered song after song on the radio, but she did it with such confidence she couldn't help but appreciate it.

They were four hours into their seven-hour drive, and Harlow couldn't believe how much fun she was having. Audrey was funny, smart, and passionate. Every story she told was punctuated with elaborate hand gestures, dramatic facial expressions, and perfect comedic timing. They talked about what it was like for Audrey to become an overnight success in the film industry. They talked about how she'd graduated early from high school, and how she never got the chance to go to prom—although they both agreed the Academy Awards were much better. She talked about her and Kylie as teenagers and their first crushes. Harlow could listen to her talk for hours, and she planned on doing just that.

They pulled into a gas station, and Harlow pulled two baseball hats from the back seat of the car. She pulled one down low over her eyes and handed the other to Audrey before she jumped out to pump the gas.

Audrey put the hat on and leaned over the driver's seat and through the open window. "I'm going to use the bathroom. Do you want anything?"

Harlow leaned toward the window. "The incredible Audrey Knox is going to use a gas station bathroom?"

Audrey smacked her hand. "I'm also getting Doritos. You writing a tell-all?"

"Your Dorito secret is safe with me." She winked at her.

Harlow watched Audrey hurry inside. She smiled to herself when she considered what the next few days could bring. Usually, she'd be thinking about how to get Audrey into bed. Harlow's relationships, or lack thereof, were based on mutual physical satisfaction. That wasn't the case with Audrey, though. Harlow was excited to get to know her better, beyond the bedroom. It was enough just to be in her presence. Though, she wouldn't kick Audrey out of bed, either.

The man on the pump opposite her kept peeking around the machine. He looked like he recognized her but couldn't quite place her yet. And just like that, his eyes changed. He knew exactly who she was.

He put the pump back in its cradle. "Hey, are you Harlow Thorne?"

Harlow had already surveyed the area, and there was no one else at the pumps. The likelihood of this turning into a spectacle was low.

She stuck her hand out. "Nice to meet you."

He fumbled with the phone he was trying to pull from his pocket. "Can I take a picture with you? My friends will never believe I met you."

She waved him over. "Sure."

He wrapped his hand around her waist and pulled her unnecessarily close. "You're even more beautiful in person. I bet you hear that all the time."

She smiled and looked at the camera. "It was nice meeting you."

"Will you sign this?" He pulled a receipt from his pocket. "It's all I have, sorry." He dove into his car and tore apart his glovebox, she assumed to find a pen.

She signed the piece of paper and handed it back to him just as Audrey was walking toward the car. "Drive safe."

"Holy shit, you're Audrey Knox." He pointed at her.

Audrey waved at him like he was a friend she hadn't seen in years. "Hi there."

He didn't speak. He simply pointed to his phone and back to Audrey.

"Of course." She stood next to him and smiled for the picture.

"Where you two headed?" He messed with the hat on his head.

"San Francisco," Audrey said without missing a beat as she opened the car door. "Have a nice day."

All he could do was stare as they drove away. Harlow watched in her rearview to make sure he didn't follow them. When he finally disappeared, she relaxed into her seat.

"San Francisco?"

Audrey shrugged. "I'm nice—not stupid." She pulled open the bag. "Dorito?"

Harlow took a chip. "I don't think I've ever known anyone like you. It's nice to be with someone who knows how the game works, you know? Someone who isn't into you as a way up the ladder or whatever."

Harlow slipped her hand into Audrey's. It was the first time since they started the trip that she had dared to touch her. She didn't want Audrey thinking this whole thing was a ploy to sleep with her. She held her hand now because she was compelled to touch her. She wanted the emotional connection she had with Audrey to be proven with touch. She wanted Audrey to feel it too. Her decision was affirmed when she glanced over, and Audrey was smiling at their clasped fingers.

CHAPTER FOURTEEN

Audrey felt like one of those cats with suction cups on their paws when they pulled onto 17 Mile Drive. The homes were magnificent. Some were perched against the cliffs, while others were set slightly back along the hillside. All were designed to take in the breathtaking views this part of the Pacific Ocean had to offer. Cypress trees dotted the cliff edges, and she was made speechless by the grandiose beauty surrounding her.

They pulled onto a cobblestone driveway, and it only took a few seconds for the house to come into full view. Slim flagstone, wood, and sleek metal finishes made up the exterior design. The windows were so large, they started on the first floor and stretched up to the second. The lights were already on, allowing her to see inside before exiting the car.

"I had my security team turn everything on before we arrived. I like them to do a sweep of the house before I get here."

Audrey was surprised that Harlow looked slightly embarrassed at her statement. "I think that's smart. I had a stalker once. It was terrifying. That's when I moved to a house with a gate. My mother thinks I should use security full-time, but I'm just not there yet."

Harlow pulled a small device from the glovebox and punched a few buttons, opening the garage door. "I have full security on tour because I go so many places I'm not familiar with and I like them to check this house before I get here. I don't get to come as often as I like, and I'm always a little worried about what will be waiting for me, and that includes paparazzi. But once it's clear, I like to be on my own without all the people around."

Audrey got out of the car and grabbed her bag from the trunk. She followed Harlow into the house, more nervous now that they had reached their destination. She was going to spend three nights here alone with Harlow, and although she was well aware of that when she'd agreed to come—actually being there was a whole different thing.

It made her feel slightly better to see Harlow looking more nervous than she'd ever been in her presence. She rubbed the back of her neck and stood in the kitchen. She looked utterly unsure about what she should do next, and it was both adorable and sexy.

"Do you want anything to drink?" Harlow pointed to the fridge. "It should be fully stocked."

"Sure. Whatever you have is fine." She pointed to the stairs. "Do you mind if I go freshen up a bit?"

Harlow pulled glasses down from the cabinet. "Sure. Feel free to take whatever room you'd like." She didn't make eye contact as she continued to move around the kitchen.

Audrey was keenly aware that Harlow hadn't instructed her to put her things in the master bedroom. That fact put her slightly more at ease. It took some of the pressure off what this trip could possibly mean. Granted, Audrey hadn't ruled out taking their relationship to the next level. In fact, she was hoping that was the direction it was heading. But this small gesture assured her that Harlow wasn't making any assumptions.

The rooms were gorgeous. Each had tasteful furniture, decorated with light, earthy colors. Every room had expansive windows that faced the ocean. There was no bad choice. She chose the one next to the master bedroom. It had a sliding glass door that led out onto a large deck and a bathroom with a bathtub.

Audrey put her clothes in drawers. She hated living out of a bag, and this small task helped make her feel more relaxed. She went into the bathroom and splashed water on her face. Harlow had her all out of sorts. She was exceptionally comfortable around her but still superbly nervous. It was like all of her senses were on high alert. *She's just a woman. You like being around her. Just let whatever is going to happen, happen.*

Audrey walked out onto the deck and breathed in the cool Pacific air. The view was spectacular. The air smelled like salt and cypress.

She could understand why Harlow came here to relax before her tours. It was meditative.

"I decided to buy this house after standing on this deck," Harlow said from behind her. She handed her a glass of wine. "It was the most peaceful place I'd ever seen."

Audrey took the glass. "I agree. It's incredible." She sipped her wine. "How long have you owned it?"

Harlow motioned to the couch. "I was twenty-three. So, six years. Sometimes I come up here for months at a time when I'm not recording or on tour."

"Do you bring Casper with you?" Audrey crossed her legs and angled herself so she could look at Harlow. She loved looking at Harlow.

Harlow sipped her whiskey. "It's hard to get Casper away from the city, but he comes up and visits if he's gone too long without seeing me."

"Will you tell me about your family?" It felt like a wall between them, and she hated not being able to know something so personal, even if she had no right to feel that way.

Harlow's face changed, showing her discomfort. "My father drank too much. He had a mean tongue and an even meaner backhand." She took a deep breath. "After he drank himself to death, my mom went off the deep end. She was never really the same. I've never been sure if it was because she loved him or because she didn't know what to do with her freedom."

Audrey wanted to touch her, but Harlow seemed like a frightened animal. One wrong move could send her running, and that was the last thing she wanted. "That must have been really hard on you and Casper."

Harlow swirled her whiskey, seeming transfixed by the amber liquid. "Casper and I took off when we were seventeen. I packed our bags, and we hopped on a bus to Los Angeles in the middle of the night, and we never looked back. We both worked odd jobs, lived in motels, did whatever we had to do to get by. We did that for about a year. That's when Dominic found me singing down on the corner of Sunset and Vine." She took a long swallow from her glass. "I don't know what we would've done without him. He taught Casper how to be a real music producer, and he recorded my first three songs to help get my name out there."

"That's why you're so determined to help Shauna."

Harlow shrugged. "She's also very talented, but yes, that's one of the reasons."

The sun was starting to set, and the shimmer from the ocean cast Harlow in a beautiful golden glow. Audrey reached up and ran her finger down Harlow's cheek. "I'm so sorry you had to endure all of that."

"I'm here now, so I got the last laugh." Harlow smiled, but not with her eyes. "It's their loss."

Audrey could see the unease clouding Harlow's features. The last thing she wanted to do was force her into a conversation she didn't want to have. She decided to forge ahead into safer territory.

"So, whose idea was it to give you this bad girl reputation? Casper or Dominic?" Audrey raised an eyebrow.

"Who said I'm a bad girl?" Harlow raised a corner of her mouth in a sexy grin.

"Everyone."

Harlow smiled knowingly. "It was never my intention to be labeled as anything. I spend time with the people I want, when I want, and then some of those people make up stories that suit their narrative. Just because I go out with a woman a few times doesn't mean I've really broken their heart, no matter what they say. They sell these stories with the spin they want because I don't fill in the blanks for them."

"But you've never filled in the blanks about anyone."

"That's true," Harlow said. "Once you start giving any type of answer, they expect answers to everything. Plus, I've never dated anyone important enough to deal with the scrutiny."

Audrey twirled the ends of Harlow's hair, loving how soft it felt against her fingertips. "I see the way the paparazzi wait for you everywhere. You can't even get coffee without being photographed. I don't understand how you've managed to keep so much private."

Harlow shrugged. "If you don't answer questions, they don't have anything to work with. And the only person I'm ever really with is Casper. If I'm out with anyone else, I'm not much on public displays of affection, so there's nothing definitive." She stood and walked to the door. "Dinner should be here soon. I'm starving."

Audrey followed her. "That still doesn't answer my question. How do you manage to keep people from selling stories about you? I understand that some wouldn't want to, but there have been a few out there." She grinned sheepishly. "Not that I read the pap rags, of course."

"I spend a lot of time at the Rainbow. Most people there are in the closet or are just super private like I am. They have a vested interest in not saying anything. I like it that way. It takes a lot of the complications out of it."

The Rainbow. The most exclusive gay club in all of Hollywood. Audrey had never been there, but she was always fascinated by it. She knew lots of closeted influential people spent time there, which was one reason she never went. She couldn't handle the thought of meeting someone and being forced back into the closet to make a relationship work. It was clear Harlow felt the opposite. What did that mean for what was growing between them?

Harlow loved throwing Audrey off her game, and she knew she'd done it just by the look on Audrey's face. Audrey's life was so structured and planned; it was good for her to be thrown a curveball every now and then.

"I've heard they have a strict paparazzi policy, but I've seen people photographed near the building. Never you, though. Why is that?" Audrey walked into the kitchen and poured another glass of wine.

Harlow got the pizza and salads she had delivered from the front porch. She always used a fake name when ordering, and this time she used Sally McSallerson. She was supremely pleased by her humor.

She put the pizza on the counter and pulled plates down from the cabinet. Audrey was staring at her intently, obviously waiting for her to answer.

Harlow handed her a plate and fork. "I wear a disguise to get in. Once you're in, you don't need one."

Audrey put salad on her plate. "What kind of disguise?"

Harlow shrugged. "Like a wig."

"A wig?"

Harlow took a bite of her pizza. "Yes, a wig. Why is that so hard to believe?"

"Because I've seen you in wigs. I can't believe you're fooling anyone."

"Maybe you see me more clearly than most people." Harlow hadn't meant to sound quite so deep, but there was no other way to phrase it. She felt seen when Audrey looked at her—maybe more so than she ever had before.

Audrey blushed. "Your house is gorgeous. When do I get the full tour?"

"Right after dinner."

Dinner conversation was easy. Things always felt easy with Audrey, and Harlow was growing to really appreciate that about her. Audrey seemed to wear her heart on her sleeve, and Harlow didn't understand how she'd managed to hang on to that through all her success. Audrey could effortlessly switch between being the girl-next-door to Audrey Knox—world-famous actress. There were layers to her, and the more Harlow peeled back, the more fascinated she became.

Harlow ended the tour of the house in the backyard by the pool. "Would you like to go swimming?"

Audrey smiled and cocked her head. "In our swimsuits this time?"

"If you insist," Harlow said. She loved making Audrey blush, and her comment had the desired effect.

Audrey tried to hide her smile. "Okay. I'll be right down. I'll grab more wine and whiskey on my way out."

Harlow changed into her swimsuit and headed back downstairs. She was nervous, more nervous than she thought she'd be at the idea of swimming with Audrey again. But that shouldn't have surprised her. Everything about Audrey made her feel differently than she was used to feeling. It was invigorating and terrifying. She still wasn't sure if they were friends or if this was heading in a different direction. No. That wasn't true. She knew where she wanted this to head. She knew she wanted more. She wanted Audrey. She just wasn't sure how to make that happen. Getting a woman into bed was one thing—getting a woman into something more substantial was entirely different. It wasn't a situation she'd ever encountered before. She didn't want

Audrey to be like the others, but she wasn't sure she was built for anything serious. Taking things to a deeper level wasn't in her muscle memory, and there was good reason for that.

Harlow was seriously considering googling the question as she opened the sliding glass door. Audrey was there waiting in her black bikini, a drink in each hand. Her body was solid proof of the hours she spent in the gym getting ready for her most recent action movie. Harlow felt a slight buzzing in her head. *Jesus.*

Harlow took the glass Audrey offered. "Thank you."

Audrey cleared her throat and sipped her wine. "It's the least I can do. You did cook dinner." She smirked and raised an eyebrow.

Harlow laughed and was thankful for the reprieve of humor with Audrey being near her with so little clothing. Audrey walked into the pool and moved over to the end to see the ocean.

Harlow turned on her outdoor sound system and followed her. "This is my favorite spot in the pool."

"I see why. You can stare at the ocean without having to be in the saltwater or worried about sharks or jellyfish or tar."

"Exactly."

Audrey turned her head to listen to the music. "We aren't listening to your new album?"

"Do you think I listen to my own music?" She laughed.

Audrey shrugged. "It's a great album. I think it's my favorite." She put her forearms on the edge of the infinity pool and looked out. "I'd love to listen to you play tomorrow. If you don't mind."

"I can't think of anything I wouldn't give you." Harlow stopped breathing momentarily. She hadn't meant to say that. As true as it might be, she hadn't wanted to reveal that just yet. Or ever. Probably ever.

Audrey stared at her. Harlow watched the pulse in her neck, rapidly beating against her skin. She desperately wanted to put her mouth on it. Audrey reached for her, placing her hand on her upper thigh. She tried not to shudder at the way her fingertips moved up to her waist. Audrey's hand moved so excruciatingly slow along her skin, she thought she might start to sweat from the need building like a tornado inside her. But Harlow didn't want to rush her. She wanted Audrey to go at her own pace, whatever that meant. Audrey was watching her intently, gauging Harlow's reaction to her touch.

Audrey took a small step forward, and Harlow could feel her breath against her cheek. "I always feel a little desperate around you."

Harlow weakened at her words and the flush through her body was instant. "Sometimes, when we're near each other, my hands shake from holding back."

Audrey slid her hands up Harlow's arms and around her neck. "Why do you hold back?"

Harlow was struggling to string words together to make a sentence. "I'm not sure I'm what you want."

"Harlow." Audrey dipped her head, and Harlow felt the softness of her lips, barely touching hers. "Kiss me."

Harlow's response was instinctive. She moved against Audrey's waiting mouth. All the anticipation that had been building, all the need, all the desire, all the longing, spilled out. The kiss felt like getting to the top of the roller coaster, right before the world fell out from under you. Audrey pulled her tighter against her body. Harlow was astonished by the way her mind and body seemed to collapse. She was disarmed and at the same time enchanted. But there was nothing ordinary about what was happening to her. She knew things would never be the same after this. She would never be the same.

Audrey backed up against the wall of the pool and pulled Harlow with her. Harlow was searching for the last bit of restraint she'd tucked away. She didn't want this to be like any other time she'd found herself in the throes of craving.

Audrey put her forehead against Harlow's, panting. "I don't know what you do to me." She kissed her again, groaning softly.

Harlow took Audrey's legs and wrapped them around her waist. She needed to be closer to her. Audrey ran her mouth along Harlow's neck to her ear, biting and tugging on her earlobe. Harlow was smoldering with arousal, about to explode into a full conflagration that would consume her entirely. The feel of Audrey's bare skin against her own, the way she shuddered with each little exploration— it was euphoric. If she didn't hit the pause button soon, there would be no turning back. She wanted more for their first time than to be in a pool. She wanted more for Audrey.

Harlow leaned back and kissed Audrey's forehead. "We should slow down."

Audrey's eyes were hazy with need, and now a bit of confusion. "Slow down?"

Harlow kissed her. "If this goes much further, I'm not sure we'll be able to stop."

Audrey cupped Harlow's face. "Do you want to stop?"

Harlow leaned in to kiss her but stopped herself. "No, I don't. But everything has been so wonderful, and I'd like that to be perfect too."

Audrey's confused look melted into a smile. "You're much sweeter than you let anyone think."

Harlow ran her hand through Audrey's wet hair. "Let's go on a date tomorrow."

Audrey kissed her. "I'd like that."

Harlow reluctantly let her go. "Pick you up at nine for breakfast?"

Audrey rested her forehead against Harlow's chest before looking up at her. "I'll be here." She kissed her cheek, letting her mouth linger. "Good night, Harlow."

Harlow watched Audrey walk out of the pool and into the house. She let herself fall backward into the water. The liquid washed over her, cooling her flushed body. Audrey was so much more than she'd anticipated. She was so much more than she'd ever imagined. The fog she didn't even know she'd been stumbling through was beginning to lift.

CHAPTER FIFTEEN

Audrey's phone lit up next to her bed with a text message at seven the next morning. She saw it was Kylie and called her immediately.

"Morning."

Kylie gasped. "Oh my gosh. You called me, so I assume you aren't lying in bed next to her. Tell me everything. *Why* aren't you lying in bed next to her?"

Audrey smiled and put a hand over her face, still feeling the remnants of a wonderful evening. "All we did was kiss." She sat up and propped herself against the headboard. "I mean, it was probably the best kiss of my life, but that's all that happened. She said she wanted to take it slow."

"How do you feel?"

Audrey felt her face flush, and she tried not to smile like a smitten teenager. "I feel…I don't know, lighter? I feel happy, and I'm excited about the rest of this trip."

"She looks like she'd be a great kisser. You know how some people just have that look? I've always thought that about her."

Audrey got out of bed and walked out onto the balcony. Her heart jumped when she saw Harlow jogging along the shoreline. "So, you've thought about kissing her?" She laughed.

"I may be straight, but I'm not dead."

Audrey watched Harlow move next to the water. She reminded her of a tiger—graceful and powerful. "Well, I can assure you that your imagination is on point. You may even be underestimating it."

Kylie sighed. "I guess I'll live vicariously through you for the time being. What are you two doing today?"

Audrey smiled up into the morning sun. "I'm not sure. She's taking me on a date."

"So, you're sleeping with her tonight?"

Audrey laughed. "I've always loved your no-nonsense approach." She watched Harlow peel off her shirt and use it to dry off her face. Her stomach flipped, and little prickles appeared on her skin. "Probably. I'm not sure I'll be able to stop myself."

Kylie squealed. "I'm going to need all the details. Even if you come upon one, and are like, maybe I should skip it. Don't. Do not skip it."

Audrey walked back into her room and started pulling clothes from the dresser. "Anything exciting going on there?"

She could hear Kylie flipping through some papers. "Jane sent over several scripts with notes on which ones she thinks you should take." She could hear the frustration in Kylie's voice. "I don't know why she still does that to you. You've never made a bad choice."

"She's my agent. It's her job."

"She also called to see if you made it there safely."

Audrey turned on the shower. "That's weird. I texted her and said we'd arrived."

"Did she ask you for the address of where you're staying? She asked me, and I hate when she does that."

"What did you tell her?" Audrey stripped off her clothes and put her hand under the water to check the temperature.

"That I didn't know."

"Thank you." The last thing she needed was for Jane to get some harebrained idea of having her and Harlow photographed together. She wasn't sure she'd go that far, but she wasn't convinced she wouldn't, either. Jane had laser focus when it came to getting press.

"Of course. Put on sunscreen, and, Audrey?"

"Yeah?"

"It's okay to be happy."

Audrey smiled. "I love you. I'll call you later."

Audrey showered and started to get ready for the day. This was the first time since she could remember that she didn't know exactly where she was going, who she'd see, and what would be expected from her. It was freeing, and she wasn't sure if that was because of her lack of knowledge or thanks to Harlow.

Finally getting to kiss Harlow had been everything she'd thought it would be. Harlow was passionate while still being gentle. She made Audrey feel desired while still being patient. And that kiss—Jesus. Audrey could have stayed in that moment, with those feelings, for hours. Probably longer. Definitely longer.

The chemistry between them was like nothing Audrey had ever experienced. It felt like electricity coursing through her. Every touch, every bit of anticipation, every silent look—it was enough to make Audrey long for Harlow in a way she never had. *The problem with chemistry is it sometimes blows up in your face.* She shook off the thought, remembering Kylie's words. *It's okay to be happy.*

Harlow had woken up right before five. The energy coursing through her wouldn't let her stay in bed, so she decided to exercise it out of her system. She'd managed to lift weights, run seven miles, shower, and cook breakfast by the time Audrey came down the stairs at fifteen minutes to nine.

"Did you sleep well?" Harlow pushed a cup of coffee across the breakfast bar and put fruit and eggs next to it. "I figured I couldn't go wrong with eggs and fruit. Kind of hard to mess that up."

Audrey's eyes lit up when she saw the coffee. "You cook too?"

Harlow slung the kitchen towel over her shoulder. "I wouldn't call eggs cooking, but yes, I can cook. My menu is pretty limited. I got by as a kid throwing things together with what we had in the house."

Audrey looked slightly pained. "You were kind of the parent, weren't you?"

This wasn't how she wanted to start the morning. She'd said it without thinking because she was becoming used to not guarding herself around Audrey.

Harlow took a sip of her coffee. "I make a pretty kick-ass Pop-Tart too, if you're interested."

Audrey speared a piece of watermelon with her fork. "You're an expert deflector when it comes to your family."

"It's just not something I like discussing. There's a lot of demons shoved in my proverbial closets." Harlow wasn't sure how else to explain it, so she landed on the truth.

"I find that hard to believe. You're one of the most famous pop stars on the planet. If there were anything that bad, someone would've said something by now." Audrey raised an eyebrow as if to prove a point.

Harlow looked into her coffee cup. "It's not that they're that bad to anyone else, but they're bad to me. Any time family stuff gets printed it's pretty brief because there's not much to tell. Drunk dead dad, absent mom. Not exactly gripping stuff, and my mom hasn't talked to the press so far, so they have nothing else. The issues I had with my parents were a struggle Casper and I mostly faced on our own, and we've got our demons from it. I don't want that negativity in my life now."

Audrey swallowed a bite of eggs. "That must have been terribly isolating."

Harlow took a piece of fruit from Audrey's plate and popped it in her mouth. "It was. I'm not sure I would've survived without Casper. No matter how bad things were, at least we had each other."

Audrey reached over and took her hand. Her eyes were earnest, and Harlow felt her heart swell. "I can't imagine what that must have been like for you. I'm so sorry."

Harlow put her hand over Audrey's. "It was a long time ago."

"If you ever want to talk about it, I'm here. Please know that." Audrey squeezed her hand.

"Thank you," Harlow said.

Harlow straightened and tapped the counter a few times. She'd been looking forward to this since Audrey had left the pool the night before. She wanted to shake off this dreary sidetrack into her sad history.

"I'm really looking forward to spending the day with you."

Audrey finished up the last of her breakfast. "You going to tell me where you're taking me?"

Harlow smiled but didn't say anything. She was taking the chance this would be an activity Audrey loved as much as she did. It was a quick fifteen-minute drive to the harbor, which was a good thing since

Audrey peppered her with questions about their destination the whole time. She'd find out soon enough, but it was still a fun game to play.

They pulled into the parking lot, and Audrey looked around quickly. "Are you taking me on a boat?"

Harlow pointed to the pier where her favorite captain was waiting. "Yes, but more specifically, we're going whale watching."

Audrey stared at her for so long, Harlow thought she might have made a mistake. That thought was dispelled when Audrey grabbed her face and kissed her. It was probably intended to be a quick thank you, but the kiss became more fervent, and Harlow had half a mind to blow off the excursion and take Audrey back to the house.

A handful of kisses passed before Harlow pulled back. "We either need to get on the boat or go back to the house."

Audrey kissed her again and smiled. "Let's get on the boat. I've always wanted to do this." She unbuckled her seat belt and turned to look at her. "You're incredibly thoughtful."

"Thank you," Harlow said, her heart swelling even more. She loved making Audrey happy.

Captain Emily Hill was waiting for them when they climbed aboard. She came over and took the two small bags Harlow had brought with her and helped Audrey step down into the rocking vessel.

"I was beginning to wonder if you were blowing me off." Emily used her hand to block the morning sun from her eyes.

"Have I ever?" Harlow hugged her.

"I wouldn't blame you if you did for Audrey Knox," Emily whispered.

Harlow patted her back in response. "Thanks for fitting this into your schedule. I know you're busy this time of year."

"I always have time for you." Emily turned her attention to Audrey and stuck her hand out. "It's a pleasure to meet you. I'm Emily Hill."

Audrey took her hand and smiled broadly. "Audrey Knox. It's a pleasure to meet you, and thank you for taking us."

Emily started untying the ropes from the dock and getting the boat ready to leave the harbor. Harlow watched Audrey look on with amazement. She seemed to be studying Emily, wanting to take in everything she was doing. She wondered if this kind of unbridled curiosity was unique to Audrey or a trait common among actors.

Either way, Harlow found it endearing. She liked that Audrey was still in love with the world around her. Their lifestyles made it easy to become jaded, or worse, cynical. Audrey wasn't either of those things.

Harlow stood against the railing, watching the water lap against the side of the boat as they started moving. The song she'd been working on started to scratch at her. The melody was coming in small increments, and she never knew when her brain would produce the next clue. She hummed to herself, thinking it would make a perfect bridge.

Audrey slid her arm around her waist and snuggled into her shoulder. It was as if she knew Harlow was working on something because she watched her but never interrupted. Harlow wasn't sure if she was being rude by not saying anything, but when her mind got to this place, she could lose her train of thought if she didn't see it through. Harlow pulled out her cell phone and hummed the bridge into her voice memos.

Audrey kissed her cheek after she'd put the phone back in her pocket. "I always wondered how you came up with your music. I love watching it happen. Does it always come to you in obscure moments?"

Harlow shook her head. "It comes to me in all different ways. I have hundreds of partial thoughts scribbled on napkins. There are thousands of short voice memos on my phone with bits and pieces of everything I've ever worked on."

"Well, for what it's worth, I really liked the part I just heard."

"Thanks," Harlow said, feeling a bit embarrassed. "I think I've always had a bit of imposter syndrome. I'm always worried the last one was a fluke, and the next won't live up to expectations."

"Seven albums, five number one hits, twenty-five songs in the top ten, and ten Grammys says you are definitely not a fluke. Especially when you take into account that you're the first woman to win album of the year more than once for your solo recordings. You took home album of the year at twenty, making you the youngest person ever to win that award." Audrey blushed when she stopped talking and turned her attention back to the water.

It pleased Harlow to hear Audrey ramble off her accomplishments. Not because she wanted praise or because she wanted Audrey to be impressed, but because it meant Audrey had spent time learning about her.

Harlow put her hand under Audrey's chin and tilted it up so she could see her. "You have two Oscar nominations, three Golden Globe wins, and are the highest-grossing action heroine of all time." She kissed her. "I guess we've kept track of each other for quite some time."

"You're better than I ever imagined you'd be," Audrey said against Harlow's lips.

"You're exactly who I thought you'd be."

"Humpback on the starboard side," Emily yelled.

The whale was magnificent. It had to be at least fifty feet, and its flippers seemed to take up a third of its body. The whale circled the boat like it was the one doing the watching. It rubbed its enormous body against the side of the boat, turning on its side and sticking its flipper in the air. The experience was pure magic, and Harlow was beside herself. She'd been whale watching before but had never seen one this close.

Audrey seemed to be in awe. She was glued to the side of the boat, watching the whale's antics. It seemed almost playful, and Audrey had taken to shouting welcoming phrases at the creature.

They spent the next few hours enjoying the glistening ocean and gorgeous Monterey coastline. Harlow had planned ahead and brought them a picnic lunch and some local wine. As the day started to disappear into the coastal skyline, Harlow pulled out her camera. She wanted to capture this time with Audrey. She wanted these pictures as tangible memories to take with her on tour. She wanted something to hold in her hands when the inevitable feeling of isolation pushed against her on night number seventy-five in a random hotel room, in a city she couldn't wander through. She needed to be able to remember how real this moment felt.

Audrey leaned against the boat railing. The way she smiled and looked up at the sky accentuated her neck and shoulders. Harlow thought of all the movies she'd seen Audrey in over the years. She was undoubtedly stunning and photogenic, but she'd never looked more beautiful than she did now. Harlow felt lucky to exist with her like this. She was thankful that Audrey had been open to letting her in, and she was also slightly petrified that she'd ruin it somehow.

"You look deep in thought," Audrey said. She walked over and slid her arms around Harlow's neck. "What are you thinking about?"

"How lucky I am to be here with you." Harlow didn't know if she sounded ridiculous or cheesy, and it didn't matter. She wanted Audrey to know exactly how she was feeling.

Audrey looked stunned. "I don't think I'll ever get used to your sudden bursts of honesty." She kissed her. "It's so refreshing."

The sky clapped loudly, and Emily waved to get their attention. "We have to head back. There's a small storm coming in."

Harlow nodded her understanding. She was disappointed they'd have to cut their trip an hour short, but she was looking forward to spending the evening alone with Audrey.

Chapter Sixteen

Audrey watched the rain cascading down the side of the car window. The car was quiet except for the swishing motion of the wipers against the windshield. She loved watching the streetlights dance against the raindrops, creating their own colors and movements. Harlow's hand rested on her leg, and Audrey thought about how right it all felt. She should be terrified, but the more time she spent with Harlow, the more comfortable she was feeling with the idea of falling. She was falling for Harlow.

They pulled into the garage, and Audrey leaned her head against the seat. "Will you play for me?"

Harlow put the back of her fingers against Audrey's cheek. "After we take showers. Your skin is ice cold."

Audrey kissed her hand. "Deal."

After her shower, she changed into jeans and a sweater. She pulled her hair up in a loose bun and headed down to the small recording studio near the pool. The space was warm and cozy. Half of the room was devoted to recording equipment, a couch, and shelves stuffed with records. The other half of the room, which was sectioned off by a glass barrier, had several instruments, microphones, and a few chairs.

Audrey ran her fingers over the edges of the records, wanting a glimpse into Harlow's inspiration. Harlow's taste in music was vast. The artists ranged from Billie Holiday to Patsy Cline, and a thousand in between. Audrey's fingers thumped against the spines of the records, and she couldn't help but wonder about their significance to Harlow. These records meant something. They weren't kept in her house where she could listen to them at her leisure. They were intentionally here—at her hideaway.

"Do you have a favorite?" Harlow leaned against the doorjamb.

Audrey's chest warmed at the sound of Harlow's raspy voice. "I'm afraid I haven't had the same exposure to music as you."

Harlow pushed herself off the jamb and walked toward her. "You don't need to be a musician to have a favorite artist."

Audrey pulled *Tapestry* by Carole King from the shelf. "This one reminds me of being a kid."

Harlow took the record from her and flipped it over. "Bit young for this, no?"

Audrey shoved her shoulder. "My mom listened to it on repeat. I must have heard this record a million times."

"It's a classic." She pulled another darkened spine from the shelf and handed it to Audrey. "*Bella Donna* by Stevie Nicks is one of my favorites."

Audrey stared at Stevie Nicks holding a white cockatoo. "Why?"

Harlow grabbed one of the several guitars hanging on the wall and sat on the piano bench. "I had the most fun playing it." She pulled a guitar pick from her pocket. "I taught myself to play the guitar and piano by listening and playing. I know all of these records by heart."

Audrey looked at the shelves again. "You know every song on every record?"

Harlow laughed. "Pretty much. We couldn't afford music lessons, so this is how I learned. I got my first guitar and keyboard from a secondhand store after washing cars, mowing lawns, and recycling glass bottles for a year."

Audrey sat on the couch facing Harlow. "Play me your favorite song."

Harlow smiled and strummed down the guitar once. "This was originally recorded by Fleetwood Mac, and later redone by the Dixie Chicks—or the Chicks as they're known now."

Harlow's fingers moved across the guitar with ease and intention. It was like watching an artist beginning to paint a canvass. There was tenderness in her voice as the lyrics to "Landslide" fell from her lips. Audrey was familiar with the song, but this was a different experience altogether. Harlow had changed some of the inflections at the end of the words and extended vowels that seemed to add more texture to the song.

Harlow seemed to slip into the lyrics. She could tell by watching her that they not only held some unseen value but that she was able to transport herself to a memory attached to the harmony. It was then that she realized listening to Harlow sing was like being able to peek inside her soul. There was vulnerability and innocence woven through her attachment to the music. It was beautiful.

Harlow put the guitar down and turned to face the piano. Audrey recognized the chords to "A Thousand Years." It sounded different without the violins in the background. It was almost haunting. With just the piano, the words that echoed promises of forever and trepidation seemed even more personal.

Audrey pushed herself off the couch, needing to be closer to Harlow. The urgency she was feeling was confounding. She understood what it was like to be someone else. In her younger years, it had been difficult to separate her experiences from the people she played. It was one of the reasons she'd been adamant about coming out—she needed to know who she was. She'd played a woman feverishly drawn to a man. She'd forced herself to put her mind into a fictitious character who felt as if their existence hinged on being able to touch the other person. It wasn't until this moment that she'd ever had a glimpse of how strong that genuine emotion could be. The invisible string drawing her to Harlow was stronger than anything she could've imagined.

She sat next to Harlow on the piano bench. Harlow smiled as her fingers continued to glide along the ivory keys. Audrey felt her body temperature rise under Harlow's attention. She put her hand on Harlow's leg. Her pulse quickened when Harlow moved closer. Audrey pushed Harlow's blond hair away from her neck, her hand finally settling against the perfect curvature. She watched closely as the pulse point under Harlow's tender skin picked up speed. It was intoxicating to realize she had this effect on Harlow. Audrey wanted Harlow to feel what she was feeling. She wanted to know that what was happening between them was mutual. She wanted to know if Harlow felt as undone and put together as she did when they were this close to each other.

"I love watching you play," Audrey whispered against Harlow's ear.

Harlow shivered slightly. "I love it when you watch me."

Audrey's hand fell away from Harlow's neck and she slid it under her sweatshirt. She ran her fingers back and forth across her spine. "How does it make you feel?"

"It's like being on fire and pulled into the ocean at the same time." Harlow turned her full attention to Audrey. Her cheeks flushed, and her eyes were slightly hazy. "You make me feel everything all at once."

Audrey couldn't handle the minuscule separation between their mouths for another second. She leaned in and ran her mouth along Harlow's lips. Harlow's breath hitched, and she pulled Audrey closer. Audrey had been kissed hundreds of times before, but those kisses had only scratched the surface. Her body reacted to Harlow's need, and she allowed herself to be pulled in.

The kissing from the previous night had been some of the best Audrey ever experienced, but it had nothing on this. Harlow's passion that always smoldered right below the surface seemed to spill out of her, and Audrey loved being on the receiving end. Her lips were tender and forceful. Staying in control had always come easily to Audrey, but that was quickly slipping away under Harlow's soft and purposeful actions.

Harlow's thumbs moved over her cheeks and down to her neck. The movement felt so soft and sweet, as if Harlow was memorizing the way she felt. Each stroke increased her need. She wanted Harlow to devour her.

Harlow pulled Audrey up, placing her against the piano keys. The barrage of random notes that thrummed out of the instrument mimicked the urgency Audrey felt growing inside her. Harlow ran her lips against Audrey's jawline and along her neck. Audrey loved the way she kissed and nipped the sensitive skin on her neckline. She pulled at the bottom of Harlow's sweatshirt, hating the barriers of clothing that separated their bodies. Audrey wanted to feel all of her. Harlow obliged by reaching behind her head and pulling off the hoodie. Audrey took a moment to appreciate what she'd just revealed as Harlow dropped the garment next to her. Harlow was an exquisite combination of strength and femininity. Her curves and lines were like a sculpture, and Audrey wanted to run her hands over her like an artist.

Harlow stepped between Audrey's legs again and slid her hands under Audrey's sweater. She pulled it off and let it fall next to her discarded sweatshirt. Audrey watched Harlow's face as she traced the outside of her breast with the back of her hand. Harlow's breathing had increased, and the change in her body language was painfully sexy.

Audrey used her legs to pull Harlow against her. When their bare skin finally touched, waves of arousal crashed through her. She gave her mind over to her senses and allowed herself to be devoured. The fevered kissing, the soft moans, the feel of Harlow's hands on her body—it was like falling without the worry of landing.

Harlow unbuttoned Audrey's jeans and slid them down her legs while the keys of the piano continued to give in to her weight by proclaiming different notes. Harlow kissed her way up the inside of her thigh until Harlow bit down slightly through her underwear. The anticipation of what was to come caused Audrey's hips to buck slightly, and Harlow grinned.

She slid Audrey's underwear down while kissing her lower abdomen, and then she skimmed her hands up and down the expanse of Audrey's body as she moved her mouth between her legs. Audrey slid one of her hands into Harlow's hair as her mouth finally connected with her sex. She could hear herself whimpering, and with each swipe of Harlow's tongue, her breathing became more desperate. Harlow continued with her rhythmic movements as she slid her fingers inside, pressing into her. Audrey looked down the length of her body. Her chest and stomach expanded and collapsed with more urgency, and there were small droplets of sweat starting to bead on her exposed skin.

Harlow continued to increase the speed and the pressure—pushing Audrey closer to the edge. She didn't want it to end. She wanted to stay in this heightened state of arousal for as long as possible. But her body wasn't going to let that happen. It climbed to the threshold of orgasm and went tumbling over the side. Her legs shook as she pushed herself harder into Harlow. The release was explosive, and she let her head drop back as she cried out Harlow's name.

Harlow stood and held her, keeping her from collapsing to the ground. Audrey blinked, trying desperately to regain her senses. She buried her face into Harlow's neck, loving the way her salty skin tasted against her lips. When she was finally able to get her breathing under control, she pushed Harlow backward toward the couch.

Harlow's legs hit the front of the couch, and she fell back, taking Audrey with her. They both laughed as Audrey continued to kiss her. Audrey made quick work of Harlow's jeans and underwear. She lay on top of her, marveling at the way their bodies seemed to fit so perfectly together. Harlow's eyes tracked her every move. She loved having her undivided attention, but not as much as she loved watching Harlow's face change as she slid her hand between her legs.

Harlow's head pushed back into the couch as Audrey moved deeper inside her. She could've watched Harlow's descent into euphoria for hours, but she couldn't keep herself from kissing her. As Harlow moved under her, Audrey found herself growing closer to another orgasm. She'd wanted to return the pleasure Harlow had awarded her, but seeing and feeling her so turned on was undoing her all over again. Harlow raked her nails down Audrey's back as their orgasms swallowed them both.

Audrey put her head on Harlow's chest, loving the way her rapidly beating heart sounded. Harlow pushed Audrey's damp hair away from her forehead as she kissed the top of her head. They lay there together in silence for several minutes.

Harlow kissed her shoulder. "That was—"

"I know," Audrey said as she tenderly kissed her chest.

Audrey wanted to stay awake. She wanted to talk about what was going to happen next. It wasn't that she needed Harlow to commit to her, but their lives were complicated and very public. She wanted to know if this was the beginning of something, or if Harlow saw it differently. But instead, she let herself be soothed to sleep by the gentle stroke of Harlow's hand on her back.

CHAPTER SEVENTEEN

Harlow listened to the rain continue to pelt the windows of her small studio. Audrey had drifted off to sleep, and Harlow was allowing herself to enjoy their closeness. She wasn't sure what any of this meant for either of them. Her love life was littered with one-night stands and near misses. She'd intentionally never gotten close to anyone, but she was pretty sure that wasn't what she wanted with Audrey. She was compelled to be near her. She didn't know what to do with any of that.

Harlow moved delicately off the couch, careful not to wake Audrey. She pulled on her jeans and sweatshirt, then padded barefoot into the glassed-off room and shut the door behind her. She wanted to reconcile her growing feelings with her innate desire to bolt at the first sign of real intimacy. She picked up the headphones from the keyboard and slid them over her ears.

Her face ran hot when she started playing, thinking about the piano on the other side of the glass and what had taken place there just over an hour ago. She knew next to nothing about being in a relationship or truly caring about someone, but she wanted to try. She just didn't understand how to navigate those waters. Harlow continued to develop the melody to the song she'd been working on for weeks. This next album would be a peek inside her heart that she'd never shown to the world before, and it had everything to do with the woman lying naked twenty feet from her.

"Should I take it personally that you left me on the couch?" Audrey's voice filled her headphones.

Harlow looked through the glass and smiled. "Not at all. I guess I was feeling inspired."

"Should I leave you alone?"

Harlow took her headphones off and waved for her to come inside the room. Audrey had put her clothes back on and was adorable in all her nervousness. Her hair was messy, and her skin was still rosy from exertion. She looked slightly hesitant as she walked toward her, and Harlow felt guilty for having left her alone.

Audrey sat on her lap and wrapped her arms around her neck. "You okay?"

Harlow kissed her. "Better than okay." She tucked Audrey's hair behind her ear. "Do you want to go to the People's Choice Awards with me?" She'd asked without thinking and only slightly regretted it based on the look on Audrey's face.

Audrey's eyes slightly narrowed. "Is that a step you're ready to take?"

Harlow hadn't considered how to answer that question, but she knew she wanted to spend as much time with Audrey as possible. "I'll be on tour, but I'll be at the awards show. I thought it would be a good chance for us to get to see each other."

Audrey kissed Harlow's jaw. "I would love to go with you, but I already promised my mom I'd take her. She's been really looking forward to it, and I don't want to make her feel awkward by making her the third wheel."

"I understand." Harlow pushed away the tiny feeling of relief. Showing up with Audrey, publicly, would put her private life firmly in the public eye. Maybe it was better to take it slow…

"But," Audrey whispered, getting closer to Harlow's ear. "I'm all yours for the after-parties."

"Deal." Harlow pressed her lips into Audrey's and delighted at the soft moan that escaped her throat.

The way Audrey melted into her made Harlow feel as if her skin was on fire. Every flexed muscle, every tug on her lip, every caress was a blaze of its own. She was light-headed and supremely focused all at the same time. Audrey was like a drug, and she wanted more.

"Do you hear that?" Audrey asked as she tried to catch her breath.

"I don't hear anything," Harlow said as she greedily caught Audrey's mouth with her own.

Audrey put a hand on Harlow's chest and pushed her back. "Seriously, I think someone is here."

Harlow tilted her head, but they were in a soundproof room, and it was difficult to hear anything. She glanced over at the door Audrey had left cracked open. She saw a shadow and then heard someone curse.

"What the hell." Harlow stood and put Audrey behind her. She slid the light controls for the mixing room up to high. She hadn't been expecting to see him but was relieved. "What the hell, Casper?"

He had the decency to look apologetic as he came into the recording room. "I was hoping to get in and out before you saw me. I thought you'd be up at the main house." He ran his hand through his hair. "I'm really sorry." He shifted his weight back and forth. "Hey, Audrey."

"What are you doing here?" Harlow wasn't sure if she was angry or worried.

Casper usually wasn't one to drop by unannounced, and she thought it was even stranger that he would do so when he knew she was with Audrey. She didn't think he was spying on her as much as something must have taken precedence over her privacy.

"I was coming to pick up the 1959 Les Paul. We're going to auction it off for charity." Casper looked around and then pointed to the wall. "There she is."

Harlow felt a surge of anger. "I never agreed to auction it off."

Casper delicately took the guitar off the wall but didn't bother looking at her. "Yes, you did. We talked about it last week."

There had been very few items she'd been able to hold on to from their childhood, and almost all of them were in that recording studio. They were the only happy memories she had, and she wouldn't part with them for any price or any reason. The guitar her brother held was the first one she'd ever touched. It was the only tangible tether she had to the only adult who'd ever cared about her. Watching him hold it was like watching him grab a chunk of her heart, and he was willing to sell it.

"That guitar isn't going anywhere. It belonged to Grandpa, and he gave it to me." Harlow almost jumped out of her skin when Audrey took her hand but was grateful for the support.

"This guitar is worth half a million dollars." Casper didn't move from his position, but he'd taken his hands off the instrument.

"It stays here. I'd rather donate the money than part with it." She felt Audrey squeeze her hand, and she allowed herself to take a deep breath. "Why do you need it this minute anyway? Why didn't you just call me and ask me to bring it back?"

Casper flashed his smile that normally coerced her into anything. "Would you have brought it?"

"No."

"That's why I didn't ask, and they need it for the auction tomorrow."

Audrey stepped up next to her. "What charity is this for?"

Casper rolled his eyes. He seemed annoyed that Audrey involved herself in their conversation. "Foster care."

Harlow felt a pang of guilt at hearing his answer but focused on keeping her resolve.

"Which charity? There are several that focus on foster care." Audrey tilted her head, looking interested.

Casper sighed. "Look, I'm sorry I bothered you. I'll just cut them a check."

"Wait." Harlow looked around the room for another offer. She hated the idea of not providing something that had apparently been promised. "Take the Stratocaster."

Casper looked shocked. "You want to donate the Stratocaster? It's worth twice as much as Grandpa's."

Harlow shrugged. "Not to me."

Casper turned and stared at the guitar. "It's a piece of music history."

"I'd rather donate a piece of music history than our history. We're already in short supply of our own," Harlow said. She turned to Audrey, who looked understandably confused. "Bob Dylan played that Stratocaster at the Newport Folk Festival in 1965. It was the first time he'd ever performed with an electric guitar."

"And you think it's worth a million dollars?" Audrey looked as if she couldn't quite wrap her head around it.

Casper pulled it from the wall. "Maybe more." He pulled one of the guitar cases from the small closet and placed the instrument delicately inside. "You're doing a good thing, Harlow."

"You should stay the night. It's way too late to head back to LA." Harlow was still irritated by the intrusion and being effectively blindsided, but she didn't want her brother driving several hours this late at night.

Casper picked up the case. "Thanks for the offer, but I have an early day tomorrow. I'll stop and get coffee. Don't worry about me." He pointed between them. "If this is going to be a thing, we'll need to talk about what that means."

Harlow followed him to the door. "I'll walk you out."

She didn't want to spend her time arguing or fighting with Casper. She had a much more important task at hand—being with Audrey. Casper had always been prone to somewhat strange behavior, but this was odd, even for him.

"You sure everything is okay?" She touched his arm.

"Yup, all good."

"Casper, if you need to talk—"

"Everything is fine. Stop worrying so much." He looked up at the house. "You seem to have your hands full here."

"What's that supposed to mean?" She crossed her arms, irritated by his inference as well as his intrusion.

He rolled his shoulders. "Nothing. I want you to be happy."

She watched his eyes. He looked as if he was going to elaborate but changed his mind. She wanted to push him further, but she didn't want to ruin her night by fighting with her brother.

She nodded to the car. "You better get going. I don't like the idea of you being tired when you drive."

He gave her a half-smile and kissed her cheek. "I really do want you to be happy. I slip into being a manager before being your brother sometimes. I'm sorry about that."

She ran her thumb along the scruff on his face. "I'm fine. My career will be fine."

He nodded and moved to the driver's side of the car. "I'm sure you're right. See you when you get home."

She watched his car pull out of the long driveway. Something still didn't seem right, but she could deal with that when she got back to LA. Right now, Audrey was waiting for her in her bedroom. The thought made her heart race. She took the stairs two at a time and thought how this was the first time she was running toward something instead of away.

❖

Audrey watched from Harlow's balcony as she said good-bye to Casper. It had been a weird interaction, and she was trying to understand their dynamics. The last thing Audrey wanted to do was pass judgment on the most important person in Harlow's life, but she'd spent enough time studying people to know when someone was lying. His defensive posture and the way he wouldn't make eye contact were sure tells. She was instinctively protective over Harlow, but from what? Casper? She shook her head. That didn't make any sense. Casper and Harlow had depended on each other when there wasn't anyone else. Who was she to insert herself or question him?

Audrey inhaled deeply. She loved the way the pavement smelled after a rainstorm. It was the smell of earth, the coming fall, and the promise of cozy nights cuddled up on a couch. Casper's car pulled away, and Harlow turned, looking up at the balcony. Her heart caught in her chest at the way Harlow rocked back on her heels, smiling. *Damn it. She's so sexy.* Every movement seemed so effortless and cool. Audrey decided to focus on their time together instead of getting wrapped up in the strange interaction with her brother. Her time with Harlow was limited, and she resigned herself to make the most of every single second.

Audrey continued to stare into the blackness of the night. She could hear the ocean, and she let her senses take it all in. She was listening to the waves when arms came around her waist, and Harlow placed her chin on Audrey's shoulder. She leaned into Harlow, wanting to be as close as possible. It was such a simple exchange—one that a couple would share. Her heart rate picked up again at the thought.

"I'm sorry about that," Harlow whispered against her ear.

Audrey turned in Harlow's embrace and wrapped her arms around her neck. "No need to apologize. He's your brother."

"He could've called first."

Audrey kissed her jaw and smiled at the way Harlow shivered. "Now I have you all to myself again."

Harlow slid her hands under Audrey's sweater. "Are you tired?"

Audrey stepped backward out of Harlow's embrace. She pulled the sweater over her head and dropped it on the lounge chair. She let Harlow's eyes travel up and down her body. She loved the way Harlow looked at her. The hunger in Harlow's gaze sent a shiver up her spine. Audrey was sure she'd never felt more beautiful than when Harlow looked at her.

Audrey took her hand and led her through the moonlight filled room. Their last time had been rushed—a fury of need and pent-up desire. She wanted something different this time.

Audrey pulled Harlow's shirt over her head and ran her finger from her chest to her stomach. Harlow took her hand and pulled her against her. She stroked her back slowly, leaving a wake of need with each gentle pass. Harlow's breath on her neck was like a slow-burning fuse—the longer it lingered on her skin, the more explosive it began to feel.

Harlow moved her lips up Audrey's neck and finally found her mouth. Every kiss seemed better than the last. As they got to know each other better, and their exploration became more focused, the kissing seemed more intimate. Audrey loved the way Harlow would bite her lip. She loved the way Harlow's mouth devoured her own, and she loved the small noises that would escape from Harlow's throat as their intimacy intensified.

She let Harlow pull her onto the bed. Harlow ran her fingers through her hair, bringing their faces closer together. She loved the way Harlow's body moved under her own. Audrey reveled in the feel of Harlow's mouth traveling down her neck and shoulders. She used her thigh to increase the pressure between Harlow's legs. As Harlow's hips moved with need, Audrey slipped her hand between them. Harlow's fingers dug into Audrey's back as she entered her, and she watched the expression on Harlow's face grow more desperate.

Harlow adjusted to match her movements as she moved inside Audrey. The immediate heat that rippled through Audrey was overwhelming. They moved against each other, each growing closer to climax with every stroke.

"Look at me," Harlow whispered against her ear.

Audrey struggled to focus. It was proving more difficult as Harlow continued to increase the pressure between her legs. She was moving quickly toward release, and as much as she wanted to stay in the moment with Harlow, she couldn't stop the pleasure from claiming her. She bit down on Harlow's shoulder as her body completely took over, dragging Harlow over the edge with her.

She collapsed on top of Harlow and smiled against her neck. She loved the subtle taste of salt on Harlow's skin. She loved listening to Harlow try to catch her breath, and she loved the way her body slightly trembled with aftershocks of what they'd just shared.

Harlow kissed her forehead. "Come on tour with me."

Audrey tried not to smile by pressing her face into Harlow's shoulder. "I love that you want me there, but I can't. I'm in the middle of shooting, remember?"

Harlow traced circles on Audrey's back. "Fair enough. But can I talk you into coming to one of my shows?"

Audrey grabbed her chin, forcing Harlow to look at her. "I'll make it to as many as possible. I promise." She kissed her lips and rubbed her nose against Harlow's. "I want to be there."

"I'm going to hold you to that."

Audrey climbed on top of her and wrapped her arms around her neck. "You can hold me to anything you want." She kissed her again. "In fact, I have a few ideas."

Harlow's left eyebrow lifted. "Oh, really?" She rolled over, pinning Audrey to the bed. "Tell me more about that."

Audrey kissed her and let herself get lost in Harlow all over again. She didn't know what all of this meant, but that didn't seem as important as the time they had together right now.

CHAPTER EIGHTEEN

Harlow listened to the voice on the other end of the phone as she watched the sweat start to bead on Audrey's back. They'd started their day with a run along the shoreline and had been thirty minutes into lifting weights when she'd gotten a call from her booking manager. Typically, she'd be taking copious notes, but that would require her to drag her eyes and attention from Audrey in a sports bra.

"Yes, we can add a second night in Dallas, but I'm not adding a third to Phoenix. That would mean only having twelve hours off before the show in San Jose, and I don't like cutting it that close," Harlow said, hoping this would be the end of the questions.

Audrey turned her head. "When is San Jose?"

"November second," Harlow whispered.

Audrey straddled the bench Harlow was sitting on to face her. "I'll be coming to that one." She leaned forward and kissed Harlow's neck.

"Don't do any VIP promotions for San Jose. I need the whole section." Harlow was trying to focus on her booking manager, but Audrey seemed determined. "Save Los Angeles and New York too."

Audrey made her way to Harlow's ear. "Hang up the phone," she whispered.

"If you have any other questions, email them to me. I'll be back in town tomorrow, and we can finish going over any details. Thanks, Mac." Harlow clicked the end button and tossed the phone down onto her towel next to the bench.

She grabbed Audrey's face and kissed her hard. She loved how Audrey responded to her with equal need and desire. It seemed they were always on the same wavelength when it came to their arousal.

"Who are you saving Los Angeles and New York for?" Audrey asked while pulling Harlow's shirt up over her head.

"You. Who else?"

"I don't know who else you have stashed around the country waiting for you." Audrey's tone was joking, but Harlow knew there was some truth to it.

Harlow didn't want there to be any speculation or concern before she left for the tour. If there were, they'd never survive the months apart. Harlow didn't know how this would all pan out, but she knew she wanted to give them the best shot possible. Audrey was different. Her feelings for Audrey were different. Insecurities and past experiences be damned; she wanted this to work.

Harlow took Audrey's hands. "I want you, Audrey. I know that's easy to say while we're locked away here in our private bubble. I'd really like to make this work between us and see where it goes. But you need to understand how difficult that will be. Even the best relationships struggle under the distance and weight of a tour, and we have your filming schedule on top of that, too. We're very new, so it will probably be even more difficult, but—"

Audrey kissed her, effectively cutting her off her thought. "Harlow Thorne, are you asking me to be your girlfriend?"

Harlow chuckled and shook her head. "I've never asked anyone to be my girlfriend. Is that still a thing people do?"

Audrey bit her lip. "I'm not sure what people do, but that's what it sounds like you're asking." She wrapped her arms around Harlow's neck. "You do know what it means to be someone's girlfriend, right?"

Harlow pulled her closer and pretended to ponder the question. "I'm assuming there are rules involved. I'm just spitballing here, but one of them is commitment, meaning no sleeping around." She tried not to smile when Audrey raised an eyebrow. "Calling after my shows." Harlow ticked off the points on her fingers. "Spending all my free time with you."

Audrey laughed and kissed her. "Correct on the no sleeping around part. Yes, call me after your shows if you aren't too tired. Spend time with me, but no, you don't have to devote every second to me." She kissed Harlow. "Harlow, we're busy people with busy lives. I want to be with you, but it doesn't need to be a chore or an obligation. We have a zillion commitments to a zillion different people. I want to be your reprieve. I want you to talk to me when you feel lonely or lost. I want to be there for you, and I want you to let me care about you." She ran her hand down Harlow's face. "I want you to be with me what you can't be anywhere else—completely yourself."

Harlow was speechless. A lump had formed in her throat. She'd never been in a relationship before, and Audrey was offering total honesty and vulnerability. It was like a dream come true. That was the alarm bell—too good to be true usually meant it was. But that was what Audrey was offering. She nodded, unable to vocalize what she was feeling.

Audrey smacked the side of her leg playfully. "Now, let's go take a shower and then spend some time by the pool. I want to squeeze the last few hours out of this nice weather."

Harlow wiggled her eyebrows. "Take a shower with me?"

Audrey grabbed her hands and pulled her to her feet. "Obviously. That's another perk of being my girlfriend."

Harlow let Audrey lead her up the stairs and hoped for the hundredth time that she wouldn't do something foolish.

The last two days with Audrey had been the best of Harlow's life. Selling out Madison Square Garden for the first time was thrilling, to be sure, but it had nothing on how her body reacted when Audrey looked at her. All of the goals she'd set and shattered, all of the milestones achieved, all the screaming fans, paled in comparison to how everything in her seemed to hum around Audrey. But could it last? Harlow wasn't sure how their feelings would hold up under the weight of their lives, other people's expectations, or their schedules.

She also had to consider how different they were. Audrey came from a devoted family. Her support system extended beyond a sibling who had all the same demons. Audrey knew what commitment and longevity were because that was all she'd known. Harlow had the potential to be catastrophically disappointing. Then there was the whole image thing to consider. Harlow wouldn't be good for Audrey's.

People would be intrigued, sure. But once that wore off, the questions would be constant and invasive. Audrey wasn't some hookup at the Rainbow. She was an A-list celebrity, and that wasn't something Harlow had ever had to deal with before. Audrey was worth it, no question. But what if she dragged Audrey down?

Audrey buried her face into her side. "You okay?"

Harlow kissed the top of her head. "Yeah, just thinking."

Audrey propped herself up on her elbow. "About what?"

Harlow got up and shifted the logs in the fireplace, causing them to burn hotter. "How much my life is about to change." She saw the worried look on Audrey's face and decided to rephrase. "Not in a bad way. I've been able to keep my personal life relatively private because I've never been with anyone people cared to discuss. That's not the case with you." She didn't mention her insecurities about their vastly different histories because she didn't think that was fair. It was her shit to work out, not Audrey's.

Audrey nodded. "I get that. Is there a certain way you want to approach this? I want to do whatever will make it easier on you."

Harlow laid back down and pulled Audrey close. "I'm sure our managers will have some opinions."

Audrey blew out a breath. "This isn't about them. What do you want?"

Harlow answered without hesitating. "I don't care if people know we're together. I hope you don't think that." She waited to continue until Audrey acknowledged her understanding. "I just don't want to ruin your reputation in any way."

Audrey looked at her with sympathy. "Honey, I'm not worried about any of that. It's not like I've carefully curated my public persona. I've just always been me. But if it helps, we don't have to tell anyone anything. We can just hang out and let people believe what they want. We don't have to make a public proclamation."

Harlow chuckled. "You've been involved with four women since you were nineteen. Every time it happens, there are a million articles written about you and whoever they are. People set up online polls to discuss if the woman is worthy of your attention. It's not like your relationships fly under the radar. I just don't want things to be harder than they're already going to be."

Audrey pinched her side. "You've kept pretty close tabs on me for someone who cares very little about our world."

Harlow's face heated. "I've always had a bit of a crush on you."

"Well, that's adorable." Audrey kissed her cheek. "Just worry about us, and we'll deal with the rest as it comes. We don't have to confirm or deny anything until you're ready."

Harlow squeezed her hand. "I'm not trying to hide you or us away. I just want to give us a chance before everyone weighs in—for now, at least."

Audrey pulled the blanket off Harlow and got on top of her, straddling her waist. "Deal." Audrey pulled her shirt off and unclasped her bra. "Now, let me make sure you don't forget what I feel like while you're gone."

Harlow pulled Audrey down to kiss her. She'd do precisely what Audrey asked of her. She wanted to etch herself into Audrey and memorize every inch of her. She wanted to be able to pull on these moments later when the loneliness set in on the road. Audrey was like a tether to everything important and true in the world. She'd need it when they were apart and her mind started playing tricks on her. She needed these last few hours of quiet closeness as much as Audrey.

CHAPTER NINETEEN

The feeling of dread grew more intense the closer they got to Audrey's house. She wasn't ready to leave her. *Pull yourself together. You sound like a lovesick teenager.* She pushed the thoughts down. They had lives to live. Audrey had to be back on set, and Harlow was leaving for her tour. Their time in Monterey had been incredible. She'd hold on to that until they were together again. People did this all the time and under much more difficult circumstances. They had money and privilege that so many others didn't. Harlow wasn't being shipped off to war; she was simply going on tour. They'd be fine. Everything would be fine.

Harlow put the car in park at the top of Audrey's driveway. "I would come in and hang out for a bit, but I have to be at the dance studio in an hour."

Audrey grinned, remembering why they were running late. "Sorry about that. When I asked you to stop at Big Sur, I didn't think it would be that much of a detour."

Harlow laughed. "If you didn't plan on making us late, why did you haul that blanket down into the woods?"

"Okay, maybe I had some intention."

"Uh-huh." Harlow kissed her. "It's not like I'm complaining."

Audrey rested her forehead against Harlow's. "Call me when you get to Portland."

"I promise, and don't forget, I'll see you in two weeks at the People's Choice Awards."

Audrey opened the car door and got out before she got caught up and made Harlow even later. She grabbed her bag from the back seat and waved one more time before forcing herself to walk inside the house.

Before she had an opportunity to catch her breath, there were arms around her neck. She practically fell over from the surprise.

"Your mom and Jane are here. I tried to get Jane to leave, but she refused," Kylie whispered. She grabbed Audrey's shoulders and intentionally spoke much louder. "I'm so glad you made it back safely. I bet you're exhausted. You should take a shower and lie down."

Jane rounded the corner before Audrey had time to formulate a response. "You can rest after we've had a chance to chat."

Audrey dutifully followed her into the kitchen as if it wasn't her house they were in. She kissed her mom on the cheek and took a seat at the breakfast bar. Jane slid a glass of water in front of her. The silence was awkward, and Audrey shifted under the weight of everyone's eyes on her.

"So?" Jane leaned on the counter. "Let's hear it. What are we dealing with?"

Her mom smacked Jane's arm. "Oh, stop. Honey, how was your trip?"

Audrey drank almost the entire glass of water. She knew there would be questions when she returned, but she hadn't thought she'd get ambushed the second she walked in.

"It was good." Audrey put the glass down and folded her hands.

"No, we aren't going to do this. I have three more meetings today. I need to be prepared for the press. I need you to be honest with me. I need to know exactly what is happening." Jane tapped her finger on the counter. She had her determined face on, which meant she wasn't leaving until she got the information she wanted.

Audrey sighed. "Here is what I will tell you." She held her hand up when she saw Jane was going to interrupt. "This is all you're getting for now. Harlow and I have decided to explore a romantic relationship together. We will not be issuing a press release. We will be spending time together without putting a label on it. We won't be denying or confirming. Harlow will be at the People's Choice Awards, but I will still be going with my mom. I will be attending her San Jose show." She intentionally left out the other two shows Harlow had mentioned. She didn't want to give Jane any more than she had to at the moment. "Neither of us will be dating anyone else during this time. So please, stop trying to set me up with women, and don't make a big deal of this in front of the media. I don't want it ruined before it even has a real chance to get going."

Jane smiled and raised her right eyebrow. "This is very good. With your new movie and her being on the soundtrack, the press will be off the charts."

Audrey knew this was Jane's job, but it still irritated her that this was how she saw her life. But what could she say? This was exactly what she paid her to do.

"Will you be spending the night after the San Jose show? I need to make sure I have your calendar up to date." Jane had her iPad out, but Audrey didn't miss her little smirk.

Audrey lifted her chin. "Yes, but so will Kylie and my mom. I'm taking them with me."

Her mom clapped. "Oh, yay! I love Harlow's music."

Jane grabbed her briefcase from the chair. "I have to get going. I gave Kylie your updated schedule. You have several press junkets over the next few weeks that will be sewed into your shooting schedule. I also need an answer on those scripts I sent over last week. I'll expect an answer at the end of the week since I'm sure you didn't do any reading while you were away." She stopped at the door and sighed. "On a personal note, I'm happy for you." Jane left quickly, and Audrey was sure it was because she showed even the slightest bit of humanity.

When she got back in the kitchen, her glass of water had been replaced with a glass of wine. Both Kylie and her mother were looking at her anxiously. It was these moments, with the two of them, she was the most normal.

"Okay, tell us everything." Kylie scooted the barstool closer and leaned on the counter.

Audrey glanced at her mom. "I don't know about everything."

Her mom waved her off. "Oh, honey, don't worry about me. Your father and I have been married for a long time. There's a reason it's lasted."

Audrey scrunched her nose at the implication. "It was incredible. I haven't been this happy in a long time."

Kylie motioned for her to continue, and she only hesitated for a split second. The truth was, she wanted to share their trip with them.

She wanted to tell them how she was feeling and how fabulous Harlow had been. She wanted to share it all with them, if for no other reason than she could hardly contain her happiness. So she did. She told them every detail—well, almost every detail. It didn't matter what her mom said; there were some things she was better off not hearing.

When she finally finished detailing her last several days, both Kylie and her mother looked genuinely happy for her.

Her mom rubbed her arm. "I'm so happy for you, honey. And I'm very excited to see her in San Jose. Can I bring your father, or is this a girls' trip?"

Audrey thought about it before she answered. "How about this first time, it's just us. I don't want to spook her by bringing both parents. She's already met you. I don't want to make it seem like I'm looking for a lifelong commitment, and I've brought my parents along for approval."

Kylie pulled an iPad from her bag. "You know I hate to be the one to cut this short, but there were some script changes while you were gone. I think we should go over them before you're back on set tomorrow."

Audrey sighed and motioned to Kylie to give her the tablet. "Anything interesting?" She scrolled through the pages looking at the comments. "So, why does he have to rip my shirt off before we run into a building where people will be firing guns at us?"

Kylie shook her head and shrugged. "My guess would be to sell more tickets to the target audience—males eighteen to thirty-nine."

Audrey ran her hand through her hair. "Yeah, I know the spiel. These writers and directors do realize that there are women who like action films too, right?"

"I think they assume the women who like action films are the same women who'd like to watch you run into a building without a shirt." Kylie's expression was apologetic.

"That's ridiculous. Some women enjoy action films because they like action films," Audrey said.

She knew she was preaching to the choir. She'd ranted for years about her frustration with the film industry. Too often, women were used as props to lure in men and make women feel inferior. No one ever considered the work that went into it—strict diets, hours upon hours of exercise, personal trainers, personal chefs, and camera editing. The image they portrayed was virtually unobtainable unless you devoted your life to it. She was so tired of the superficial roles women were forced into. But those roles had also given her a career she loved, for the most part, and there was no denying they paid well.

Her mom sipped her wine. "Maybe it's time we revisit the topic of creating your own production company. You could pick the scripts, the parts, and the stories. You're a big enough name now. If you don't want to do these parts anymore, don't."

Audrey turned her mother's words over in her head. She'd toyed with the idea for some time but always found a reason to procrastinate. She'd always thought she'd take a project like this on later in her career, but why wait? She had the connections, the influence, and the name. She could pull a few other female names in with her—create a formidable force. There would be some pushback. Major production companies didn't like competition, and forming her own would look like a challenge. It could cause some people not to want to work on her projects, especially those bound by contracts, but it would be worth the energy.

"You know what, Mom?" Audrey came around the counter and kissed her cheek. "You're absolutely right."

"Give me a list of where to start," Kylie said.

Audrey inhaled deeply as she lifted her glass for a toast. "To strong women. May we know them, may we be them, may we raise them."

Audrey was excited in a way she hadn't felt in years about her career. The future was looking bright indeed.

Harlow caught her breath while she waited for the final run-through with her dancers to wrap up. They'd have another few days of rehearsal when they arrived in Portland, but right now they could fix any glaring mistakes prior to being on stage. Everyone looked great, and she was glad she'd left and given them the chance to practice the larger dance numbers while she'd been away.

She looked over and noticed Casper walking toward her. She rolled her shoulders and inhaled, waiting for what she assumed would be questions about her time with Audrey.

Casper handed her another bottle of water. "They look ready."

"They are ready. We're lucky to have them." She tried her best to sound pleasant, not wanting to have any serious conversations while she was trying to work.

"Harlow, about the other night—"

She cut him off before he could say anything else. "It's okay, Casper. Let's just focus on the tour now. You know how stressful the first few performances are."

He nodded. "You know I just want you to be happy, right?"

Something in his tone made her really look at him. There were dark circles under his eyes, and his skin looked blotchy. He looked incredibly stressed, and she felt guilty for having added to his discomfort and concern. She loved her brother and knew that his nagging always came from a good place. He'd always looked out for her, and she needed to give him the benefit of the doubt.

She put her hand on his shoulder. "I know, and thank you. For the record, I am happy. Very." She shook him a little. "You know I want the same for you, right?"

He smiled, but it didn't erase the concern in his expression. "I'll see you on the plane in a few hours." He kissed the side of her head. "I love you."

"I love you too." She rolled her shoulders as she watched him walk away. She usually backed off and let him tell her what was going on in his own time, but maybe she needed to push. He looked rough, and she was worried. The call came to start again, and she pushed the thought aside to concentrate on the moment.

Later, when she walked into her house, the normal hustle and bustle that was constant prior to the tour was absent. Everyone was on their way to Portland now, and she was alone. Her house was rarely empty during the day, as a portion of it doubled as her office. It was one of her tactics of avoiding the paparazzi—the less she went out, the less they had the opportunity to photograph her.

She showered, walked through the house one more time to make sure she'd grabbed everything, and headed to the car waiting in the driveway. The driver placed her bag in the trunk and opened the back passenger door. She stared at her phone, wanting to talk to Audrey. She looked at the man driving her and wondered if he'd pay attention to her phone call. Then she realized that she didn't care. She pulled up her contact information and hit the call button.

Audrey picked up after the first ring. "Hey, you." Audrey's voice was smooth and soft, and Harlow enjoyed the chills that went down her spine.

"Hey. I just wanted to say hi before I got on the plane."

"I'm glad you did. I was just thinking about you."

Harlow smiled. "Really, what were you thinking?"

Audrey hummed on the other end of the line, and Harlow felt her stomach tighten at the sound.

"I already miss you."

Harlow smiled. "I miss you too. Portland would be much more fun with you there."

Audrey laughed. "Yeah, I'm sure it gets tiresome hearing thousands of people scream your name every night. Such a drag."

Harlow glanced up at the driver to see if he was watching. "I'd much rather hear you scream my name."

"I'll see you in two weeks, and we'll see what we can do about that."

"I can't wait. I hope everything goes well on set. I promise I'll call when I can."

"Talk to you soon. Safe travels."

"Thanks, bye." Harlow clicked the end call button. She didn't want to hang up, but there wasn't really anything more to say. She just liked the reassurance she felt at hearing Audrey talk.

Her heart was still hammering when the car pulled up on the tarmac. Audrey had given her an extra jolt of energy. It was like she was under the influence of something, and maybe she was. Audrey was intoxicating, and she loved every minute of it.

Chapter Twenty

Audrey sipped her drink. "Michelle, you're one of the biggest producers in Hollywood. You've managed to bring great female film roles to the big screen year after year. Let's work together and make this a more common occurrence. We could change the way the film industry views women."

Michelle sipped from the small straw that stuck out of her vodka and soda. "Audrey, I love the idea. I've been pitching this to different people over the years, but you know how this town works. A small group of men runs it."

Audrey leaned forward. "So we bring stories they can't turn down." She slid a book across the table. "Read this and let me know where you stand."

Michelle looked at the cover. "I've never heard of this author." She took another sip of her drink and smiled. "That's your point, isn't it?"

Audrey wiggled her eyebrows. "See, you're already reading my mind, and we haven't even started working together yet."

Michelle laughed. "Okay, you have me intrigued. I'll read it and let you know if I think it would make a good script. I take it if we do this, you'll be starring in it?"

Audrey shrugged. "If there is someone better, we can use her, but I'd waive my salary for this first one."

Michelle motioned to the server to bring her another drink. "That's a hard deal to pass up, and you know it." She picked at the plate of vegetables. "Let me read the book and talk to a few contacts. I promise I'll give you an answer by the end of next week."

Audrey hadn't realized how nervous she'd been about Michelle's reaction until she got one. If she could get Michelle on board, it would offer validity to what she was trying to do, and it would help her get even more people invested. It was a great place to start.

Audrey audibly exhaled. "Thank you for taking it seriously and considering the possibility."

Michelle snapped a piece of celery off and chewed. "It's not every day Audrey Knox comes to you with an offer like this. I'd be a fool not to think about it."

Audrey was on the verge of asking Michelle about her two children when she saw Casper come out on the patio. He was with two other men, and he looked frazzled. What was more peculiar was that he was here at all. He was supposed to be on tour. Audrey knew this was the last night of the Seattle show. He shouldn't be in LA.

Michelle touched her arm, effectively dragging her out of her internal monologue. "You okay? She followed her line of sight. "You know Casper Thorne?"

Audrey didn't want to reveal too much, even to her old friend. "I'm friends with his sister. I'm just confused as to why he's here; he's supposed to be on tour."

"Isn't Harlow Thorne performing at the People's Choice Awards in a few days? Maybe he's here to make sure everything is set up for that."

Audrey nodded. "I'm sure you're right."

Casper had every reason to be in town with the award show coming up, but Audrey couldn't quite shake the feeling that something was off. He didn't look like a guy having a friendly lunch with his friends, or even just someone having a quick business chat. He looked frustrated, and his leg bounced nervously.

She'd been trying to study him without looking suspicious as she continued her conversation with Michelle. Apparently, she'd sucked at it, since he approached their table.

Casper closed one of the two buttons on his jacket and leaned down slightly. "Audrey, how nice to see you." He gave Michelle a tight smile.

The last thing she wanted Casper to think was that she was on a lunch date of some kind, so she introduced Michelle before anything else was said. "Casper, this is my friend Michelle Fleming. Michelle, this is my friend Casper Thorne. We were discussing a potential upcoming project."

The muscles in his jaw relaxed slightly, and he put his hand out. "Michelle, it's nice to meet you." He shook his finger at her. "You worked on *Bad Blood*, right?"

Michelle smiled. "That's right. That's how Audrey and I met. I was the producer. I assume you're Harlow Thorne's brother?"

"What gave it away?" Casper deployed his most charismatic smile, and Audrey saw how women would easily fall all over themselves to be on the receiving end of it.

Michelle sipped her drink and crossed her leg. "Besides your last name?" She pointed at him. "You and Harlow have identical eyes. They're hard to miss. I'm not sure there's actually a name for that color blue."

"We get that a lot," Casper said.

"Do you want to have a drink with us?" Michelle eyed the seat next to her.

Casper checked his watch. "I'd love to, but I have to be over at the Microsoft Theater in about thirty minutes. It was lovely to meet you, though." He shook Michelle's hand again and turned his attention toward Audrey. "I'll be seeing you in a few days." He leaned down and kissed Audrey's cheek.

He walked away, and Michelle fanned herself. "Jesus. It's not often that a man makes me turn my head. Don't get me wrong, I love my husband, but he's gorgeous."

"Yeah, the whole family just oozes sex. It's a bit unfair," Audrey said.

Michelle raised an eyebrow. "Do they, now?"

Audrey sipped her water, wanting to hide her smile and the blush she knew was forming on her face. "Oh, come on, I'm not the only one to make that proclamation."

Michelle smiled. "Can't argue with that."

Audrey thought Michelle might push a bit more, but she didn't. They finished their drinks and set an appointment to meet next week and discuss the project. Excitement about the possibilities made her giddy. This project could be the start of the next phase of her career, and she would get to see Harlow soon. She'd been trying to keep everything in perspective, but it was hard not to feel like everything was lining up perfectly.

❖

Harlow listened to the crowd as the small lift lowered her under the stage. She'd finished her finale and had introduced the band, but the crowd was still screaming her name. The stadium was roaring, and her adrenaline was still pumping hard.

Shauna grabbed her and hugged her when she got off the lift. "That was amazing." She kissed Harlow's cheek. "Thank you for letting me close the show with you. I've never felt anything like that."

Harlow took the towel and water handed to her. "I'd tell you that you get used to it, but I'd be lying."

Harlow waited for her dancers to come down and hugged each of them when they passed. She was eternally grateful for their contributions to the show. They made it so much more than just live music—it was a production, and they made her look good.

Harlow's tour assistant led her back to the dressing room. There were flowers and gifts all over the room, but she was only interested in finding her cell phone. She picked it up and clicked the call button.

"Hey, there." Audrey's voice was low and sleepy.

"Did I wake you?"

Audrey chuckled. "You know I don't care if you wake me. I'll talk to you whenever I get the chance. How was the show?"

Harlow smiled and tried not to sigh into the phone. "It went great. I brought Shauna out on stage with me for the final set. She loved it."

"I bet she did. That's a big opportunity for her."

"I miss you," Harlow said.

"Just a few more days, and I'll let you kiss me three times."

Harlow loved that Audrey was counting down the days. She'd started the practice as soon as she'd left for Portland, and it made her feel less out of her mind to know Audrey was doing the same.

Harlow smiled. "Just three?"

"You'll have to earn the others, superstar."

The wardrobe director walked into the dressing room. "We need your outfit, Ms. Thorne."

Harlow sighed. "I have to go."

"Harlow?" Audrey waited. "I miss you too."

"Night."

Harlow hit the end button and pulled off her outfit with the help of wardrobe. It was a complicated piece with a million sequins. It would need to be checked before the next show. If anything was broken, there was a team to fix it. There was someone readily available to do everything for her on tour if need be. It was a surreal feeling, and one she still wasn't accustomed to.

With a sigh of relief, she changed into her yoga pants and pulled on her sweatshirt. She put her hair back and stared at herself in the mirror. The transformation back into a normal person was complete. Thirty minutes ago, there had been tens of thousands of people screaming her name, and now she looked like someone leaving a gym—alone.

Harlow was escorted to a vehicle waiting at the back of the stadium. The car was quiet, and she looked out the window at the people still lingering around the stadium. They were laughing, hugging, and seemed to be having a good time. She loved being able to give them the experience, but the contrast was stark. She wanted someone to share in the excitement with her, but that wasn't possible.

It was the same at the hotel. She was slipped in through the back by private security, escorted to a special elevator, and brought to her room where she found herself alone again. She showered and went to sit by the expansive window that looked out over the city. It took hours for the energy she absorbed from the show to subside, and it hadn't yet.

She could slip out and go to a dive bar. She'd be able to blend in. She could have some normal human contact, if even for a few hours. But she stayed rooted in her chair because she knew it wasn't true. There was a trade-off for doing what she loved to do, and that was solitude. She never dared to voice these thoughts because she knew how it would sound. She would sound ungrateful, spoiled, and whiney. She was lucky, and very few ever achieved the level of fame she'd reached. But none of that changed how alone she felt at times. If Casper was away, there was no one else.

Audrey. What would Audrey think of her isolated life? Audrey had people she kept close. She had friends. She'd managed to not wall herself off from everyone and everything completely. They lived in the same kind of world, yet Harlow hadn't managed any of the vulnerability. It was easy to blame her parents. They'd inflicted a significant amount of damage on both Casper and her. But was that really fair? They were grown-ups now. They chose their lives. But the fear of getting hurt was very real. Whenever she considered the worst-case scenario, Harlow remembered what it was like to be a little girl. She'd hide in her room for hours practicing on her old guitar and keyboard. She'd drown herself in her music to not deal with reality. What if she was still doing that? What if she was using music to shield her from anything real?

Her phone rang, pulling her from her morbid internal reflection. "Hey, Casper."

"I knew you'd still be awake. How was the show?"

"Everything went perfectly. It was a great crowd." She slid her finger against the rain-covered window.

"You always do great. I'm sorry I missed it."

"That's okay. You had to be in LA," she said.

"You ready to come home for a few days?"

She wanted to tell him that she was excited to see Audrey. They'd never kept anything from each other, but that was changing. She didn't want to hear the analysis of the benefits and the risks. She was protective of their growing feelings, and she didn't want to open it to the ridicule of anyone.

"Yeah, the People's Choice Awards is always a good time."

"I'm still your date, right?"

Harlow sighed. "Of course. I would've told you if the plans had changed."

"Okay. I was just checking." He was quiet for a beat. "Everything okay?"

She smiled, hoping it would reflect in her voice. "Definitely. I'm just finally starting to get tired. I'll see you tomorrow."

She hung up and tucked herself into bed. She might be alone tonight, but tomorrow she'd be in bed with Audrey. The thought was enough to let her smile as she drifted off to sleep.

CHAPTER TWENTY-ONE

"Mom, you look beautiful. Stop messing with your dress." Audrey smacked her mom's hand for the third time since they'd gotten into the limo.

"I'm not messing. I'm adjusting." Her mom ran her hand down her leg another time. "You know I get nervous at these things."

"Well, you look flawless." Audrey squeezed her mom's hand. "I'll be there with you the whole time."

Her mom laughed. "It's you that's up for two awards, not me. I don't know what I'm going on about. How are you feeling? Are you nervous?"

Audrey stared out the window at the line of cars forming. She was excited about being nominated for Favorite Movie Actress and Favorite Face of Heroism, but she could barely control her excitement about seeing Harlow. The anticipation sparked through her, fraying her nerve endings.

"Not at all. I genuinely like everyone in my categories," Audrey said.

Her mom squeezed her hand. "Your cheeks are flushed, and your breathing is erratic. If it's not about the awards, could it possibly be because you're going to see someone tonight?"

Audrey noticed she was chewing on her lip and stopped herself, not wanting to ruin her lipstick. "We haven't interacted in public since this all started. What if she doesn't like me anymore? What if she doesn't want to be seen with me after the show? What if it just gets... weird?"

Her mom chuckled. "My goodness, you get so wrapped up in the thought of Harlow Thorne, you forget you're Audrey Knox." She kissed her cheek. "You're worth the risk, my dear. If she doesn't feel the same, that's her loss."

The limo came to a stop, and a man in a black tuxedo pulled the car door open. The reporters went quiet for a second, waiting to see who would exit the car. She gave her mom a final smile, hoping it implied the gratitude she felt. Audrey grabbed the usher's hand and stepped out of the limo into an array of flashing lights and questions being shouted from every direction.

She looked over to make sure her mom had been escorted off to the side before she made her walk down the red carpet. Most of the questions were about her dress. The designer had used her latest character as inspiration. The tight black leather, accentuated by perfectly placed silver zippers, gave her ensemble the appearance of battle gear. She'd loved it as soon as she'd seen it, and she knew her fans would feel the same way.

The red carpet line moved quickly, and it wasn't until she was almost near the end that she heard the crowd erupt with excitement. Very few celebrities could garner that kind of universal furor, and Harlow Thorne was at the top of that list.

Her pulse quickened, and just the thought of her being nearby made her skin tingle. She slowed her pace, letting the photographers at the end of the line get more time than she typically would've allotted. Harlow was wearing a form-fitting white tuxedo with a plunging shimmering silver top. She looked magnificent, and Audrey couldn't look away.

Harlow finally looked down to the end of the carpet and made eye contact with Audrey. A slight smile formed on her lips as she turned for the cameras to catch her at every angle. The entire world faded into the background as she watched Harlow move, totally at ease with the cameras and crowds.

Her mom grabbed her hand, pulling her from the moment, and they moved into the theater. Attendees were mingling, drinking champagne, and ignoring the snacks that floated around on small silver trays. No one ever ate at these things. Getting something stuck in your teeth would be a nightmare. Audrey grabbed two of the glasses and handed one to her mom.

"Did you see Harlow?" Her mom spoke into her glass.

Audrey sipped on her champagne. "How could I miss her? She looks phenomenal."

"So do you, honey. The dress highlights the post-apocalyptic theme, but you look much better without the blood all over your face."

Audrey laughed. "Thanks, Mom."

"I don't know, I kind of preferred her with the blood on her face."

Audrey recognized the voice and tried not to roll her eyes. "Hello, Tia," she said but continued to look at her mom.

"You look great tonight, Audrey." Tia squeezed between them.

"Thank you." Audrey knew Tia was waiting for her to comment on her appearance, but she wouldn't give her the satisfaction.

"So, two awards and presenting tonight. That's a big deal." Tia clearly ignored Audrey's lack of interest in the conversation.

"She's a shoo-in for both," Harlow said from behind them.

Audrey loved the warmth Harlow's voice sent through her body. "Harlow Thorne," Audrey said as she turned to face her. "Finally made it through the gauntlet, I see."

"Mrs. Knox, you look fantastic tonight." Harlow hugged her mom.

"Oh, stop. Also, I told you to call me Kathy." Her mom held on to Harlow's arms. "But you look breathtaking. I'm not sure anyone has ever looked as good in a suit as you do tonight."

Harlow eyed Tia and put her hand out to introduce herself. "I'm Harlow. It's nice to meet you."

Tia took her hand. "Tia Perkins. I'm Audrey's friend."

Audrey coughed slightly on her champagne. *The audacity.* Audrey was aware of all the eyes aimed in their direction—no doubt because everyone knew their romantic history. She slipped into acting mode and smiled at Tia. She made sure to place her hands at her sides instead of across her chest, not wanting to give off the impression that she was defensive.

Tia looked as if she would say something when her mom slid her arm through Tia's. "Tia, tell me about your latest project while we hunt down some more champagne."

"It was nice to meet you, Harlow. Audrey, call me. I'd love to meet up this weekend," Tia said, as she finally allowed Kathy to pull her away.

Audrey turned to look at Harlow. "I'm not going out with her this weekend. Or any weekend. Ever."

Harlow smiled and allowed the back of her hand to brush gently against Audrey's. "I know. Tia Perkins doesn't intimidate me."

Audrey hadn't been this close to Harlow in several weeks. She'd spent hours daydreaming about being near her again. She'd thought about touching her, kissing her, tasting her skin. Now that she was so close, it took all she had to adhere to their agreement not to out themselves in public just yet.

"I love you in a tux, by the way." Audrey made sure to let her eyes linger over Harlow a little longer to ensure the meaning of what she was saying wasn't lost.

Harlow took a small step closer, and Audrey shuddered at the breath on her ear. "I haven't been able to take my eyes off you since I got out of the car."

The lights started blinking, indicating they needed to get to their seats. Audrey didn't want to go into the show. She didn't care about the awards. She didn't care about anything but being near Harlow. That choice, however, was taken from them as one of the show's ushers approached.

"Ms. Knox, Ms. Thorne, please take your seats."

Audrey forced herself to swallow. "I'll see you in a bit then. Good luck tonight."

Harlow pressed against her fingers with a little more force. "You too."

Audrey forced herself to step away and find her mom to get to their seats. She stopped periodically to shake hands with people, but she was keenly aware of where Harlow was the whole time. One row ahead of her and three seats to the left. She briefly wondered as the lights dimmed for the opening performance if she would ever be seated beside her.

Harlow fixed the strap on her outfit as she waited for the host to introduce her. The stage director held up her fingers, indicating she had two minutes until performance time. The dancers moved behind her, joking and doing a few last-minute stretches. Harlow was trying to get in her zone. She needed to transform into who the public perceived her to be.

She heard the presenter announce her name, and the theater started cheering. One of the reasons she loved this particular awards show was because they gave tickets to fans. There were several beats of silence, allowing the fans' excitement to permeate the theater. She could picture them at the stage edge screaming, and the adrenaline jump she was always ready for flushed her system.

The theater was dark until the spotlights started thumping along with the base beat of her song. The curtain came up, and her dancers ran out on stage. They contorted themselves into different positions, mimicking the intensity of the music. She sang a brief "oh" into the microphone to ensure the ear monitor was working correctly. Then the full light show started, and she came into the first verse.

She worked her way to each end of the stage, making sure to touch as many people's hands as possible. She glanced up at the large screens on either side of the stage. Images of Audrey running through a post-apocalyptic world filled the screen. The dancers behind her mimicked the different fight scenes during the chorus.

Harlow found Audrey in the crowd. Everyone else's attention flickered between Harlow, the dancers, and the screen, but Audrey was laser-focused on her. She loved it when Audrey watched her, but there was so much charge in her stare now. Audrey was the only person in the room. She was down at her end of the stage, and it was like she was singing just to her. Flashes of her music studio slipped through her mind, and she couldn't stop smiling. Audrey had the same look on her face, and Harlow wondered if she was reliving the same memory.

She reached the end of the song, and the lights went down again. The other stage where an award would be announced lit up. Harlow jogged off the stage with the dancers. People handed her water and a towel and ushered her away to set up for the next performance.

She hurried over to the other stage, where the next category was being announced for Favorite Face of Heroism. The names were listed, and Harlow knew the cameras were honing in on each to capture their reaction to the winner. She held her breath.

"And the winner for Favorite Face of Heroism is," the announcer said, allowing for a pause to open the envelope. "Audrey Knox."

Harlow tried to hear Audrey's acceptance speech, but there was so much noise backstage, she couldn't make out the words. She waited to congratulate Audrey, unconcerned about needing to be back in her seat or whatever else the stage directors were trying to get her to do.

Audrey came backstage and walked directly toward Harlow as people pulled the award from her hands and offered their praise. "You waited for me."

Harlow hugged her. "Of course, I did. Congratulations, you were amazing in the role."

"Thank you," Audrey said as she buried her face in Harlow's neck. "Your performance was outstanding, too, by the way."

"I missed you." Harlow knew she'd been hugging her for too long, but she didn't want to release her.

Audrey ran her hands along Harlow's back. "I missed you too."

A stagehand informed them both they needed to move along, so Harlow reluctantly moved back.

Audrey kissed her cheek. "See you at the after-party."

Harlow nodded because she didn't trust her voice. She hated herself when Audrey walked away. She hated not being able to kiss her. But if she was honest with herself, that was her doing. She was the only one who could do anything about it. She only thought about running the idea past her brother for a split second. Not everything was up to Casper.

CHAPTER TWENTY-TWO

Casper, who would've normally insisted that he escort her to any public party, had made an excuse to leave. He'd seem agitated and checked his phone constantly. She was going to ask him what was going on, but she also didn't want to give him a reason to stay. She wanted to spend this time with Audrey without his interference.

Harlow had kept an eye on the entrance, hoping to catch Audrey early. That idea was foiled by a rather persistent movie producer who wanted to discuss a project he wanted her to work on the music for. *This is why you keep Casper around at these things.*

"Oh, Steve, give Ms. Thorne a break. She just won an award for the last song she worked on for a movie. Let her bask in the excitement for a few hours before you lock her into something else." Audrey stepped up next to her at the table.

Audrey's arrival was such a welcome reprieve that Harlow almost hugged her without concern for anything they'd discussed before. She'd been waiting for this time together, and now that it was here, she had very little patience for interference. It wouldn't have mattered if she'd been talking to Brad Pitt, she still would've wanted to shoo him away.

"Audrey," he said as he tipped his wine glass toward her. "Congratulations on your two wins as well. You're quite the commodity right now."

Audrey clinked her glass against his. "Do you mind if I borrow Ms. Thorne for a moment? We need to discuss some upcoming press."

Bless her.

He looked disappointed but took his leave. "Have a good evening. I'll contact your managers."

Harlow kissed Audrey on the cheek. "Thank you. Casper normally gets me out of those predicaments."

Audrey squeezed her hand. "It was a selfish move. I wanted you to myself. Although it was slightly entertaining to watch him fall all over himself." She leaned closer and kept her voice low. "But if I can get my production company off the ground, I'm going to make you promise to give me a song for our first movie."

"It was a great idea when you told me about it a few days ago, and it's an even better one now that I know you're interested in using me." She winked. "I love your dress, by the way. It makes you look every bit the badass." Harlow traced her finger up Audrey's side to her arm.

She knew the touch was more intimate than what they'd agreed to, but she didn't care. The desire to touch Audrey was overwhelming, and she didn't care what looks it elicited.

Audrey glanced at Harlow's finger with a subtle look of confusion. "I wore it hoping you'd want to take it off me."

Harlow slid her hand behind Audrey's back, pulling her closer. "Where's your mom?"

Audrey still looked confused, but she didn't protest. "She went home. She's not a fan of the after-parties." Audrey looked around. "You know people are staring at us."

Harlow nodded but couldn't stop looking at Audrey's lips. "I don't care."

"Are you sure? We can always just go back to my house. We don't have to be together in public."

Harlow contemplated her options. If she wanted to continue to avoid questions, they should leave immediately. Then she thought back to what it felt like at the show. She hadn't been able to be with Audrey the way she wanted. She hadn't been able to support her or kiss her. She didn't want that with Audrey. She didn't want to pretend she was something she wasn't. She wanted Audrey, and she didn't care who knew it. And Audrey knew what she was getting into.

Harlow rested her cheek against Audrey's. "I've been reconsidering that whole agreement. I don't mind answering a few questions if you don't."

Audrey smiled against her cheek. "I don't mind at all." She took Harlow's hand. "How about a drink?"

Audrey tugged Harlow through the crowd to a table near the bar. Harlow was accustomed to people staring at her when she was in their proximity. She was used to the whispers and the pointing, but this felt different. This would be the first time she'd be publicly linked to anyone, and it wouldn't just be speculation. It didn't feel the way she thought it would. She'd pictured herself being uncomfortable, or at least a little more timid. But Audrey made her feel brave, even emboldened. She just hoped it would be the same for her.

She still wasn't ready to make a public announcement to define what they were to one another. She fiercely guarded her personal life and wanted to keep it that way. She knew the questions would start as they always did when she was spotted with someone. She expected it, and so did Audrey—that's how their lives worked. But she didn't want their relationship to overshadow Audrey's movie or her tour.

Audrey handed her a whiskey. "You okay?"

Harlow took a sip of the amber liquid and let it warm her throat. "I just don't want us being together in public to derail anything for either of us." She wished she could take it back as soon as she said it. It sounded shallow and heartless—even if that wasn't how she meant it.

Audrey raised her left eyebrow and leaned closer. "What could possibly go wrong? The press becoming overly obsessed and not covering my movie or your tour and only focusing on whether we're together?"

Harlow sighed in relief. "I was scared you'd think I was shallow. But of course, you get it."

Audrey glanced to the other side of the room. "When Tia and I got together, she ended up getting three television spots because of the increased press coverage." There was a bit of pain and irritation in her eyes.

"I don't want to be on television, nor do I ever want to be in a movie."

Audrey smiled as she ran her hand down Harlow's arm. "Perfect. I don't want to sing in front of thousands of people."

"Look at us, solving all the hard problems up front."

"And people say relationships are hard," Audrey said as she smiled. She took the glass from Harlow's hand and set it on the table. "Come dance with me."

A few hours later, they were waiting in the glass-enclosed lobby for their cars. Harlow had dreaded this moment all night. She had no desire to be away from Audrey for a minute more than she had to be, but they hadn't discussed what would happen at the end of the night. It wasn't like in Monterey, where they were holed up from the rest of the world. Paparazzi cameras were flashing nonstop, and there were plenty of people watching, undoubtedly wondering if they'd get in the same vehicle.

Audrey glanced at the paparazzi and tucked her hair behind her ear. She looked as if she wanted to say something but didn't. Harlow realized she probably didn't want to push her to do something she wasn't comfortable with in public.

Harlow grabbed her hand. "Come home with me."

Audrey's smile was immediate. "Do you want me to meet you there?"

Harlow felt no hesitation now. "No, my driver will take us."

The driver opened the back passenger door, and Audrey and Harlow hurried into the car, ignoring the questions about where they were going together. The driver said it would be thirty minutes to get to Harlow's place and rolled up the privacy barrier.

"How are you feeling? You okay?" Audrey's face was full of concern.

It hurt Harlow to think Audrey was feeling unsure about how she felt about her or the decision to spend time together in public. There were millions of words available to articulate her feelings. She could string several of them together in a sentence and hope her point was made, but it didn't seem sufficient.

She slid her hand behind Audrey's neck and pulled her closer. "My only regret is not kissing you as soon as I saw you in this dress."

Audrey smiled as she kissed her. The kiss was sweet and slow. It was filled with a tenderness that Harlow couldn't quite pinpoint. Audrey deepened it, pulling Harlow further into the moment. She'd wanted to be this close to Audrey all night, and now she couldn't wait until they got back to her place.

Audrey pulled away and picked up her purse. "Sorry. This thing won't stop buzzing." She pulled out her phone.

"Everything okay?" Harlow gently rubbed Audrey's arm.

Audrey turned the phone off and put it back in her purse. "Just my agent telling me to look at Twitter."

"Do you need to check it?" Harlow's pulse quickened, thinking about what people could already be saying.

Audrey ran her hand over Harlow's face and through her hair. "Not tonight. We only have a few hours. I'll deal with it tomorrow."

Harlow watched Audrey's eyes. She needed to know if that sentiment was sincere. All she saw looking back was blatant honesty and desire. She leaned into Audrey's palm and kissed her wrist.

"What time do you have to leave tomorrow?" Audrey whispered.

"I have to be on my plane by seven."

Audrey shifted her wrist to bring the gold watch face around to the front. "You have five hours to make sure I don't forget you while you're gone."

Harlow laughed. "Is that so?"

Audrey kissed her. "Wasting time, superstar."

The car rolled to a stop, and the driver came around to open the door. "Have a pleasant evening, Ms. Thorne."

"You too, Thomas. I'll see you in the morning," she said to him, but she couldn't pull her eyes away from Audrey.

The low light inside her room cast shadows across Audrey's face. Harlow had always thought Audrey was beautiful, but there was something different when they were alone. Her flawless features had been a part of her quick rise to fame. Her long neck and perfect jawline seemed like the work of an artist. Her pursuit of movie stardom in the genre of action films had sculpted her body like a goddess. But when they were alone together, she softened. Like every protective wall fell away to reveal the gentle, sweet beauty underneath that she reserved just for Harlow.

Audrey slid her hands down the front of Harlow's jacket and released the front button. She pushed it off her shoulders and let it fall to the floor. Harlow watched as Audrey's pulse quickened under the skin of her neck as she pulled Harlow's shirt over her head. Harlow reached around Audrey's back and slid the zipper down. Audrey stepped out of her dress to reveal her black lace bra and underwear.

Harlow's emotions were on overdrive as Audrey pulled her in to kiss her. She loved how her soft skin felt pressed against her body. Harlow had been with dozens of beautiful women over the years, but none of them compared to this. She had never been so utterly dominated by someone's touch or presence. She didn't ever want it to stop.

She hadn't tasted Audrey in weeks, and the sweetness on her lips was better than she'd remembered. She tasted like champagne and chocolate, like desire and home. Her skin was soft and warm. Harlow ran her lips down the soft expanse of her neck to her shoulders. She smiled against Audrey's skin when she felt her shudder.

"I don't think I'll ever get enough of you touching me," Audrey said as she ran her hands through Harlow's hair.

Audrey pulled her down onto the bed and took one of her nipples in her mouth. Harlow closed her eyes and groaned at the excruciating pleasure that surged through her body. She bit down on Audrey's shoulder as her hand slid down between her legs.

"I missed you." Harlow managed to choke out between breaths.

Audrey slid her fingers inside Harlow. "Show me."

She pushed against Audrey, and everything in her felt like it was lit on fire as Audrey started her gentle rhythm. The orgasm was building inside her, but it was much too fast. She wanted more of Audrey. She wanted all of her. She maneuvered their bodies and forced Audrey onto her back. She pulled away and smiled at the groan of protest that escaped Audrey's lips.

She slid her mouth over Audrey's ribs toward her stomach. She quivered and moved against her as she continued her exploration down her body. When she finally reached Audrey's sex, she heard Audrey whimper.

"Put your mouth on me."

Harlow did as she was told and was rewarded with a gasp. She slid her tongue along her hot center, loving every blissful second. She drew it out as long as she could, but Audrey's body was urging her to move faster. Her hips moved under her mouth, begging for more. Harlow knew with a bit more pressure she'd push Audrey over the edge, and when she begged for release, Harlow did just that. Audrey's tumble into her orgasm dragged Harlow along. She'd never climaxed while pleasuring someone else, but she was quickly discovering that Audrey offered her an array of firsts that went far beyond the physical.

She climbed up next to her and continued to lazily stroke Audrey's flushed skin. She kissed the back of her neck and loved the quiet hum Audrey offered. She knew there would be more of this tonight. She could already feel her arousal building again, but she wanted to enjoy all the moments she had with Audrey. These times in between, where they lingered somewhere between love and passion, were some of her favorites. Audrey had made Harlow want things she never thought she could have.

CHAPTER TWENTY-THREE

Audrey drew small circles on Harlow's back as she listened to her rhythmic breathing. She looked over at the neon numbers glowing next to her and sighed. She picked up Harlow's hand and kissed her knuckles.

They'd only fallen asleep an hour before, and Audrey knew she was going to be wrecked for the remainder of the day. She smiled as she buried her face deeper into the pillow. She'd be blissfully wrecked and wouldn't change a single second of it. Sex with Harlow was fantastic, but more than the sex was becoming addictive. The way Harlow looked underneath her when she came. The primal possessiveness that spilled out when Harlow would bite down on her shoulder, too overcome with desire to hold back. The way she'd say her name when she was right on the brink. Audrey loved all of it and couldn't get enough.

Harlow turned her head to look at her. "What time is it?"

Audrey kissed her forehead. "We need to get up if you're going to make your plane."

Harlow scooted up and buried her face in Audrey's neck. "Seven days until San Jose."

"I wouldn't miss it." Audrey forced herself into a sitting position.

"You better not. Those tickets are expensive." Harlow slid behind her and wrapped her arms around her. She kissed her shoulder. "You'd be costing me."

Audrey laughed and kissed her cheek. "I don't want to be the reason you end up destitute."

"I know. I'd have to go live in your pool house." Harlow released her and walked to her closet.

Audrey felt the absence of her body and wished for the millionth time they had more time together. She made her way over to the bathroom and splashed cold water on her face. Harlow pulled a drawer open and handed her a toothbrush.

"Thank you." Audrey eyed Harlow up and down. "Put some clothes on before I make you late."

Harlow smiled and handed her sweats and a shirt. "I figured you'd want these to wear home. As hot as that dress is, I bet you don't want to put it on right now." She walked past her. "Don't follow me into the shower, or I'll never get out of here on time."

"I could think of worse reasons to be late," Audrey said as Harlow stepped into the large shower. "There's enough room for three people in there."

"Six actually," Harlow said and laughed teasingly.

Audrey pulled on the clothes Harlow had given her. "Funny. You're very funny."

"What are you doing this week?"

"I have some press to do, and I find out if my production idea is going to get off the ground."

Harlow stepped out of the shower and pulled a large towel from the rack. "Of course it will." She kissed Audrey's cheek as she walked into her closet. "You're Audrey fucking Knox. People will line up to work with you."

"I appreciate it, but wanting to work with me and wanting to fund a project are two very different things."

Harlow came out of her closet in jeans and a T-shirt. "I think you can do anything."

Audrey hugged her. "Thank you, but it's not you that I need to convince."

"Come with me. I want to show you something."

Harlow took her hand and walked her down the stairs and into a large room. There was a sizable white screen on the front wall and twelve black recliners in three lines. A movie theater popcorn machine sat next to a drink cooler, and there were shelves of candy stacked on the other side.

Harlow pointed to the left wall. "What do you see there?"

Audrey looked at the movie posters and put her hand over her chest. "You mean aside from having your own movie theater? You have posters of every movie I've been in." Audrey stepped closer to look at them.

Harlow put her arm around her. "I realize now that it may seem creepy." She chuckled. "But I swear I had no idea we'd ever be in this situation. I just wanted to show you that you have devoted fans—people who've followed you through your whole career. Those movie people know that. You're a good investment. Your name attached to a project helps it sell. Have a little faith in yourself. I have faith in you."

Audrey hugged her. "Thank you." She pulled back to look at Harlow. "And it is a little creepy now."

Harlow shrugged. "What can I say? You've always been my celebrity crush."

Audrey kissed her for being adorable. She kissed her for being sweet. But mostly, she kissed her for saying precisely what she needed to hear at that moment.

Harlow's phone buzzed. "We have to get going."

Audrey found herself sitting as close to Harlow as possible on the drive to her house. She hadn't planned on missing Harlow as much as she did—as much as she knew she would in a few minutes, but that was the truth. Harlow made her feel special in a way she didn't think possible. She was normal with her, special with her and seen by her.

Harlow rested her forehead against Audrey's when the car stopped in front of her door. "Thank you for last night."

Audrey smiled. "Which part?"

Harlow kissed her. "All of it. And for giving me more than three kisses."

"You're so welcome." Audrey reached for the door. "I'll see you soon."

Harlow grabbed her hand before she got out of the car. "Audrey." Audrey stopped and looked at her. "Go into those meetings knowing it will be their loss if they don't choose to work with you. Don't let anyone sell you on accepting less than what you want."

Audrey put her hands on Harlow's cheeks and kissed her. "Thank you for being you."

Audrey watched as Harlow's car pulled away, and she forced herself to take a deep breath. Kylie was sitting on the couch tying her running shoes when she walked in the front door with a massive smile on her face.

Audrey flopped down on the couch next to her. "Morning."

Kylie gently kicked her side. "How was your night?"

"I won both categories."

Kylie pinched her leg. "I saw, but that wasn't what I was talking about."

Audrey sighed. "It was wonderful, and my God, sex with her gets better every time."

Kylie clapped. "Those are the details I want."

"That's all the details you're getting." She pointed to Kylie's table. "Jane wanted me to look at Twitter. How bad is it?"

Kylie typed a few words on the keyboard and handed the tablet to Audrey. "Ten thousand Twitter mentions."

Audrey scrolled through and tried not to cringe when she passed some of the more hateful comments. "Well, no one can confirm anything. It's all speculation." She allowed herself a few moments to study some of the pictures. Her black dress and Harlow's white tux were a fantastic contrast, but that wasn't the only thing she noticed. She studied the expression on Harlow's face in one of the candid shots someone had captured. She remembered the moment well. Harlow had made a funny comment about how much they must have paid for the centerpieces, and Audrey laughed. Harlow's eyes were focused entirely on her, as though Audrey was the only person in the room. If she hadn't known where they were in this picture, she'd assume they were like any other couple in the world caught in a perfect moment. She smiled at the memory.

Kylie nodded and took the tablet back. "Do you think Harlow is ready for this? She's always been so private." She pointed to the screen. "This is the opposite of that."

Audrey leaned her head back on the couch and looked at Kylie. "She says she's okay, but a thought exercise is vastly different from reality."

"Jane sent me a list of responses to questions you'll probably get today. You have two interviews, and the first one is in three hours. "

Audrey pushed herself off the couch. "Go on your run. I'll take a shower, and when you're ready, we can get going."

"Hey," Kylie said. "For what it's worth, you look incredibly happy in these pictures from last night."

"I am happy, thank you."

Audrey headed toward the stairs to take a shower. She was happy—supremely. Harlow was happy, for the moment. Now, they just had to make sure that the rest of the world didn't derail that for them.

❖

Harlow had managed to put Casper off for the entire flight, feigning exhaustion. Unfortunately, the flight was only an hour. He hadn't bothered to make eye contact with her until they were safely in the car on the way to the hotel.

"Did you have a good night?" Casper's tone implied that he wasn't actually curious about her night.

"Yes. Did you?" She pulled her hair back because she needed something to do with her hands.

"My night doesn't matter. Have you looked at social media?" He held up his phone.

Harlow sighed. "No, but I'm sure you're going to fill me in."

He tossed her the phone. "I told you we'd figure all this out, but we needed a plan. Going out with Audrey in public isn't a plan—it's a statement."

Harlow rolled her eyes. "So what if it is? Does it really matter? It's not like being seen with Audrey will tank my ticket sales. People will ask questions, but they always do. We aren't proclaiming that we're together. I haven't sworn my devotion to her in public." She sighed. Casper had no idea how much time she'd spent thinking this through. The more she turned it over in her head, the less it bothered her. Yes, she'd always been private, but nothing had changed. She was far more concerned about what her reputation could do to Audrey than vice versa.

Casper rubbed his face. "And what if this doesn't work out? You'll be the person who hurt sweet Audrey Knox. I bet there will be an over-under on you two in Vegas. Remember when what's-his-name cheated on and divorced Sandra Bullock?"

She opened a bottle of water and drank half the contents before answering. "I think you're getting a little ahead of yourself, Casper. We've been seen together once, and you already have me married, cheating, and running."

"Damn it, Low. You aren't built for anything else, and we both know it. I know you like her, but what is the point of all this really?" He pointed at her. "A teenage crush?"

"Just because I've never been involved with someone long-term doesn't mean I can't learn to be." She knew she was raising her voice, but she didn't care. His assertion hurt.

"I'm looking out for you like I've always done. She's one of America's sweethearts, and you don't want to be on the wrong end of that. Look how the tides turned on her ex. She ran around saying all kinds of negative things about Audrey. People pondered it for what, like ten seconds? Now it has been hit job after hit job in the media, and the word is no one will hire her."

The car rolled to a stop at the back of the hotel, and she unbuckled her seat belt. "We aren't confirming anything. We're letting people get used to seeing us in public. We're spending time together. We'll announce our relationship when we have to and not a second before. Jesus, we're not even totally sure what it is, yet." She threw his phone back at him. "Not that it is anyone's business."

He followed her into the hotel. "We aren't done talking about this."

She ignored him and continued to the service elevator. She understood that Casper had a job to do—a job she paid him to do, but this was ridiculous. At the very least, he could've taken a full minute to be her brother instead of whatever this was.

He closed the hotel door behind them. "You're being reckless. Do you have any idea how many people are impacted by your decisions? It's not just you. You have an entire team of people you employ. There are millions of young women who look up to you."

She turned and shoved her finger in his chest. "Don't do that. Don't you dare put all that on me. I'm entitled to live my life. I'm entitled to be happy." She pushed him farther back. "I've followed all the rules. I've been everything everyone ever wanted me to be. I get to have something that makes me happy." She swallowed against the knot in her throat. "Just because we haven't been built for something doesn't mean we can't change. That we can't be more. That's not fair, Cas."

He stared at her for so long she was sure the argument was going to escalate to another level. She was trying to get her breathing under control. Her anger was simmering right on the surface. She'd never pushed back against her brother. She hadn't had a reason to until now.

He stood and grabbed her, wrapping her in a hug. "You're right. I'm sorry."

She reluctantly hugged him back. "I'm right?"

He stepped back and held her at arm's length. "You deserve to be happy. I want you to be happy." He ran his hand through his hair. "I guess I've just been feeling a bit out of the loop, and I'm not used to that. I'm sorry."

She sat down on the bed. "I *have* thought it through. I know you don't think so, but I have."

He sat next to her and bumped her shoulder with his own. "It's not that I don't think you're capable of more. I just don't want to see you get hurt. I'd hate to think the first time you actually take a leap, you end up hurt and blasted by the press. You're more fragile than people think." She stared at him and opened her mouth to answer, and he held up his hand. "It's not your or Audrey's fault. It's just one of the costs no one ever thinks about." He kissed her forehead. "I love you, Low. Take a nap, and I'll see you at the stadium in a few hours."

He walked out of the room, and she let herself fall back onto the bed. She was angry that her personal life was up for debate. She was frustrated that her brother thought it was his place to weigh in on her decisions. Mostly, she was irritated that any of this had to be discussed.

She picked up her phone and smiled when she saw a text message from Audrey. *I miss you more than words can express. Good luck tonight. Xoxoxo.*

Audrey was absolutely worth it. Whatever was going to happen, Harlow was ready to face it head-on if it meant having Audrey. There was no doubt in her mind, no matter what her brother said.

Chapter Twenty-four

Audrey closed her eyes as the makeup artist put the finishing touches on her lipstick. Lights in a television studio were always brighter and hotter than those on a movie set. She understood it was a necessity, but she couldn't help but feel as if they were a little hotter today. It also could have something to do with the fact that she'd only slept for an hour and had to change her wardrobe a few times to make sure the bite mark Harlow had left on her shoulder wouldn't be seen. *Totally worth it.*

The countdown ended, and the host plastered on her television smile. "Welcome back. I'm thrilled to have Audrey Knox here with me today." The host turned her attention to Audrey. "Audrey, congratulations on your two People's Choice Awards last night. You must be delighted."

Audrey smiled. "It's always exciting to win an award that is decided by the fans. I'm so grateful for all the support I've received, not just this year but throughout my whole career. I have amazing fans."

Behind the host, pictures of the awards show flashed on a large television screen. "How cool was it to have Harlow Thorne performing a song from your new movie?"

Here it comes.

Audrey nodded. "Harlow is incredible, and we were all so appreciative that she agreed to be part of the project."

"It seems like you two have become pretty good friends. Is that because of the film?"

Audrey clasped her hands in her lap. "Yes. We met because of the film and became friends. I enjoy spending time with her."

The host turned and looked at the pictures. "You two seem very cozy." An image of the two of them leaving the award show holding hands appeared on the screen. "Is there more than friendship brewing there?"

Audrey hated that she had to laugh, but she did. "Harlow and I like spending time together, but that's all I'm going to say."

The host leaned in, pretending it was just the two of them in the conversation. "Does that mean you're both still single?"

Audrey laughed again and shook her head. "If I have any public announcements to make, I'll let you know."

Twenty minutes later, Audrey unhooked her microphone, thanked the host, and walked to the green room where Kylie was waiting.

Kylie pushed her glasses up her nose. "Well, that went pretty well."

Audrey started pulling off her clothes to change into jeans. "I think so. She didn't spend the whole time focused on Harlow and me. At least I got to talk about the movie."

There was a knock on the door, and Kylie pulled it open. It was Alicia, the host of the entertainment show who'd just done the interview.

"I just wanted to thank you again for doing the show. I'm sorry about all the Harlow questions, but with the way Twitter was reacting, I had to ask."

Audrey waved her off. "No big deal. Thanks for a good interview."

Alicia handed her a card. "My cell is on the back. I'd love to take you out for a drink." She took a step closer. "Are you free Saturday?"

Kylie stepped up beside her. "She's out of town from Saturday through Monday."

Alicia nodded at Kylie and turned her attention back to Audrey. "The next weekend?" Audrey hesitated long enough for her to continue. "Give me a call if you're free. It doesn't have to be anything serious."

"I will, thanks," Audrey said.

Kylie looked at her with raised eyebrows after the door shut. "You know that's going to keep happening if everyone continues to think you're single."

Audrey picked up her bag and swung it over her shoulder. "So? I don't have to agree to go out with everyone that asks."

"No, of course, you don't. But it will add fuel to the fire about you and Harlow the longer you don't answer questions."

"We're taking it a day at a time."

Kylie nodded. "I know that, but the vague answers will only work for so long."

Audrey didn't respond because she wasn't sure what else to say. Kylie was right, but this was what they'd agreed to, and it was still too new to push it.

Kylie handed her the phone. "Speak of the devil."

Audrey read the text message. *You looked amazing during the interview. I'm heading to the stadium. I'll call you tomorrow.*

"Got to love live television." Audrey handed the phone back to Kylie.

Audrey had agreed to deflect questions because it was what Harlow wanted, but Kylie was right. It wouldn't hold up forever. At times Harlow was filled with confidence that bordered on cockiness, and then at others, she was like a terrified girl afraid it would all be taken away in a heartbeat. Audrey wanted her to feel safe. She just needed to figure out a way to make that happen.

One of Harlow's favorite parts of touring was the meet and greet. There was something magical about the palpable excitement exuded from the fans she had personal interaction with—even if it was only for a minute or two. If it were up to her, she'd spend longer than the time allotted, but that decision hadn't been hers for years.

A young girl came back into the staged area and burst into tears. "I can't believe I'm meeting you."

Harlow hugged her. "Thank you for coming."

The girl's hands were shaking. "Your music means so much to me. It got me through some of the hardest times in my life."

Harlow grabbed her hands. "And you have no idea how much you mean to me."

The young girl handed her a small rainbow pin. "My best friend got this for me the day I moved in with her because my parents threw me out of the house."

Harlow had to grit her teeth to keep from crying. "Are you safe now?"

The girl nodded. "Yes. I'm doing much better. I just wanted you to have this. I know you don't specifically sing about women, but sometimes it feels like you do. Thank you."

Harlow hugged the young woman, and tears nearly fell when she saw the scars along her wrists. "I want you to hang on to your pin. How about instead I give you something?" She waved to her tour manager. "She's going to give you two VIP tickets to the next show. We're going to take care of your hotel and getting you there too." She waited for her manager to nod. "You're enough. Don't let anyone tell you differently."

The young girl continued crying and nodding her understanding. "I don't know what to say."

"What's your name?"

"Monica."

Harlow hugged her again. "I'll see you on Saturday, Monica."

Later that night, when Harlow stood on the stage listening to the twenty thousand fans screaming her name, all she could think about was how many more Monicas were out there. Casper had talked about the negative impacts of her being in a public relationship, but what about the positive? Visibility was important. Knowing there were people like you out there was important. She'd been so concerned about what questions could mean for her career and privacy, she'd never considered what more public relationships would mean to the LGBTQ+ community—especially the youth.

She sat at the large black piano that had been wheeled out on stage. "This song is for my new friend, Monica."

Harlow sang one of her most famous songs and intentionally changed the pronouns to she/her. It wasn't difficult. The song had been written about a woman. She'd just never had a reason to proclaim as much. She needed to be more like Monica.

Casper handed her a water bottle when she stepped off stage. "Nice show."

She took it and gulped down as much as she could with her limited breath. "Thanks."

She waited for him to comment on the final song of the night, but he didn't. "I need to head back to LA."

"Everything okay?" Harlow was relieved he wasn't going to make an issue out of what just happened, but she was concerned he was leaving.

"Nothing I can't handle."

She grabbed his arm. "What's going on?"

He looked like he wasn't going to answer at first, but he didn't. "Just some stuff with a contract I need to be there for."

He was lying, she could see it in his eyes, but Harlow released his arm. "I'll see you in San Jose."

"I'll be there." He kissed her cheek and left.

The drive back to the hotel was even lonelier than normal. She turned the conversation with Casper over in her head several times. Something was going on with him, and she had no idea if she should be concerned.

Still distracted, she showered and called Audrey. "Hey."

"Hey, superstar," Audrey said, her voice much more enthusiastic than she'd expected for two in the morning.

"Why are you still awake?"

Audrey squealed. "I got that author under contract to write the screenplay—it's the first step in creating my own production company. We still need to get the funding, but I have several possibilities lined up, and they're looking really good. I was going to wait until I saw you to tell you, but I'm just too excited. I've been celebrating with Kylie. How was your show?"

Harlow wanted to tell her about Casper and her unease when he left, but she decided not to burden Audrey. She was so excited about her project, and the last thing she wanted to do was bring her down.

"I'm so happy for you. I knew you could do it."

"Thank you for having faith in me." Audrey squealed again. "I'm so excited about this. It will be a game changer for my career."

"You deserve it. I'm proud of you."

"I can't wait to see you. We can celebrate together."

"Absolutely. I'll see you in two days."

It sounded like Audrey brought the phone closer to her mouth. "I miss you. I can't wait to kiss you."

Harlow smiled as she tucked herself in under the sheets. "I miss you too. Congratulations. Now, go continue the celebration. I'll see you soon."

"Don't forget the kissing. I want lots of kissing."

Harlow switched off the light. "All the kissing."

"Night, Harlow."

"Good night, Audrey."

Harlow plugged her phone into the charger and closed her eyes. She tried to focus on Audrey and on the look on Monica's face when she gave her the tickets. That's what she wanted to see, but she couldn't get Casper out of her mind. She needed to find out what was really going on with him because she had a feeling it wasn't good.

Chapter Twenty-five

Audrey was amazed as the limo waited to pull into the VIP entrance at the SAP Center in San Jose. There were thousands of people in line waiting for their turn to enter. People were decked out in creatively decorated shirts, many were holding signs, and others bounced around with extraordinary excitement.

"How long has it been since you've been to a concert?" Kylie looked amused.

Audrey shook her head. "At least a decade." She pointed to the bouncing fans. "Is it always like this?"

Her mom joined her at the window. "I haven't seen anything like this since Elvis."

Audrey bumped her mom. "You're not old enough to have ever seen Elvis."

"No, but I watched him on television when I was a little girl. Your grandma used to say he had the devil in his hips."

Audrey laughed, picturing her long passed grandmother saying exactly that. "She would've fainted seeing Harlow dance around the stage."

The car stopped, and two men in suits opened the door. "We're here to escort you and your party in, Ms. Knox."

Audrey stepped out of the vehicle. It took only a few moments for the people at the end of the line to recognize her. Many started yelling, waving, and pointing. Audrey waved back and was going to walk over to take selfies, but the security detail had other plans. They stepped between her and the growing crowd, directing her toward the door.

The larger of the two men leaned down to talk to her. "If you're going to stop for photos, we need advance notice to block off the area."

Audrey nodded. "Sorry about that. I hadn't thought about it."

"We'll talk to your people before you arrive next time," he said.

Next time. Audrey wondered how much Harlow's security detail knew about their relationship. She'd clearly filled them in to some extent, but she didn't know the scope of their duties. She made a mental note to ask Harlow if this was the norm so she knew what to expect next time.

The security guards led them through the bowels of the arena. There were hundreds of people scampering around. Huge metal boxes on wheels, people talking into headsets, and carts full of sparkling clothes moved past them.

The taller man pushed a door open and showed them into a small room. "We'll come to get you right before the concert starts." He pointed to a phone in the corner. "If you need anything, just pick up the receiver."

The room didn't look like it belonged with all the organized chaos taking place just a few feet away. There were large leather couches, a glass table, a full bar, snacks, and framed posters of Harlow at different concerts on the walls.

Kylie walked to the corner of the room and pulled a bottle of champagne from the bucket. "This is way better than anything you get on set." She pulled three glasses from the shelf. "Maybe she'll give me a job."

"I clearly went into the wrong artistic field." Audrey took the glass Kylie offered.

Her mom sipped from the glass. "Oh, honey, you have a terrible voice. It would've never worked out for you."

"Thanks, Mom," Audrey said and tried not to laugh.

Her mom shrugged. "It's true." She picked up a half sandwich from the tray. "I can't wait to see the show. I know every single song by heart."

Audrey took another sip of champagne. Her nerves were starting to fray from the anticipation of seeing Harlow. This level of excitement over a person was new to her, and her body didn't know how to handle it. It made her jittery and a little on edge. She was undoubtedly looking forward to seeing the concert, but mostly she wanted to be able to hug Harlow. She missed touching her, seeing her, and being near her.

The phone rang, and Kylie held up a finger. "Hello?" She paused for a second, listening to whoever was on the other line. "Thank you." She hung up the phone and smiled widely at Audrey. "Harlow is on her way down."

Audrey's heart rate increased exponentially. She didn't know why her body reacted like a teenager at the mere mention of her name, but that's precisely what happened. It was like being seventeen all over again. She checked her reflection in the mirror on the wall and ran her hands through her hair.

The door opened, and Harlow stepped inside. She was wearing a shimmering black V-neck bodysuit. Her black leather boots came right above her knees, and her blond hair hung over her shoulders. She looked absolutely stunning, but Audrey's favorite part was the way her beautiful blue eyes gleamed with excitement when they landed on her. Harlow seemed to have her own gravitational pull, and Audrey was firmly in her orbit.

Harlow held her arms open. "Hey, beautiful."

Audrey hugged her and inhaled as deeply as possible. "I missed you." She kissed her cheek. "You look incredible."

Harlow hugged both Kylie and her mom. "You guys have everything you need?"

Kylie raised her glass. "I was just telling Audrey that I should try to get a job with you."

Harlow held Audrey's hand as she continued to chat with her mom and Kylie. The simple gesture meant more to her than she could explain. It gave her a sense of normalcy, even if their lives were anything but that.

The door opened, and a frantic looking woman popped her head inside. "We need to get you in position, Harlow."

Harlow put a finger under Audrey's chin and tilted her head up to kiss her. "See you soon."

The smaller guard appeared again. "I'll take you to your seats."

They followed him through several corridors before they stopped at a large roped-off section on the arena's floor. The noise was incredible. The volume of screaming fans was enough to shake the walls. Thousands of tiny lights were littered throughout the crowd. People in the surrounding areas noticed their presence and started taking pictures of her with their phones.

"Do you want me to get security to have them stop?" Kylie yelled into her ear.

Audrey shook her head. "No, it's okay. They're here to have fun, just like us. They aren't hurting anyone."

The lights on the stage went completely out, and the screaming intensified another ten levels. Harlow's voice came through the speakers, singing the first line to her most popular song from the new album. The massive doors that hid the stage décor started to slide open, and bright white light spilled into the arena. Fog machines poured their contents out along the stage, and Harlow's silhouette appeared on the one-hundred-foot screen. The lighting strips that adorned the stage rails started flickering red to match the beat.

Harlow appeared on center stage, and the music went silent. She sang the first line one last time, the lights flashed in an array of colors, and pyrotechnics exploded above the stage. The song continued, and Harlow walked the stage like a cat. Her movements were perfectly timed, eloquent, and sexy as hell.

Her mom hugged her. "She's even better than I thought she'd be."

Audrey joined her mom and Kylie in singing along. She was keenly aware of the people still staring at her, taking pictures, and probably recording her. A part of her wondered what would be plastered all over Twitter, Instagram, Facebook, and any other platform she wasn't thinking of at the moment. The other part of her didn't care. She didn't care who knew she was at the concert, or that she was enjoying herself. She was proud of Harlow, and she didn't care who knew it.

Harlow only had forty-five seconds to change into her next outfit. The people who helped her could probably join the NASCAR Circuit with their precision. Shauna stepped up next to her on the platform, waiting for it to take them up for the next song.

"You're in a good mood tonight," Shauna said as she fixed her jacket.

Harlow fluffed her hair. "The show is going great."

"You sure it doesn't have to do with Audrey Knox sitting in the VIP section?" Shauna raised an eyebrow.

Harlow smiled as the lift started taking them to stage level. Her mood had everything to do with Audrey. She'd been looking forward to seeing her all week, but she hadn't been prepared for the way her body reacted to seeing her standing in the lounge. Audrey looked gorgeous in her short red dress that exposed her stomach and shoulders. But she looked even better, dancing and singing along to the music. Harlow had never performed for a single person, but that's how it felt on stage with Audrey in the audience. It didn't matter that there were seventeen thousand people in the arena. Audrey was all she could see.

Harlow performed the next two songs with Shauna. She'd vastly improved in the short amount of time they'd been on tour together, and Harlow knew she was going places. She was happy to be part of her growth. There was nothing quite like being able to hone your skills on stage, and she knew Shauna would be better off for the experience. There hadn't been any weirdness or awkward moments since the brief kiss they'd shared, and she was grateful for that. She wanted Shauna's experience on tour to be a positive one.

Harlow sat at the piano just as she did every night of her tour. She played as she spoke to the crowd about how thankful she was for each of them attending. She talked about love, hope, and heartbreak. She gave them little glimpses into her songwriting and how she came up with her ideas. She glanced over at Audrey and couldn't help but smile at her. At that moment, she decided to be a little more honest than she usually was with her fans.

Harlow let her fingers glide across the keys. "I wrote this next song when I was sixteen. The inspiration came from someone I went to high school with, and I was beyond smitten." The crowd laughed. "I was sure I'd never fall that hard again." She looked over at Audrey. "I was wrong."

She finished the show and hurried to the dressing room to change. All she could think about was being with Audrey. She'd spent the whole night staring at her from the stage, and now she only had a few hours to devote to her. She called her security team and directed them to bring Audrey to her dressing room. The wardrobe team helped her out of her outfit and inspected it for damage.

Audrey knocked on the door and entered when the wardrobe director pulled it open. "Hi."

Harlow pulled up her track pants. "Hi." She looked at the wardrobe director. "I think that's everything."

She checked the items on the rack and nodded. "We'll get these taken care of by tomorrow." She pushed the rack past Audrey and shut the door.

Audrey was in her arms before she had a chance to put her T-shirt on. "You were incredible." She kissed her hard. "I can't tell you how long I've wanted to do that."

"I'm so glad you made it," Harlow said and kissed her again. "I loved having you here."

Audrey ran her hands up Harlow's stomach and over her chest. "Do you know how much I've wanted you all night?"

Harlow picked her up and put her on the vanity. "I think I have a pretty good idea." She kissed her neck and worked her way up to her ear.

Audrey wrapped her legs around Harlow's back, pulling her closer. "My mom and Kylie are waiting."

Harlow pulled her head back. "Okay, we can get going."

Audrey pulled her back in. "No, don't you dare. I just need a little more urgency out of you."

Harlow slid her hand between Audrey's legs. "How much urgency?"

Audrey mimicked Harlow's movements and pushed hard against Harlow's center, causing her to gasp. They matched each other's rhythm until they were both breathing heavily. It was as if Harlow's body had been waiting for her all her life. Her reaction was so strong, she could barely stay upright. Each stroke brought her closer to the edge, causing her whole body to tremble. The force and sound of Audrey's breath on her neck increased until it hitched, and Audrey bit down on her shoulder and cried out. Harlow rested her head against Audrey's, waiting for the shuddering to subside. She'd never come so fast or with so little effort.

Audrey turned Harlow's face toward her and kissed her softly. The kiss was sweet and full of longing. If Harlow was still holding anything back, it broke away at that moment. She had no defenses left when it came to Audrey Knox. She'd never belonged to anyone—not completely. She did now.

Chapter Twenty-six

Audrey tentatively touched Harlow's hand as they walked, unsure how much PDA Harlow was comfortable with, and smiled when Harlow intertwined their fingers. The small gesture was another step forward in their relationship, and it made Audrey happy.

The security guard used his body to block them from the screaming fans and flash photography as he opened the door to the car. "We've called ahead to the restaurant. They're expecting us. After dinner, we'll escort you back to the hotel."

"Thanks, Greg," Harlow said as she climbed in the car.

Audrey grabbed Harlow's hand as soon as they were seated. "What's the other security guy's name?"

Harlow pointed to the driver. "That's Jim. They've both been with me for ten years."

Audrey's mom was practically vibrating with excitement. "Harlow, that was an amazing show. Thank you so much for having us. Truly, you were extraordinary."

Harlow turned to look at her. "Thank you, Kathy. I appreciate you all coming. I'm sorry you all have to leave so quickly."

"Audrey, you should really just spend the night."

Kylie jumped in. "Nope. Can't do it. I know that was the original plan, but we had to move things around. We have the first read through for the new film tomorrow morning, and then two meetings in the afternoon." She used the back of her hand to touch Audrey's cheek. "Are you feeling okay? You feel warm."

Audrey felt the burn of embarrassment flush her neck up to her forehead. "I feel great." She smiled, hoping to dissuade any further questioning.

The last thing she wanted to do was dwell on the subject or draw more attention to herself and have her mom realize she'd just had a quickie in an arena dressing room. Harlow squeezed her leg, and a jolt of excitement shot through her. Audrey shifted in her seat to be closer to Harlow. The heat from her body, the way it felt pressed against her, the way she smelled—Audrey had limited time to imprint this moment into her memory. It would be three weeks before she saw her again, and she'd need this anchor to get through.

The car pulled up outside the restaurant, and Audrey was relieved to see no paparazzi waiting outside. Greg got out of the car and went into the building. He emerged a few minutes later and pulled the car door open. They were escorted inside and into a small room in the back of the building.

The dinner conversation was light and fun. Audrey enjoyed being able to sit with Harlow and touch her during casual conversation. She watched fondly as her mom and Kiley interacted with her. It appeared they were nearly as enamored with Harlow as she was. Harlow was an attentive listener, funny, and engaging. Audrey knew she'd fallen hard for her, but it all came into crystal clear focus during this one meal. A sense of contentment overwhelmed her senses. Her three favorite women surrounded her, and she would've been perfectly happy to let the night stretch on into the early morning hours.

"I hate to do this," Kylie said as she checked her watch. "We need to get to the airport. We told the pilot we'd be there in an hour."

"Greg will take you there," Harlow said.

Kylie and her mom hugged Harlow good-bye. More accurately, her mom hugged Harlow and rocked her back and forth several times before finally releasing her. Audrey would've been embarrassed had it not been so cute to see her fawn over her.

Greg dipped his head in from the back entrance. "You should say good-bye inside. There are photographers here now."

"Thanks, Greg." Harlow took her hands and kissed her knuckles. "I'm going to miss you."

Audrey hugged her more forcefully than usual. "Me too." She breathed as much of Harlow in as she could muster.

"The American Music Awards are in three weeks."

Audrey wrapped her arms around her neck. "I know. I'm presenting."

"Go with me." Harlow ran her hands up and down Audrey's back.

"I'd go anywhere with you."

Harlow kissed her, and Audrey felt every nerve ending in her body burn. She absorbed the last drops she could out of their time together. Reluctantly, she took a step backward. If she was going to get to the plane on time, she couldn't put it off any longer.

Audrey opened the door and was met with flashing cameras and people shouting questions. Greg did his best to shield her, but she was sure they managed to get a few shots. She watched as Harlow climbed into the car behind hers and was relieved they only had to make it a few feet.

Kylie held up her phone as the car pulled away. "You two are trending again. The speculation about whether or not you're together is off the charts. Want to hear the couple name they've given you?"

Her mom leaned over Kylie's shoulder. "Oh, hashtag Audlow. That's cute. It could be worse." Her mom rubbed her shoulder.

"What are the chances the speculation will die down?" Audrey stared out the car window, wishing she was still with Harlow.

"Zero," Kylie said. "Are you worried?"

"Just about Harlow. You know I'm not bothered by it."

"I'm sure everything will be fine, honey. Harlow is no stranger to the press. She can handle it," her mom said.

Audrey took her mother's words to heart. She was right. Harlow wasn't new to this business, and she'd managed to stay at the top of her game for years. She needed to trust in her and what she knew they had together. There wasn't another option besides giving her up, and that wasn't going to happen.

Kylie closed her tablet and took a deep breath. "So there's something that I've meant to talk to you about, and I've kind of been putting it off, but I can't anymore."

Audrey felt her defenses go up. She leaned forward. "Is everything okay?"

Kylie held her hands up. "Oh gosh, yes, everything is fine." She smiled. "I didn't mean to make that sound so dramatic, sorry."

Audrey leaned back and let out a breath. "What's up?"

"I finished my screenplay." She pulled the tablet up against her chest. "I sent it out to a few studios, and I have a meeting tomorrow."

Audrey grabbed Kylie and wrapped her in a hug. Her heart swelled with excitement. "Oh my God, that's fantastic." She kissed her cheek. "I'm so excited for you. You have to let me read it."

"I don't want any favors, seriously. I'm not asking you for anything with this." Kylie's expression was serious and slightly worried.

Audrey grabbed her hands. "Kylie, you're my best friend. I want to read it because I love you, and I want to support you in whatever you choose."

Kylie's face softened, and she scrunched her nose. "Okay, I'll give you a copy." She grabbed her hand. "But I want your honest feedback. Don't sugarcoat it for me."

"I won't. I promise."

Audrey leaned back and let her head rest. Everything was trending toward the positive for not just her, but her best friend too. She couldn't have created a better scene had she written it herself. She was excited to see what the next few days, weeks, and months would bring for all of them.

Harlow pushed herself out of the lap pool and sat on the edge. It was rare that she had a day off, but she was going to take advantage. All that was on her schedule today was to get a massage, and then she was going to barricade herself in her hotel room and finish the book she'd started months ago. She pulled off her goggles and laughed to herself, thinking about how much had changed since her last tour.

During the last tour, days off included disappearing into a dive bar in disguise and having a random one-night stand. Now, just the thought of that made her uneasy. She wouldn't risk what she was building with Audrey for any form of emotionless escapism. *Look how far you've come.*

She dried off, pulled on her track pants, and slipped her feet into her flip-flops. She'd just thrown her towel in the bin when she heard someone open the door.

"Hey," Casper said from across the room. "I've been looking for you."

"You found me." She was still irritated by his erratic behavior, but she hugged him anyway. "I just finished doing laps. Come up to my room in half an hour. I need to shower."

He put his hands in his pockets, looking nervous. "I need to talk to you."

"Can it wait until after I shower?"

"I um—I don't think it can."

She put a hand on his shoulder. "Okay, come upstairs with me. Whatever it is, we'll figure it out together."

He nodded and dutifully followed her to the elevator. She wanted to make small talk to ease whatever was bothering him so much, but she couldn't. It was clear by his body language; there was something seriously wrong, and it had her anxiety spiking off the charts.

"Is Audrey okay?" She didn't realize her voice would shake until the words had left her mouth.

"What?" He looked surprised by the question. "As far as I know. This has nothing to do with Audrey."

She allowed herself to take a deep breath. There was nothing wrong with Audrey. Her anxiety subsided slightly. She could handle anything else Casper had to say. *Unless he's sick. Fuck. Don't let him be sick.*

Harlow sat on the bed as she watched Casper pace. "What's going on?"

Casper was moving like every muscle in his body was twitching. "I fucked up, Low." He shook his arms. "I fucked up real bad, and I can't fix it."

Harlow had never seen him like this, and it was making her incredibly uneasy. "Just tell me what's going on, and we can figure it out together. I'm sure it isn't as bad as you're imagining."

He ran his hands through his hair. "I got into some trouble gambling."

"Okay." She tried to keep her voice even, but she knew there was more.

"It's been escalating for a long time. I owed this guy in Vegas a lot of money. When I couldn't pay it all, he said I could work it off instead." He sat down. His face had turned a dark shade of red, and tears started to stream down his cheeks. "At first, it started with just a few small runs. It all seemed simple enough. I'd load one case onto a tour truck and deliver it to whoever when we got to a tour stop."

Harlow felt like she was having an out-of-body experience. She could see herself listening to him. Her chest was rising and falling rapidly, and her knuckles were white against the end of the bed. She could see it all unfolding, and she wanted to shake herself. She wanted this to be a dream—she wanted it to be anything but what was happening.

"What was in the cases, Casper?" She was surprised her voice didn't break as she spoke. He didn't answer right away, and her patience was on a razor's edge. "What was in the cases?" He said nothing but continued to sob. She got off the bed and pushed him. "Answer me right now, Casper."

He fell to the floor. "Fentanyl patches."

She sat on the chair, feeling as if her legs would give out from underneath her. Her head pounded, causing even the slightest noise in the room to drum against her temples. Her skin felt clammy as she began to sweat. Her stomach turned, threatening to expel what little was in it.

"I'm sorry. I'm so sorry. I know how bad I fucked up, but—"

"Why now?" She glared at him. "What happened that you waited until now to tell me?"

"One of the guys I delivered to was arrested," he whispered. "I think I'm going to be in big trouble."

She searched his face and realized she didn't know him anymore. In a matter of six minutes, he'd gone from being the most important person in her life to someone she didn't recognize. She searched her heart, hoping to find the remains of the love she had for him, but at the moment, all she could feel was anger and disappointment.

"The guitar you took from Monterey wasn't for a fundraiser, was it?"

He shook his head, looking defeated. "No. It was for more gambling debts. I couldn't pay him back with work until the tour started. I just...Low, I used the tour trucks. If it gets out, it could fall on you, too."

There should've been burning rage. Disgust. Shame. Betrayal. All those emotions were present, but the rage was nowhere to be found.

She stood and walked to the door. "Turn yourself in." She pulled it open. "You're off the tour. I can't have you anywhere near it, and you need to get help."

He stood. "Please don't do this. We can figure something else out."

She shook her head. "There isn't any other option, Casper. You've left me no other choice. Please leave. I'm too upset to even look at you right now. I need to be alone."

Normal people would've cried. Normal people would've called a lawyer to help the only person they'd ever trusted. Harlow stripped off her swimsuit and turned on the shower. She let the spray cascade down her trembling body as she considered all the elements that led her here. She'd spent her whole life being disappointed by people— her father, her mother, people in her small town, and now her brother. They'd promised they'd never hurt one another. They swore to protect each other. But not only had he not protected her, but he'd also potentially put her in the firing line too. The part that hurt the most was that he didn't trust her enough to ask for help. But then, when he had come to her, she'd turned him away. So maybe he was right. She slid to the bottom of the shower and let the tears fall.

CHAPTER TWENTY-SEVEN

Audrey wasn't sure what to make of the text message. She read it four more times as she patted her face down from her run. Her initial reaction to seeing a text message from Casper asking if they could talk was concern for Harlow, but she knew it was misplaced after rapid reflection. If something had happened to Harlow, Casper wouldn't want to talk. No. This came from a place of the in-between. Casper was either trying to decide something, or he wanted to issue a warning of some kind. *Or he could be planning a surprise birthday party. Jesus. Paranoid much?* She texted him back and was floored when he was at her house less than three minutes later.

She pulled the door open. "Were you just sitting outside my house?"

His arms were crossed, and he wouldn't look her in the eye. "Something like that. Can I come in?"

She stepped out of the doorway and waved him inside. "Sure."

She led him to the kitchen and poured herself a glass of water. "Want anything to drink?"

"Do you have anything stronger than water?" Casper fidgeted as he looked around the room.

Audrey pulled the whiskey out of the cabinet. "Strong enough?"

He nodded and looked impatient as she poured him three fingers of whiskey. He gulped it down and took the bottle from her hand. He poured himself another few fingers and clasped the tumbler like it tethered him to reality. She wasn't going to pretend this was normal by placating him with small talk. Casper had come here for a reason, and she would stand here until he was ready to share.

He stared down at the glass. "Have you spoken with Harlow?"

Audrey leaned down on the breakfast bar. "Not since yesterday. She said she was going to swim some laps. She has a show today, and I don't usually hear from her until after."

He sipped his whiskey. "I need your help." He still wouldn't make eye contact. "I fucked up pretty bad, and now I'm worried it's going to blow back on Harlow."

"I'm going to need more information than that."

She listened to him detail the last several years of his life. She listened to the rise and fall of his gambling career between football, boxing, MMA, horse races, and even airline flights. When all was said and done, he'd been in the hole for millions. Each time he tried to regain his footing, he fell even further behind. Each bet promised a better outcome than the last, but he could never win back enough to cover his losses. Even the short-term victories were quickly squandered because of the false bravado brought on by momentary triumph.

She watched him slowly break down as he explained the extent to which he owed the bookie and what he'd agreed to do to subsidize his losses. She could see it unfolding with each sentence. The bookie was in a win-win situation—forgiving debts just to have them rack up again with abandon. He finally reached the point in his story where he revealed the reason for his abrupt appearance at her home—Harlow's reaction. The pain he was in was palpable, and she couldn't help but feel a little bad for him, even though he'd gotten himself into this mess.

She was careful with her tone, not wanting to shame him further. "What is it exactly that you want me to do?"

He poured more whiskey into his glass. "Tell her to forgive me. Tell her I'm sorry. Make her see that I didn't do this to hurt her."

She reached across the counter and put her hand on his. "Forgiveness doesn't come from force. If and when it comes, it will be because Harlow has decided to give it to you."

"If I turn myself in, *she'll* be investigated. It will ruin her career. You have to make her see that."

She squeezed his hand. "That's not my decision to make."

He scoffed. "So you don't care what happens to her, is that it? Are you willing to watch her burn down her life for a stupid choice I made? I thought you cared about her?"

"Casper," she said and waited until he looked at her to continue. "You've put Harlow in an impossible situation. If you don't turn yourself in and get caught, she'll be in the middle. If you do turn yourself in, she'll be investigated, but the truth will come out. You want me to absolve you for what you've done, and I can't do that. You've done this, and you need to fix it."

He shook his head. "I'll go to jail."

"Probably." She came around the counter and sat next to him, taking his hands. "You need to talk to a lawyer. If you're really worried about your sister, you need to get out in front of this. She's got a team of people in her corner. Use them, and make things right."

"What if she never forgives me?" He wiped at his tears.

"She may not, but does that mean you shouldn't do the right thing?"

He sighed. "The right thing for who?"

"Only you can answer that."

He finished the rest of the whiskey and stood. "I gotta get going." He stopped at the door. "I really do love her."

Audrey crossed her arms. "I know. She loves you too. And that's why I know you'll do the right thing."

Casper got into the back seat of the car that had been waiting out front. Her heart broke as the car pulled away. Harlow had been through so much, and she'd view this as nothing short of outright betrayal. Casper and Harlow had sworn an allegiance to each other that she knew Harlow viewed as impenetrable. This would splinter her fragile heart, and Audrey wasn't sure if she'd let anyone close enough to help hold the pieces together—not even her.

"I know your heart is in the right place, but I really don't want to talk about it." Harlow swirled the ice cubes around in her glass. "He shouldn't have dragged you into it at all."

"I understand you don't want to talk about it, but I want you to know it's okay not to be okay." Audrey sounded concerned.

Harlow hated the sound of pity. She hated even more that it was falling from Audrey's lips. It was the last thing she wanted Audrey to feel when she thought about her. This was exactly what she'd been worried about. Dragging Audrey's reputation into the gutter would be unforgivable. She should've gone with her instincts. Hell, she should've listened when Casper told her it was a bad idea. Although, clearly, he had his own reasons for thinking so.

"Are you still going with me to the American Music Awards?"

"Harlow, of course I am. I'm here to support you."

"I want you to go to spend time with me, not because you're trying to keep an eye on me." Harlow knew she sounded angrier than she intended, but she couldn't help her reaction.

"I'm going with you because I wouldn't miss the chance to spend five minutes with you, much less several hours."

That mollified her a little, but not much. "I need to get to bed. I have an early flight to Phoenix tomorrow."

"Okay," Audrey said. "I worked both the New York and Los Angeles shows into my shooting schedule. I didn't want you to think I forgot."

Harlow's chest clenched from Audrey's thoughtfulness. "Thank you," she whispered. "I love having you there."

"I was thinking, since the New York show is right before Christmas, maybe you'd like to come back with me and spend the holiday with my family and me."

"I, um—" Harlow's heart raced at the idea of such an intimate gathering when her life could spiral out of control any second.

"No pressure at all. Just thought I would put it out there. Don't feel obligated." Audrey sounded panicked.

"I'd like that."

This was the first Christmas, or any holiday, Harlow would spend away from Casper. The realization burned like hot wax on an open sore. This was going to be her new reality, and she needed to do her best to cope. She'd planned on walling herself up in a hotel room and drinking until she didn't remember Casper's name, but this was a much better option.

"Okay, perfect." Audrey sounded excited, and Harlow was glad she could give that to her.

"I'll talk to you soon," Harlow said.

"Night, Harlow."

"Night."

Harlow turned off the lights and tried to put the conflicting emotions out of her mind. Part of her felt as if she was dying. The section of her heart that Casper had punctured burned. She was overwhelmed by a sense of betrayal for what he'd done and concern for his well-being. She ignored the incessant pleas for understanding he'd been lobbing at her in texts, voice mails, and emails. It wasn't that she didn't have compassion for the addiction he was struggling with—it was that instead of asking her for help, he'd put them both in line for serious trouble.

She hadn't spoken with Casper since he'd told her what happened. She didn't know what he was planning to do or how to handle it. The truth was, she didn't want to know. She still wasn't sure how she'd manage it if the police came to her to ask questions or if she should be trying to find him a lawyer. She'd reacted based on gut instinct—to get as far away from the problem as possible. The struggle now was knowing if that was the right thing to do or if she should be handling it differently.

Part of her wanted to help get him into rehab for his addiction. That part of her would've done exactly that had he come to her when the issue first arose. But he chose to take that possibility away when he submerged himself in the other aspect—the aspect that could land him in jail for years and do serious damage to her reputation.

She closed her eyes and tried to imagine what life would look like without Casper. She couldn't. She couldn't imagine any part of her life without him in it, but at what cost? And what about Audrey? The blowback could hurt her new production company, let alone her reputation. She couldn't be tied to a musician who was accused of drug running, could she? Just as she'd always feared, her roots based in addiction and fear were going to pull them all under. She held the pillow over her face and screamed into it. *Damn you, Casper.*

CHAPTER TWENTY-EIGHT

A udrey caught a glimpse of Jane impatiently tapping her foot at the edge of the sound stage. She'd been at rehearsal for the last several hours and couldn't imagine what could have her so wound up. Jane was brash and imposing, but she was always professional. This type of behavior was out of character.

Audrey hurried over as soon as the rehearsal wrapped. "What's up?"

Jane grabbed her arm and dragged her over to a quiet corner. "I changed my mind about you dating Harlow. I don't think it's a good idea."

Audrey pulled her arm away. "I'm sorry, what?"

Jane forcefully ran her hand through her hair. "I just got off the phone with a friend of mine at the Los Angeles Police Department. Casper Thorne turned himself in for drug trafficking. He was apparently using Harlow's tour bus as a cover. This will *not* be good for your image."

Audrey subconsciously put her hand against her chest, her heart aching for Harlow. "When is this going public? Has anyone warned Harlow?"

Jane looked annoyed by the question. "I don't know, and that's none of our concern. You need to get out of this relationship."

"I'm not going to do that."

The vein on Jane's forehead started to bulge. "We've based your entire career on being a good girl with a wholesome image. We've honed it so well people don't care about you being a lesbian. But they won't tolerate this."

Audrey wanted to say that she couldn't believe what Jane was saying, but that wasn't true. This was precisely what she'd expect to hear. She wasn't paid to care about Audrey's feelings, mental health, or what she felt was fair. Jane was paid to make Audrey marketable. She was paid to get Audrey the best jobs possible and to help build her brand. Audrey had always known she was a product, but it was crystallized in that moment.

"I don't care what they'll tolerate. I'm not leaving Harlow."

Jane pressed her lips together. "You think this whole standing on principle thing is cute—it's not. You're about to age out of the young action star genre. You don't do romantic comedies, and you're attempting to launch a production company that focuses on female-driven roles, writing, and directing. You don't get to die on this hill. Don't you see what you mean to an entire generation of women?"

Audrey crossed her arms. "And who exactly would I be if I abandoned someone when they needed me the most? It's not all about public perception. It's also about whether or not I can look in the mirror. Harlow didn't do anything wrong. These were her brother's choices, and I'm not going to punish her for them."

Jane grabbed her arm. "You talk about truth like it matters. Public perception is all that matters. I've seen people lose their careers for less."

Audrey pulled away. "The answer is no." She turned to leave. "I will not change my values for public perception."

Jane called out after her. "Don't say I didn't warn you."

Audrey ignored her as she continued to her car. It wasn't that Jane was wrong; it was that it didn't matter. People were going to have their opinions. People always did. But she wasn't going to let their version of the story dictate how she conducted herself. She refused to hang Harlow out to dry regardless of the implications. People could take what they wanted from that, but she was going to remain true to herself, and damn if she'd be yet another person to let Harlow down.

Harlow gripped the arms of the makeup chair. Her heart felt like it was hammering in her throat, and she'd been nauseous all day. She'd gotten on a plane early in the morning to be back in Los

Angeles for the American Music Awards. She'd arrived at her home and was patiently waiting for the stylists and makeup artists to work their magic. She'd done all of this on autopilot because she couldn't manage anything more.

The story broke that morning, and she knew it would change her life forever. It started first on ABC, then CNN, and now it was on every major media outlet. Her brother's addiction, his role in the drug operation, and the questions about her knowledge of it. She second-guessed every decision she'd made. She imagined her brother sitting by himself in a jail cell. She pictured what he must be thinking, feeling, and how alone he probably felt. It would be easy to say he did this to himself, but that would be absolving her of any wrongdoing. She'd failed him as a sister. She'd known something was wrong, but she'd stuck her head in the sand like she always did and figured he'd tell her what was wrong in his own time. She should've sat him down and made him talk to her.

She could've handled the situation a million different ways. She could've gotten him help, a lawyer, or she could've just hugged him. She did none of those things. She'd thrown him out because of old reactions to betrayal and loss.

Her phone buzzed, and she hesitated before looking at it. Relief swept over her when she saw it was a message from Kylie. *I'm at your house. Can I come in?*

Kylie waited patiently as the stylists put the finishing touches on her eyes. She looked concerned but not rushed. She was obviously waiting for them to be alone to talk, and Harlow wasn't sure if she could handle whatever news she was bringing. Could it be that Audrey was canceling their date? She wouldn't blame her. Getting sucked into whatever vortex was swirling would be a lot for anyone. Audrey owed her nothing.

"Everything okay?" Harlow turned to face her once the stylists had left.

Kylie surprised her by hugging her. "Are you okay?"

Harlow returned the embrace. "That depends on how you define okay." She leaned back to look at Kylie. "I assume you're here to tell me Audrey isn't going with me to the AMAs."

"What?" Kylie looked confused. "No. Audrey sent me here to help you. You don't have anyone to help manage everything right now. I'm here to fill that void until you can find someone. You're on tour, and you need help."

Harlow hadn't realized how close she was to tears until the burning in her throat started. "She's not leaving me?" She sat on the bed.

Kylie sat next to her and put her hand on her shoulder. "Quite the opposite. Now, tell me how I can help."

Harlow searched her eyes and found nothing but understanding. "I'm not really sure. I've never been in this situation before."

Kylie handed her a piece of paper. "I've formulated questions I think you'll be asked, along with some canned responses. If you don't like any of them, I can change the wording around. But I think it's best to be prepared, and as vague as possible. The other option is to say absolutely nothing. You can let them pepper you, and not give them a response." She looked as if she wanted to say more but stopped herself.

"Go ahead. Tell me what you're thinking," Harlow said.

"I also think we should contact the police and say you're willing to cooperate with whatever they need. It would be best if you also talked to a lawyer. You need to make sure you understand what you should and shouldn't say prior to talking to the police."

Harlow nodded. "I spoke with my lawyer on the plane ride here. I'm going to be speaking with the police tomorrow morning. He requested they come here, so I don't get photographed going into the police station."

"Good." Kylie rubbed her shoulder. "Do we need to make any changes to upcoming tour dates? If you want to give me your tour manager's number, I can talk to them and handle whatever needs to be done. I can also work on getting you a replacement for Casper, or I don't mind filling in until you find someone."

Harlow wrote down her manager's number and handed it over. "I hope that's not necessary regarding the tour because it's pretty well set, and my tour manager should be able to handle anything left. As far as you helping me out with other stuff, I really appreciate it. I'm interviewing a few people at the end of the week that my tour manager recommended to handle the stuff Casper usually handles. But if there's anything you can think of that I need to focus on, let me know."

Kylie shrugged. "I have no idea how this will pan out." She stood. "How about you look over those questions and answers? You'll meet with the police tomorrow, and then you can make any necessary decisions after. You don't have to have everything figured out tonight, or tomorrow for that matter. I'm here until you find someone else."

Harlow stood and looked at herself in the mirror. The reflection staring back at her didn't align with how she was feeling. Her dress was beautiful. Her makeup was flawless, and her hair was perfect. She looked poised and confident. In reality, she was going to shatter. The fourteen-year-old girl she used to be with nothing in front of her but uncertainty and fear took center stage. She'd intended to leave that girl in the past. The truth was, she was there the whole time, hiding in the shadows of the spotlight and fame.

"Let's go pick up Audrey," Harlow said as she continued to stare at herself in the mirror. Audrey had sent Kylie over to help her. She wasn't avoiding her, and right now, that was something special. If she could just force her demons behind her, maybe she could believe that she and Audrey would be okay in the long run.

Audrey would make her feel better. She could use her as an anchor. Audrey was a reminder of what was right and what she had to look forward to. She needed that now more than ever.

CHAPTER TWENTY-NINE

Harlow was rubbing her thumb into her palm. It was a nervous habit, and Audrey hurt for her. If she had it her way, they wouldn't be going to this awards show. She wanted to drag Harlow into the safety of her home and hold her until she wasn't scared anymore. She wanted to reassure her that everything would be all right. She wanted to protect her. But Harlow not appearing at the American Music Awards would raise more questions than it was worth. There would be speculation, rumors, and it could possibly cast doubt on the truth. So she'd go with her, stand with her, and try her best to be the support she knew she needed.

Audrey grabbed Harlow's hand. "Hey, everything is going to be okay. I'm here with you."

Harlow looked over with a faint smile. "I didn't tell you how gorgeous you look."

Audrey kissed her knuckles. "You clean up nicely too, superstar."

Kylie leaned forward in her seat. "Okay, remember you don't have to answer every question. If you do answer anything, keep it vague and keep moving down the carpet."

The car door opened, and Audrey made sure to exit first. She waved to the crowd and smiled broadly. The camera flashes were rapid and consuming. It wasn't a sensation she'd ever really get used to, but it was consistent, which was weirdly reassuring in its own way.

She reached back and took Harlow's hand, helping her out of the limo. The flashing lights intensified, and the yelling from reporters increased.

"Are you here together?"

"Are you two dating?"

"Harlow, how is your brother?"

"Did you know about the drugs?"

"Harlow, are you dating women now?"

"Audrey, what do your parents think of Harlow?"

Audrey felt Harlow freeze next to her. She smiled and continued to wave to the people who lined the red carpet. Harlow followed suit and never let go of Audrey's hand. She knew Harlow was a bubbling ball of anxiety by how hard she was squeezing her hand, but her face didn't show it. Her smile had the same relaxed ease to it that it always had. If she could keep it up for another hundred feet, they'd make it inside without a major incident.

Harlow put her arm around her waist, and Audrey turned into her. The photographers asked them to pose in different positions, and they adjusted slightly.

"Harlow, will what's happening with your brother affect the tour?"

Harlow changed positions to show her other side.

"Harlow, did you know what your brother was doing?"

Harlow put her hand on her waist and posed for the camera.

"Audrey, how long have you two been dating?"

Audrey turned to show the back of her dress.

"Harlow, does addiction run in your family?"

Audrey felt Harlow tense next to her. She saw a small bead of sweat trickle down her hairline. Audrey took her hand, which made Harlow look at her. She waited until Harlow made eye contact with her, and she smiled. She wanted Harlow to know she wasn't alone. Audrey was on her side, and she wasn't going anywhere.

"You don't owe them an explanation," Audrey whispered.

Harlow kissed her cheek. "Thank you."

When they finally got inside, Harlow was visibly relieved. It was as if she'd been holding her breath the whole time, and she was finally able to exhale.

"I can't thank you enough." Harlow hugged her.

"You don't have to thank me."

A frantic young woman speaking into a headset approached. "Miss Thorne, we need you backstage to get ready for the opening."

"I'll see you soon," Harlow said as she disappeared through one of the side doors.

"She'll be okay." Kylie bumped Audrey's shoulder with her own.

"Jesus," Audrey said. "Where did you come from?"

Kylie laughed. "I came in right after you guys. You just don't notice anything else when Harlow is around."

Audrey linked her arm with Kylie's as they walked into the main theater. "I'm just worried about her. I appreciate you offering to help her out through all this."

"No thanks needed. I'm happy to help. I know how much she means to you."

Audrey looked around to see if anyone was listening to them. "Do you think I'm doing the right thing?"

Kylie tilted her head. "I think you're being you. Does anything else really matter?"

Audrey knew the answer to the question before she asked. She knew Kylie would support her, but she still wanted the confirmation from her oldest friend. In the world she lived in, there were very few people she could count on for candor, and she always valued Kylie's.

They found their designated seats, and she was delighted to see Harlow would be next to her for the show. She knew that had been Kylie's handiwork.

"Remind me to give you a raise," she leaned over and told Kylie.

"Done and done."

Audrey bumped her. "I've meant to talk to you about your screenplay." Kylie's eyebrows raised to her hairline. "It's phenomenal. Honestly, I think it's one of the best things I've ever read."

Tears welled in Kylie's eyes. "You're not just saying that?"

Audrey hugged her. "Absolutely not. I can't begin to tell you how much I enjoyed it. I know you're shopping it around, and I don't want to hold you back from big money, but I'd love to produce it."

Kylie squeezed her arms. "I don't care about money. I want to see it on the big screen. That's all that matters to me. You just picked up a project. Are you sure you'd have room for this one as well?"

"We can figure something out; I know we can. I also think you should keep meeting with the big names. It's always a good idea to generate buzz about a project. You really need to weigh your options, and my small production company may not end up being the best choice for you." Audrey hoped she sounded as sincere as she felt.

This was a significant accomplishment for Kylie, and she wanted her to make the best choice possible. It wasn't personal; it was business. She hoped she'd choose her company but would understand if she went in a different direction.

They spent the next thirty minutes exchanging pleasantries with the people in their section. No one asked her about Harlow's situation, for which she was grateful. They all knew how painful it was to have your personal life exposed to the world. It was an exchange you made for being successful. People had what seemed to be unfettered access to every aspect of your life. No question was out of bounds, and there were no lines people wouldn't cross to gain even more access. In exchange, you were paid a lot of money to do what you loved. It was a fine line to walk. The public was fickle, and it could all be taken away in an instant. People tended to think celebrities were untouchable, but it wasn't the case. A well-placed rumor could put someone on borrowed time.

They flashed the lights, indicating that the show would be starting momentarily. The fans placed next to the stage started screaming in anticipation. They waved their glow sticks, and the crowd buzzed with their shared excitement.

The host took the stage to do her opening monologue. She covered the year in music, poked fun at a few people in the audience, and covered recent political events. Audrey knew she was funny because everyone in the theater was laughing, but she couldn't focus. Her mind was with Harlow. She pictured her getting ready behind the sliding doors of the stage. Was she nervous or taking refuge in the routine of getting ready to perform? She hoped that was the case.

The doors slipped open and shirtless men came onto the stage in lines, following the drumbeat. Harlow's voice filled the theater, but they couldn't see her. The flashing lights and the screaming fans overwhelmed her senses. Harlow finally stepped on stage in a sheer gold bodysuit. Sequins covered the entirety of the fabric, reflecting the bright lights that followed her around the stage. She could watch Harlow perform a million times, and it wouldn't be enough.

Harlow seemed fearless on stage. The way she interacted with the fans, the music, and her surrounding was almost poetic. Audrey thought about the looming details that swirled outside the theater walls and hoped it wouldn't impact her career the way Jane thought it might. She couldn't imagine a version of the world where Harlow wasn't singing and entertaining. She couldn't imagine Harlow without that outlet. It would be like taking a part of her soul.

Audrey had been lost in a haze of what-ifs through the entirety of the performance and was only able to snap out of it when she heard the theater erupt with a roar of applause. There was an inexplicable feeling of pride as Harlow exited the stage. Watching Harlow was like watching real magic, and she was lucky to know her. It wasn't a feeling Audrey was accustomed to, and she wondered why she'd lived without it for so long.

She watched the next few award presentations with bated anticipation. She couldn't wait for Harlow to be next to her again. She wanted to hug her and tell her what a fantastic job she'd done. She wanted to be near her to make sure she was okay. As confident as Harlow appeared on stage, there was still a fragility about her, and Audrey wanted to protect her.

At the dedicated break to move people in the audience around, Harlow hurried back to her seat. Audrey grabbed her and hugged her without thinking, considering who was watching or whether or not cameras aimed at them. Harlow tensed at first and then seemed to melt into the embrace. It warmed Audrey's chest to feel Harlow give in to her in public. She kissed the side of her cheek, loving the hint of salt that clung to her skin.

"You were incredible, as always."

Harlow smiled and hugged her again. "Thank you."

They took their seats, and Audrey's stomach fluttered as Harlow took her hand. The warming sensation that exploded through her body brought with it a realization—she was falling in love with Harlow Thorne. Audrey glanced over at Harlow when the realization struck. There was no way her internal thoughts had somehow escaped into Harlow's mind, but she watched her profile to be sure. Obviously, Harlow remained unaware of the epiphany, but it lingered in Audrey's mouth like it wanted to escape. Audrey pushed it away. She wouldn't add something else to Harlow's growing plate of unforeseen circumstances. Instead, she held her hand a little tighter, happy to simply be in her presence.

❖

Harlow wanted nothing more than for this night to be over. Casper's absence was acute, making the whole event even more daunting. The only reason she hadn't canceled was because the negative press associated with such a decision would've been worse than the actual event. She probably would've disappeared immediately following her performance had it not been for Audrey. Her presence gave her strength. But how long could she expect to draw on her?

She didn't win album of the year and almost wept with relief from not having to go up on stage. She knew people were looking at her differently tonight, and that would probably be the norm for the foreseeable future. She hated that so much of her life would now be based on the public's whims and opinions. She'd worked incredibly hard to crawl out of the in-between, where a little bad press could derail all your aspirations. Clearly, that was never really true. She'd tricked herself into thinking it was because she enjoyed the sense of safety it gave her. There was no such thing as real safety, not in her profession.

She grew queasy as she realized they were going to have to go back out through the same gauntlet they'd entered. Her body felt clammy, and her heart was fluttering in a weird rhythm. She glanced over at Audrey, who looked concerned.

"Are you okay?" Audrey whispered against her ear.

Harlow shook her head and regretted it as another wave of nausea ravaged her. "I don't think I can make it back through those reporters."

Audrey gently put both hands on Harlow's face. "I'll take care of it." She disappeared out of her peripheral to speak with Kylie.

Harlow took a few deep breaths as she waited. She'd never had a panic attack, but maybe that's what this was. She tempered her breathing and did her best to focus on a point across the room. A room that suddenly felt a fraction of the size it had twenty minutes before. *What is happening to me?*

Audrey grabbed her hand and pulled her into the bowels of the theater. She walked her down a long hallway, which Harlow assumed would lead to the outside. It was becoming slightly easier to breathe the farther away they got from the hordes of people. Embarrassment over what was happening hit her next, and she wanted to curl up in a tiny ball and disappear.

Audrey rubbed soothing circles on her back. "Kylie is getting the car to come around. Everything will be okay. We're going to get out of here."

Harlow wanted to speak, but she couldn't. At the least, she could offer up a thank-you. Audrey had anticipated what she needed and made it happen. She was a steadfast presence, and Harlow didn't have the words to express how much she appreciated that about her. Audrey was strong and brave and reassuring. She was everything Harlow couldn't be.

Kylie knocked on the door, and Audrey popped it open, scanning the area. She waved for Harlow to follow her, and she practically fell into the car. She stared at her trembling hands and willed them to stop. She couldn't feel or act like this over a few reporters. This wasn't sustainable.

"Do you want me to come home with you?" Audrey turned fully to face her.

"Yes," Harlow managed.

She tried to focus on the streetlights as they whizzed by the window. She heard Kylie talking to Audrey about canceling her shoot the next day. Harlow wanted to protest. She didn't want to keep Audrey from her work. She didn't want to pull her down into this pit of sorrow, but she said nothing. She said nothing because she was selfish. She wanted Audrey there with her when she talked to the police. She needed her there. She knew she wasn't behaving the way a considerate person should, but she didn't care. The shame of that realization brought tears to her eyes.

Audrey went to work when they arrived at Harlow's house. She turned on the bathtub and pulled Harlow to her feet. She unzipped Harlow's dress and removed her bra and underwear. She watched as though from a distance, paradoxically numb and in too much pain to speak. Once she got Harlow in the tub, she lit several candles around the bathroom and turned on soft music.

The warm water was soothing. Harlow felt the stress dissipate only to be replaced with sadness. The urge to cry was overwhelming, and there was nothing she could do to stop it. The tears came like a tsunami, swamping her, pulling her under. It was infuriating to be so helpless. This was what she got for caring too much, for letting people in. Trust was nothing but quicksand.

"Can I get you anything?" Audrey leaned against the doorframe.

Harlow wanted too many things. She wanted her brother to be safe. She wanted him to have made different decisions. She wanted to have been raised with better coping skills. She wanted to wave a magic wand and for this all to be better. But she couldn't say any of those things without sounding like a child, so she shook her head and let herself sink deeper into the tub, hoping it would wash away the despair threatening to overwhelm her.

CHAPTER THIRTY

Audrey groggily rolled over and touched an empty spot where Harlow should've been. When the realization hit that it was empty, she pushed herself upright. Harlow hadn't been in a good place the night before, and she'd hoped a full night of rest would alleviate some of her sadness. After her bath, Harlow had crawled into bed without saying a word. She'd let Audrey hold her, but she seemed to be erecting a wall around her emotions. Audrey would climb it as often as necessary.

She finally found Harlow sitting on the back patio drinking coffee. The instant relief made her want her to run over and hug Harlow, but she didn't. She poured herself a cup of coffee and took a seat next to her. She told herself she wouldn't say anything until Harlow did, not wanting to push her before she was ready.

Harlow didn't say a word until the sun had firmly taken its place on the horizon ahead of them. "Thank you for last night. I appreciate everything you did for me and staying the night."

"I'll be here as long as you need me."

The corners of Harlow's mouth turned up, but it wasn't so much a smile as much as confirmation this was far from over. "I don't want you to miss any more shooting days because of me."

Audrey put her hand on her forearm. "You're more important than any shooting schedule."

Harlow stared at her hand for so long, Audrey almost pulled away. "I'm sorry everything is such a mess."

"It's not your fault. None of this is your fault." Audrey wanted to convey conviction in her tone.

Harlow's phone rang, pulling her from the conversation. She disappeared into the house, shutting the sliding glass door behind her. Audrey took several deep breaths as she tried to remind herself not to take her departure personally. Harlow was under an extraordinary amount of stress, and her life had just been shaken to the core. *It has nothing to do with you. All you can do is be there for her. You can't control how she reacts. You don't need to know everything she talks about.*

After getting herself fully under control, she went back inside. She needed to shower before the lawyer and police arrived. It would also give her something to do that didn't require her to have awkward interactions with Harlow. She was used to things feeling so easy and natural between them. It was more difficult than she'd expected when they weren't. It felt like every strained interaction chipped away a small piece of her heart.

She stripped off her clothes and was about to get in the shower when Harlow rounded the corner. "There you are. I was looking for you." Harlow's eyes changed when she looked at Audrey.

Audrey watched as desire replaced whatever Harlow had been dealing with before. This pleased Audrey much more than it should've given the circumstances. Passion was one of the reasons she'd fallen for Harlow. It was immensely satisfying to see it regardless of what else was happening.

"You found me." Audrey waited to get in the shower. She wanted to give Harlow her full attention. That, and she loved the way Harlow was looking at her. "Did you need something?"

Harlow grabbed her wrist and pulled Audrey against her. "I made you breakfast."

Audrey practically melted when Harlow pressed her lips against hers. This kiss was different from others they'd shared. It seemed desperate and frantic, but Audrey couldn't pinpoint the origin. There was desire there, but the desperation seemed almost primal. Audrey kissed her back with the same amount of force, determined to give Harlow whatever she needed.

Harlow's grip around her tightened, and it felt possessive. She picked her up and walked her toward the bed. Audrey wrapped her legs around her and fought the urge to whimper at Harlow's sudden desire to be in charge. She placed Audrey on the bed and climbed on top of her.

She pulled at Harlow's shirt, wanting to feel her skin. Harlow was kissing and biting Audrey's neck. There was a frenzy in her touch that hadn't been there before, and Audrey loved it. She hurriedly unbuttoned Harlow's pants and slid her hand between her legs. Harlow was in such desperate need, her hips bucked as soon as Audrey touched her. Audrey pushed deeper inside, and Harlow pressed her hips harder against her. It was like she let her whole body be consumed, and Audrey was enthralled.

Harlow slid her hand between the two of them, and Audrey almost came immediately. She tried to focus on Harlow and what her body was telling her that she desired. She wanted to give Harlow whatever she was looking for—whatever she needed, and she had a feeling it was to feel connected, no matter how frantic.

She grabbed her lower back and pressed harder into her center. Harlow's hips followed the rhythm, but it only took a few more strokes before she cried out and then collapsed on top of her. Harlow's body was trembling, and she buried her face in Audrey's neck. She made no movement to move off of her, and Audrey wasn't about to ask.

"I'm sorry that was so fast. I'm not sure what came over me."

Audrey hugged her tighter. "Don't ever apologize for something like that. I assure you, it was my pleasure."

"I feel so scattered right now. I'm not always sure how my emotions will shift."

Audrey kissed the side of her head. "It's okay, baby. It's okay."

The doorbell rang, and Harlow groaned. "No more imagining how this will turn out."

Harlow stood, fixed herself in the mirror, and splashed cold water on her face. Audrey didn't get up to get in the shower until Harlow had left. She let the warm water cascade across the tender parts of her skin where Harlow still lingered. She considered what had just happened and the few words Harlow had spoken and hoped she would let her put the scattered pieces back together.

❖

Harlow tried not to tap her foot while listening to her lawyer go over what he assumed the police would be asking. He was doing his job, but she didn't know how to articulate the gravity of how this would affect her life. For her, this was about far more than her career. Yes, that was important, but the implications for Casper weighed on her more with each passing minute.

"Do you have any questions?" Rick clicked his pen closed and placed it on the notepad in front of him.

"Is Casper okay?"

He tilted his head. "I saw him yesterday, and he's holding up."

She shook her head and opened one of the bottles of water she'd put out for the meeting. *Was this a meeting? Was it an interrogation? Did it matter?* The panic she'd been feeling in her chest loosened slightly when she heard Audrey coming down the stairs. Even if she hadn't heard her descending, she would've been able to tell by the look on Rick's face.

He stood and met her at the bottom of the stairs. "Ms. Knox, it's an absolute pleasure to meet you. I'm Rick Flemming, Harlow's attorney."

Audrey shook his hand. "It's nice to meet you, Rick. I'm going to grab some breakfast. Can I get you anything?"

He shoved his hands in his pockets and shifted his weight. "No, that's okay. I ate before I came over."

He sat back down at the table, looking categorically gleeful. "I'm a big fan of hers."

Harlow was finally able to stop shaking her leg. "Me too."

"My daughter won't believe I got to meet Audrey Knox." He shook his head as if he was still in disbelief.

Audrey ran her hand over Harlow's shoulders before she sat down next to her. It was a simple action, but it helped to calm her. She was grateful for all of Audrey's little gestures, even if she didn't deserve that kind of patience or kindness. Not with all the drama swirling around her.

Audrey speared a piece of watermelon with her fork. "So, should I be in here when the police arrive, or is it better for me to wait in the other room?"

Rick leaned forward on the table. "That's entirely up to Harlow. We're cooperating fully, so we have no reason to worry. They're just coming to ask questions. Harlow isn't a person of interest, and this is a voluntary interview. It's up to her."

Harlow was thankful at least one of them was thinking logically. She hadn't even thought to ask the question and just assumed Audrey would be there with her. She needed Audrey to be there.

"I'd like her to stay." Harlow forced down more water. She wasn't thirsty, but she needed something to do with her hands.

The police officers arrived on time, and Rick escorted them into the living room. They were pleasant as they introduced themselves and were even apologetic they had to intrude on her day. Harlow still had enough mental bandwidth to thank them for coming to her instead of making her endure the paparazzi. It felt like her heart was going to throw itself from her chest as the pleasantries drew to a close.

"Ms. Thorne," Sergeant Cox said as he pulled a small notepad from his jacket pocket. "We're here to get a better understanding of the situation involving your brother. You know that he turned himself in and admitted to trafficking Fentanyl. Now, with the amount he had, and seeing as he crossed state lines with it, he's looking at a minimum of five years in jail."

Sergeant Cox was still talking, but Harlow's head had started buzzing. Her chest felt constricted, and she could feel sweat beading at her temples. *Five years at a minimum.* Harlow started to imagine everything Casper would miss in those five years. Her breathing grew more shallow, and she thought she might faint.

Audrey grabbed her hand and squeezed. Harlow tried to focus on the sensation. If she could tether herself to Audrey's strength, she could make it through this.

"What is it exactly that you want to know, Sergeant?" Harlow was relieved that her voice sounded stronger than it felt.

"When were you first made aware of your brother's activities?"

"A few weeks ago," Harlow said.

"And you had no idea prior to that? No inkling something was wrong? No reason to think your tour bus was being used for anything other than equipment?"

Harlow blinked several times as she let the words settle. "No. I had no idea. I'm not really involved with any of the logistics in that area. Casper and the tour manager oversaw everything for transport."

Harlow shook her head. Her limbs felt incredibly heavy. "I'm sorry I can't be of more help. I really don't know anything else."

Sergeant Cox clicked his pen. "Mr. Thorne has been cooperative. This was a bit of a formality. We're trying to cover all our bases. Your brother isn't the biggest fish in this net." He glanced over at his partner, and it was the first time Harlow had bothered to notice him. "He's hesitant to divulge everything. There are certain things we need from him to move forward. We may even be able to reduce his sentence if he's helpful. Is that something you could assist us with?"

Harlow thought back to what Casper had told her that night and what the officer was saying now. He'd gotten the patches from someone. If they were going to go after his supplier, what did that mean for Casper? Was he in more danger? She felt like she was going to be sick. She'd practically forced Casper to turn himself in. What if that was a mistake? What if he got hurt?

"I can try to talk to him," Harlow whispered. That hadn't been her intention, and the words clung to the sides of her throat, not wanting to escape. "I'll see what I can do."

The officers seemed pleased by that as they simultaneously flashed her bright smiles. They took their leave, and as soon as the door shut, she was practically on top of Rick. "You need to go help Casper, and I need to see him."

"Are you sure? When this first happened, you told me not to get involved. You said *you* didn't want to be involved." Rick picked up his briefcase.

Harlow started pacing. "I'm sure. I don't know who he was working for or how dangerous they are. Casper needs all the help he can get. I want to make sure precautions are taken for him. Maybe we can get them to agree to house arrest. I'm scared something will happen to him if he has to go to prison." She opened the door, hoping to hurry him along. "Please, just do whatever you can. Let me know when I can see him. The sooner, the better."

Audrey was by her side as soon as the door closed. "Hey, it's okay."

Harlow leaned into Audrey, thankful for the support. Her feelings were bouncing all over. It was like there was a racquetball ricocheting inside her. She wasn't sure how to handle all her shifting emotions at once. She wanted it to stop.

Audrey grabbed her shoulders. "What can I do to help?"

Part of Harlow felt like collapsing onto the couch and never moving again. The other part of her wanted to run until her legs stopped working. She wasn't sure which to do or what was more effective.

She stared at Audrey, hoping to find the answer somewhere in her eyes. "I think I need to go for a run."

Audrey didn't miss a beat. "Okay, I'll go with you."

Harlow's initial instinct was to say no. She needed to get whatever this was out of her system. She needed to feel something other than dread and impending doom—even if it was exhaustion. But the expression of care and concern on Audrey's face changed her mind.

"Okay," Harlow said.

Harlow went to change into running clothes. She was grateful to have something to do, even if it was only temporary. She could focus on hammering her body to the point of exhaustion. Was it the best use of her energy? Probably not. But it was something.

CHAPTER THIRTY-ONE

Audrey followed Harlow dutifully out of the house. She seemed single-minded in her need, just as she had when they'd had sex two hours before. It felt like Harlow was trying to outrun what was going on, and Audrey was concerned. She'd learned a long time ago that if you didn't face your feelings head-on, they would blow up in your face. But now wasn't the time to have that conversation. She wanted to support her, and if that meant running thirty miles, or whatever Harlow had in mind, she'd be there.

They made it down the long winding driveway, through the gate, and straight into a wall of reporters. The look on Harlow's face was one of unmitigated anger. She pushed past their shouting questions and their large cameras and onto the street. A few tried to catch up but were quickly cut off by two of her security guards. One dutifully followed them at a slight distance in his car. Audrey matched her pace, wanting to stay close. She glanced over at Harlow, trying to think of what to say to make her feel better. But what could she say? Harlow seemed on the verge of several different emotional breaking points, and Audrey didn't want to push her over any of them. She stayed close and hoped that would be enough.

Sixty minutes later, Audrey glanced down at her watch. They'd run almost nine miles, and her legs were burning. She enjoyed running, but this was something different. She finally couldn't take it any longer, and she bent over, grabbing her knees.

Harlow stopped. "You okay?"

Between heaving breaths, Audrey managed to choke out a few words. "I can't keep up this pace."

"Then go back." There was no anger in Harlow's voice. The words seemed to be meant as a simple statement.

"I don't want to leave you alone right now." Audrey put her hands on her hips, still gasping for air.

"I don't need you here. I'll be fine. I'll call you when I get home." Harlow didn't spare her another glance as she took off down the street.

Audrey wanted to follow her, but her legs wouldn't allow it. Her body had reached its threshold. *Maybe I should have trained for that marathon with Kylie.* She flopped down on the park bench and opened her phone. There were several missed calls and texts from Jane and a few from Kylie. She hadn't answered them while they were running because she wanted Harlow to know she was completely present if she needed her.

She sent a message to Kylie asking for her to get her. Luckily, Kylie's response was almost instant. She let her thumb hover over Jane's contact for a beat, but she couldn't avoid her forever, so she hit the call button and waited for her to pick up—she only waited for two rings.

"You didn't go to the set today?" Jane's tone was lingering right around the irate tipping point.

"No, but I will be there tomorrow." Contrary to her feelings, Audrey tried to sound resolute.

"You can't just call in sick, Audrey. If you aren't there, other people can't do their jobs. It affects everything."

Audrey leaned forward on her knees. She'd long since gotten her breathing under control, but now her head was starting to pound. "They had someone read for me. I'll be there tomorrow."

"I just saw you on TMZ going for a run with Harlow. How do you think that will play with the director? The other actors? It was completely unprofessional." Jane was edging closer to the irate line. "Not to mention you're trying to start a new business. Do you think this comes off as reliable?"

Audrey pinched the bridge of her nose. "Harlow needed me."

Jane was quiet for so long Audrey checked her phone to see if the call had dropped. "Harlow needed you? That's your response? I'm sorry, but that isn't good enough."

"It was one day, Jane. We had to take a whole month off for Derek to go to rehab a year ago." Anger started to churn in her chest, but she did her best to tamp it down.

Jane let out a dramatic laugh. "Your entire image is wrapped up in being an American sweetheart. People love you because you're funny and cute and utterly devoid of scandal. Derek and other people like him get away with that behavior because it's baked into their image. You don't have that luxury."

Kylie pulled up, and Audrey hurried to get inside the car. "So you're worried about what, exactly? Me losing my fans because I took a day off to support my friend? You realize how ridiculous that sounds, right?"

"You keep expecting things to be fair—or equal, Audrey. They're not. The sooner you figure that out, the longer your career will be. I won't be able to help you if you go too far off the rails."

Audrey was beside herself. "Off the rails? Harlow got terrible news about her brother. I was there for moral support."

Jane sighed loudly. "Casper Thorne was involved in drug trafficking and sucked his sister, her tour, and her image into the mix. You want to support her, do it quietly, or your name will forever be tied to this mess. You cannot afford that right now." There were several long car horns in the background. "Listen, I have to go. Think about what I said, and make sure you're on set tomorrow." She hung up before Audrey thought to respond.

Audrey fought the urge to throw her phone out the window. She covered her face, overwhelmed by the anger, sadness, and concern raging through her.

"Do you want to talk about it?" Kylie's voice was just above a whisper, and her face was etched with concern.

Did she want to talk about it? Yes. No. She didn't know. She wasn't sure where to start. She wanted to be there for Harlow; image be damned. She wanted to be able to tell her that everything was going to be okay. But Jane wasn't wrong either. She was trying to juggle a million balls, and she was scared that if any of them dropped, they all would. Harlow was important, but so was her career. She needed to figure out a way to manage both amid the chaos.

"No, I'm fine." Audrey stared out the window and clenched her jaw, hoping it would stop the tears that were welling at the edge of her eyes.

Kylie rubbed her arm. "If you're not, I'm here."

"Thanks."

Audrey thought about having Kylie take her to Harlow's, but she didn't. Harlow didn't want her there. In fact, Harlow had almost seemed relieved to go without her. Anxiety started to build in her chest. What if Harlow decided a relationship, especially one where she had to deal with more press, wasn't what she wanted right now? She told herself that it wasn't personal—wanting space was a completely normal reaction. Harlow had a lot to process with everything going on. All Audrey could do was hope that when the dust settled a bit, she'd still want her there.

❖

Harlow paced the length of her pool with her cell clutched tightly in her hand. Her lawyer had said to expect a call from her brother, and the waiting was killing her. Her stomach had been churning, and there was a burning sensation at the back of her throat.

The phone rang, and she picked it up before the first ring ended. "Hello?"

"Hey, Low." Casper sounded exhausted. "How are you?"

She had a million things she wanted to say, but now she could only muster two words. "I'm sorry."

"You didn't do anything wrong, Low. I'm sorry. I'm sorry I dragged you into this mess, and I'm sorry it's impacting you."

"Are you okay? Are you safe?" Harlow needed to know the answer before she could move forward with anything else.

"As good as can be expected." He was quiet for what seemed like a full minute. "Where are you?"

"Home."

"You need to get back on the road. This can't affect the tour."

Harlow wanted to ask him how it could not affect the tour. She could hardly think of anything but him. She couldn't concentrate. The paparazzi weren't following her around for fun pictures—they were hammering her with questions at every opportunity. Plus, it wasn't just the added external stress she was feeling. Casper had betrayed her. He'd risked everything she'd built—they'd built. She was alone, and she'd never dealt with that before. Casper had always been there, on her side.

"Have you decided what you're going to do?" She didn't want to talk about music, worried she'd reveal how she was feeling toward him.

"Not yet. We're waiting for the prosecutor to make his offer."

She leaned on her railing that overlooked Los Angeles. "When this is over, are you going to get help?" There was a long pause. "You have a gambling addiction. You need help."

"It's not an addiction. I just had a really unlucky streak. I was going to turn it around. I just needed more time."

Images of her father flooded her mind. She remembered finding him covered in his own vomit. Listening to him yell at and beat their mother. She could still smell the gin on his breath when he'd grab her and force her to converse with him during his fleeting moments of parental intrusion. She remembered the crying, the meaningless apologies, the broken promises, and the way her mother gave in to him at every turn. She remembered when he broke her guitar one night in a fit of rage because she'd left it downstairs instead of in her room. She remembered all of it. She choked on those memories now as she listened to Casper spin a different version of the same addiction.

"No," she said, her voice even. "You need to get help. Jesus, Casp. Don't be Dad."

"You're overreacting, Low. Yes, I fucked up with the drugs—big time. But the gambling thing is under control."

Harlow had never understood when people talked about how they could feel their hearts literally breaking. She got it now. Her chest burned with such ferocity she had to put her hand against it to make sure it didn't burst from her chest. She tried to speak, but the words caught in her throat, intertwined with disappointment and pain.

"Look around you, Casper. Look where you are and keep telling yourself that. If you can really say that after all that's happened, you're further gone than I thought. I have to go." She hung up before he could say anything.

She slid down the glass wall and turned her phone off, not wanting to talk to anyone. Then, she let her tears come. Her body shook and lurched, mimicking the rollercoaster that seemed to gobble up every available emotion.

CHAPTER THIRTY-TWO

Audrey tamped down her annoyance toward her costar. This was the sixth time they'd taken a break for him to go over his lines. To be fair, he at least acted embarrassed by his mental lapse, but she wasn't in the mindset to deal with it.

She flopped down on the chair and took the water offered to her as she checked her phone for the hundredth time that day. It had been twelve hours since she'd heard from Harlow, but it felt like twelve years. There'd been no response to her texts or calls, but she didn't want to simply show up at Harlow's place if she really didn't want to talk to anyone. She handed the phone back to Kylie with more indignation than she'd intended.

"Everything okay?" Kylie tucked the phone into her hip pack.

"Yup. Everything is great." She winced at the anger in her voice. "Sorry, it's not your fault."

"It's okay. You're under a lot of stress."

Audrey rubbed her temples, hoping to push some pressure away. "Regardless, I shouldn't take it out on you." Kylie's eyebrows shot up as she scrolled through her phone. "What? What is it?" Kylie glanced over at the stagehands resetting the stage. "Show me. I need to know."

Kylie handed her the phone. "Could be nothing. You know how these sites are always just chasing a story."

Audrey read the headline. *Harlow Thorne Has the Worst Performance of Her Career*. She scanned the article. *Could this be the end of the Queen of Pop? Harlow forgot several words to her songs while on stage Friday night. When asked about her brother's impending conviction, Ms. Thorne became so enraged she pushed one of the reporters from* Teen Jams *to the ground. Ms. Thorne, who normally stops for photographs and autographs with her fans, hurried past wearing an oversized sweatshirt and dark sunglasses.*

Audrey handed the phone back to Kylie. "I need to get to Boston."

Kylie leaned against her chair. "You still have six days of shooting left."

"I don't care. I need to get out there. I'll be back tomorrow for the four o'clock call time." Audrey tossed the water bottle onto her chair and went back to her blocked position.

Jane's words played through her mind as she took her position. She knew what her opinion would be, and she didn't care. She wasn't going to let Harlow go through this alone. She loved her. *Shit. Love?* Was she in love with Harlow? She was playing with the words in her head, but she already knew the answer. Yes, she loved Harlow. She'd known it the first time they'd kissed. Everything after had just confirmed what her heart had known the whole time. She'd make it back in time for her call time tomorrow. She could be there for Harlow and still keep the ship steady with her career. She needed to be there.

Harlow opened and closed her hands in her dressing room. She stared at the way they were trembling and willed them to stop. This performance had been worse than the last. She'd missed dance steps, her voice was off-key, and every time she tried to let the energy of the arena wash it away, she was racked with an overwhelming feeling of imposter syndrome. She didn't know how to change it, and worse, she didn't know how to escape it.

Someone knocked on the door, and she yelled for them to go away. She couldn't do any interviews, and she'd canceled the VIP meet and greet. The knock came again, and she squeezed the vanity table to keep the anxiety at bay. The door opened, the person obviously not caring about her request. Harlow turned to yell, but the words fell short when she saw Audrey come into the room.

Harlow fell into the offered hug. "You're here."

Audrey ran her hands up and down her back. "Of course, I'm here, sweetheart."

The simple endearment cracked whatever weak barrier she'd managed to assemble. A sob escaped, and she buried her face in Audrey's neck. "I don't know what's happening with me."

Audrey walked her over to the couch. "Talk to me." She put a gentle hand on Harlow's face. "I'm here."

Harlow leaned into her touch. "I feel so lost. I feel so alone." Everything she'd been feeling was right on the verge of pouring out of her, but she wanted desperately to keep it buried. "How long can you stay?"

Audrey intertwined their fingers. "I'm on an eleven a.m. flight. I have a four o'clock call time."

Harlow didn't want to show her disappointment. It wasn't fair to feel that way. Audrey had a life and job she had to do, and Harlow wasn't her responsibility. She'd flown across the country to see her for a few hours, which was remarkable. She needed to appreciate that.

"I'm glad you're here."

Audrey put her forehead against hers. "Do you want to get out of here?"

Harlow nodded as she wiped away the tears that had started falling. "Yes."

Audrey went to the door, and she could hear her discussing something with the security guards. Harlow had doubled their presence since this all started. She wasn't worried about her safety, but she used them as a shield against the rest of the world. Harlow thought about what she must look like to Audrey. She was a blubbering, lost, mess. *Perfect.*

"They're bringing the car around," Audrey said from the doorway.

Harlow pushed herself off the couch and took Audrey's hand. She let the security team form a human shield around her as they made their way to the car in the back of the arena. As soon as they were outside, the camera flashes started. Next came the insistent questions, which seemed amped up by Audrey's presence next to her. She wanted to apologize but stopped herself when Audrey squeezed her hand more tightly. They couldn't get inside the car fast enough. Lately, Harlow had felt as if the air was thinner without the protection cars or walls offered her. It was hard to breathe, and she hated it.

They didn't speak on the way back to the hotel, but Audrey sat close, stroking the back of her hand with her thumb. She was appreciative of her support but couldn't help the growing sensation of guilt, consuming her idle thoughts. Audrey was going to spend twelve hours flying in a twenty-hour period, in the middle of her shooting schedule, because Harlow couldn't hold her shit together.

Inside the hotel room, Audrey started to strip Harlow's clothes from her body. Harlow slowed her hands. "Audrey, I can't—"

"I want you to take a bath to relax." Audrey kissed her cheek. "As gorgeous as you are, sex isn't what you need right now. Let me take care of you."

Harlow agreed and slipped into the warm water. She watched Audrey move around the bathroom, arranging different items. Part of her wanted Audrey to climb into the bath, hold her, and tell her everything would be okay. The other part of her didn't want Audrey to see her like this. The whole world was looking at her with either disgust or pity, and she couldn't handle that from Audrey as well.

As it turned out, the decision wasn't up to her. Audrey put on classical music, dimmed the lights, and slipped out of the bathroom. Harlow was left with Chopin and her thoughts. She considered her brother again and thought about what he must be going through. She picked and pulled at her empathy, wanting desperately to drag it to the forefront of her mind. But it felt as if it was snagged on something. That something being the addiction that ran rampant in the family and one her brother had so skillfully ignored. Maybe ignore wasn't the right word—denied might be better. Casper was fooling himself into thinking he didn't need help, even when his life was in danger. How could he still be in such denial when he'd dug a hole this deep?

Harlow's stomach turned, and she felt as if the walls were closing in on her again. It became slightly more difficult to breathe, and her heart was racing. She wanted it to go away. She wanted to feel better. She wanted everything back the way it had been before she found out what was happening. But that was a lie too. Her brother had been struggling for months, possibly years, and she'd been clueless. Maybe if she'd found out sooner, maybe if she'd been paying more attention, maybe if she'd been a better sister…

Maybe. Maybe. Maybe.

She slid beneath the waterline. The warm water swallowed her whole, allowing her to feel lighter and quieter. How long could she stay under? Could the warmth and the calm fix everything? Perhaps for good?

Her lungs railed against her hesitation. They screamed for oxygen, and her brain urged her to the surface. It was a survival instinct—it had to be. An involuntary response to keep pushing forward even when your psyche and emotions were ready for it to be over. Who would really miss her? Casper had made it clear there were things more important than what they'd built. Her fans? They'd move on to the next pop icon in a month. Audrey. She couldn't bear the thought of her wondering if there was something she could have done differently or if she could've prevented it.

Harlow sucked in a mouthful of air and ran her hands over her hair. She blinked the water out of her eyes, momentarily stunned by the thoughts she'd just allowed in. She was both afraid and ashamed. She was morphing into a version of herself she didn't recognize and one she didn't like. She was fragile, and she hated it. She hated herself, and she hated her genetic line for cursing her brother.

"You okay in there?" Audrey knocked on the door but didn't open it.

"Yes. I'll be out in a minute." Harlow covered her face and was grateful the bath had made her tears and water indistinguishable from one another.

She wrapped the towel around her body and stared at herself in the mirror. Her eyes, the same shade of blue she shared with her brother, glared back at her. She wasn't sure if she was strong enough to deal with this. She'd always had Casper. She'd always depended on Casper. Casper was her beacon, her guiding light. What did she do now, with no light to guide her?

Audrey stared out the forty-fifth-floor hotel room. Boston was one of her favorite cities, and it was gorgeous at night. She loved the holiday lights and the delicate dusting of snow that covered the rooftops and the streets. She imagined wandering the streets with Harlow, drinking coffee and ducking into stores to get warm. She let the happy images play through her mind because it was easier than focusing on the pain and sorrow she saw in Harlow's eyes. Harlow was struggling, and she didn't know how to fix it or how to help. She didn't know because the reality was—this wasn't hers to fix.

Harlow came out of the bathroom and pulled on sweats and a shirt without looking at her. Audrey didn't want to push, so she continued her examination of the sleepy city below. She closed her eyes and allowed herself to exhale when Harlow wrapped her arms around her middle and rested her head on her shoulder.

"Thank you for coming."

Audrey stroked Harlow's forearms. "I'm sorry I can't be here longer."

"Will you lie down with me?"

Audrey turned in Harlow's embrace and ran her hands over her face. "Whatever you need."

Audrey pulled the covers up over them and settled against her back. She wrapped her arms around her, pulling her close. Harlow had always seemed larger than life. She was one of those people who radiated confidence, and her eyes had always said she knew a secret no one else was privy to. It had seemed like Harlow had the world figured out, and she couldn't divulge it because it would take the fun out of discovering it for yourself. That spark was dimmed now, and Audrey would do anything to give it back to her.

She kissed the back of Harlow's head. "I'm here if you want to talk."

Harlow's muscles relaxed. "Did you really think I was an arrogant prick the first time you saw me?"

"Hmmm," Audrey mused. "You're assuming the first time I saw you was in that greeting line." She chuckled. "The first time I saw you in person wasn't the same night you masterfully weaseled your way into dinner."

For the first time since Audrey had arrived, Harlow laughed. "That was Kylie's doing. I was just smart enough to agree."

Audrey pulled her closer. "I saw you at a breast cancer charity event three years ago." Audrey stroked her side. "You were so cool and seemed so aloof. I never considered approaching you, but I did watch you from a distance all night. You had on a black dress that fit you so well, it looked like body paint." She sighed. "You spent the evening chatting with Rebecca Chase, but she never had your full attention. I remember feeling kind of bad for her." She laughed to herself. "I remember thinking you were the most confident, beautiful woman I'd ever seen."

Harlow rolled over to face her. "You were in a navy blue tuxedo that night. Your hair was in a Dutch braid, and you wore diamond earrings. I didn't talk to you because you were there with a date who *did* have your attention. Although, to be honest, I couldn't tell you her name." She kissed Audrey softly. "I knew you were the most interesting and beautiful woman in that room, and that fact still stands."

Audrey's chest swelled. She knew Harlow was struggling. She knew she shouldn't be falling harder for her with every sentence she spoke. She knew her energy should be focused on helping her get through the turmoil in her life. She knew it, but she couldn't help herself. Harlow's face was half-lit by the moonlight, and the soft glow made her seem more delicate than she ever had before. Her feelings simmered in her throat. The words to describe how she felt and what Harlow meant to her begged to be put into the universe. Audrey pulled them back and told herself Harlow didn't need another complication. She didn't need another set of feelings to examine. It was enough to be here with her.

"I would've left with you that night had you asked," Audrey said it without thinking. She wished she hadn't but only for a fleeting second once she saw the look on Harlow's face.

"Well, I'll add that to my list of regrets then." Harlow rolled to her back and pulled Audrey's head down to her chest. "Get some sleep." She kissed the top of her head.

Audrey listened to Harlow's heart beat surely beneath her ear. She knew there was more to talk about, and she knew Harlow had avoided it. But she wasn't going to push. She'd come here to be whatever Harlow needed, and maybe this was it. She let herself be lulled to sleep by Harlow's breathing and the promise that tomorrow would be a new day.

CHAPTER THIRTY-THREE

The realization that it was Audrey pressed up against her as she woke brought the first sense of calm Harlow had felt in several weeks. She'd been an emotional wreck the night before, but Audrey had a way of centering her. She calmed the storm that always brewed right beneath her surface—which she realized wasn't entirely fair. Audrey brought her a sense of peace and calm, but what did she have to offer? She'd brought Audrey nothing but turmoil and made her life more difficult. Harlow squeezed her eyes shut, desperately wanting to push the thoughts away.

She masterfully extracted herself from Audrey's embrace and headed to the bathroom. She splashed cold water on her face and reminded herself that Audrey was there because she wanted to be, not out of obligation. On her way back to bed, Audrey's phone dinged, and she glanced at it. She noticed there were twenty-three missed text messages. She picked it up to give it to Audrey and couldn't help but notice the last few from Jane.

You're in Boston?!

I thought we talked about this?

You can't afford to have a public relationship with her right now. She's distracting you, and she's bad for your image.

Bile formed in the back of her throat. Her face heated, and her hands started to tremble. *Jesus. What are you doing to her?* Her first instinct was to be mad at Jane, but she wasn't wrong. Harlow had been having the same thoughts. At least Jane was brave enough to say it out loud. Harlow was selfish. She couldn't bear the thought of not having Audrey, so she was willing to sacrifice her. *You're a great person.*

She hadn't realized Audrey was awake until she took the phone from her hands. She read through the messages and tossed the phone on the bed. "I know that look, and don't you say what I know you're about to say."

"She's not wrong, Audrey."

"I will not have my personal life dictated by my *agent*. I'm a grown woman, and I can make my own decisions. Neither you, nor Jane, will make them for me." She grabbed Harlow's face and forced her to make eye contact. "Do you hear me? Public opinion is fickle. It changes each news cycle. I get a choice, and I choose you. Don't you dare be like everyone else and try to take choices away from me."

Harlow nodded her understanding. "I just don't want to—"

"Don't, Harlow," she said. "Just don't." She kissed Harlow on the side of the mouth. "I'm going to take a shower, and then you have to feed me. I'm starving."

Harlow only let her hand go when she couldn't stretch any farther. "You got it."

Harlow waited until she heard the water turn on and then did something she never did. She googled herself. The number of articles was astounding: opinion pieces, quizzes, articles on mainstream media sites, and hashtags. Her stomach roiled. *Fuck.* She chewed on her thumb while she looked at the blinking cursor in the search bar. She only hesitated for a moment, glancing back at the bathroom door before she typed in Audrey's name. She was on the verge of pressing the enter key when her phone rang.

She glanced down at the caller ID. "Hey, Rick. What's up?"

Her lawyer's voice was always the essence of calm. He could be standing in the middle of a burning building and sound like he was ordering coffee. "You have a minute?"

She closed her laptop and rolled over on her back. "Sure." She tried to ignore the prickling sensation that worked its way up her body. She was uncomfortable, and she would give anything for this all to be over.

"We heard back from the prosecutor. He offered Casper house arrest and community service to give up his contact."

"And what did Casper say?" Her heart had lodged itself in her throat, making it difficult to breathe.

"He said he needed a few days to think about it."

"He what?" Harlow was on her feet in an instant. "Why would he do that? Does he realize what could happen to him in jail? Is he even thinking about his life—about what this all means?"

"The judge is releasing him for pretrial home confinement. I'm picking him up this afternoon, but, Harlow, he only has a few days to make his decision. I've already advised that he take the deal, but he's hesitant. He thinks he can beat this in court and not risk turning on the supplier." Rick sounded apologetic.

The familiar drumming of a headache formed behind her eyes. Casper was being reckless at best. He was putting his safety and well-being aside, and for what? It certainly wasn't her. How had so much changed and she'd not been aware? She didn't understand how everything had gotten so out of control so quickly.

"I'm coming home." She heard the slightest quiver in her voice and hoped he wasn't astute enough to notice.

"Okay. I'll check in with you tomorrow to see if there's anything you need."

"Thanks, Rick," Harlow said. She stared out the window and did her best to fight back the tears that were threatening to escape. God, she was so tired of crying.

She didn't hear the bathroom door open and jumped when Audrey put her hand on her shoulder. "You okay?"

Harlow's insides tightened. "I, um—I'm not sure. I need to go home."

Audrey frowned. "What's going on?"

Harlow explained the conversation she'd just had with Rick. She observed Audrey, hoping she'd agree with her choice to go home, but there was none. There was concern and confusion, but not agreement.

"Are you sure you should go home?" Audrey seemed tentative when she put her hand on Harlow's arm. "I just don't want you to make any decisions you can't undo. Canceling more tour dates would be—"

Harlow didn't want her to finish her sentence. "He's my brother. I need to be there."

Audrey nodded slowly, apparently considering her next words carefully. "I understand, but is being there the best thing for *you*?"

Harlow stepped back, needing some distance. "I can't just continue with my life as if nothing has happened. The media is all over me, my brother is on the verge of prison, he's ignoring his addiction, and to be honest—my performances have sucked. So do I need to be there? Audrey, I know this is hard for you to comprehend, but Casper and I only have each other. We didn't grow up like you."

"What does that mean?"

Harlow could see what was unfolding, but she couldn't stop herself. "Please, Audrey, name one hardship you've faced in your life. You have no idea what it's like to be us. You have no idea what it took to get us where we are, and I'm not going to abandon him now that things are hard again."

Audrey crossed her arms, her expression clouded with hurt. "Is that what you think of me?"

Stop now. Just keep your mouth shut.

"Let's be honest. If we were both ordinary people and we'd met in our everyday lives, you wouldn't have given me a second glance. I would've never been good enough for you or your family. I was nothing but poor trash from a shit background." Harlow pinched the inside of her arm to keep herself from crying.

Audrey looked dumbfounded. "That's just not true. You have no idea what would've happened had we met in a different life because we don't have other lives. I don't care about your awards, your record sales, or whatever else. I care about you, Harlow. I think I've proven that."

All of Harlow's insecurities poured from somewhere dark inside her, and there was nothing she could do to stop it. "I do know what would've happened, Audrey. Your dad, the day trader, and your mom, the nurse, would've kept you sheltered from people like me. People who grew up spending their weekends either visiting someone in jail or waiting in line at a food pantry." She squeezed her fists, the urge to hit something overwhelming her. "Your biggest struggle was what, exactly? What Christmas list to send to which relative? You cannot possibly fathom what I'm feeling or going through because you have nothing to compare it to."

Audrey tried to reach for her, but Harlow stepped away. "Then explain it to me, Harlow. We may not have a lot of the same childhood experiences, but that doesn't mean I don't care or want to understand. It certainly doesn't mean that I don't want to be there for you."

Harlow shook her head. "You have no idea how bad this can get. You don't know what addiction can do to a family. You have no idea how fast it can shred everything. It will literally come in like a tsunami and take out everything in its path. Do you think you're strong enough to withstand that? You think *we're* strong enough? My career is already toast. You can't let yours go too."

Tears streamed down Audrey's cheeks. "You haven't let me try. You're just deciding I can't handle it? You're going to give up on something special because something else is hard?"

I know. I'm sorry. I don't know what I'm saying because everything is so jumbled in my head, I can't tell up from down right now. "I think you should go. I don't think this is going to work."

Audrey put her hands on her cheeks. "You don't mean that."

You're right. I don't. I love you, and I'm terrified I'll fuck it all up like everything else I've ever had. "Please go. I have other things to deal with in my life right now." Harlow stepped away from her touch and felt the loss immediately.

Audrey wiped the tears from her face. She walked over to the corner of the room and grabbed her bag. Harlow fought the urge to grab her and tell her to stay. She wanted to tell her how she felt. She wanted to ask her to be patient and to make her understand everything she was feeling. She wanted to explain that the idea of losing her felt so tangible, she didn't think she'd be able to handle it when it finally happened. She wanted to explain that she wasn't strong enough. She'd never be strong enough.

Audrey stopped at the door and turned to look at her. The pain etched on her face cracked Harlow's heart open, and she knew it was a look that would haunt her dreams forever.

"Harlow, I—" She bit her lip. "I'm sorry I couldn't be what you needed." She left before Harlow could utter a word.

Harlow fell to her knees when the door shut. She covered her mouth and tried to muffle the sob that crept from the depths of her soul. She knew herself well enough to know what she'd just done, but she wasn't brave enough to do anything about it. She knew without consideration, there wouldn't be a day for the rest of her life where she wouldn't long for Audrey, and she hated herself for it. But there was no way on earth she'd take Audrey down with her.

Audrey went through the rest of her day on autopilot. She made it to the set with time to spare and trudged through familiar motions.

She acknowledged the director's recommendations and made adjustments. She went through minor script changes, and she made notes for the next day. She did all that was required of her, but she didn't feel truly present for any of it. Harlow's words were stuck on repeat in her head.

When she arrived home, her mom and Kylie were waiting. She'd briefly contemplated telling them to go but fell into their arms before her brain caught up with her actions. She didn't know how long she'd spent crying before she was able to get herself under control, but it was long enough to produce a headache that pinched the space between her eyes.

Kylie kissed the side of her head, her arms wrapped around Audrey's shoulders. "I don't know what to say, sweetie."

Audrey spun the stem of the wine glass they'd handed her. "It was like a switch in her flipped. I never meant to make her feel like I was better than her. I'm not even sure where she got that from."

Her mom reached across the breakfast bar and took her hand. "Harlow isn't used to feeling love from anyone but her brother, and that's a mess right now. She isn't sure what it looks like. This has nothing to do with you."

Audrey squeezed her mom's hand. "But is she wrong? Would I have noticed her if I wasn't me, and she wasn't her?"

"That's not a fair question, honey. You two are who you are. It's a pointless thought experiment to pretend otherwise."

"I don't know, Mom. Harlow has been through so much, and I just pretended like it didn't matter because she became who she was meant to be. I never thought about what it all meant and how it shaped her."

"Okay, let me ask you this," Kylie said. "Has her family history ever bothered you? Did you run at the first sign of adversity?"

"Of course not." Audrey knew she'd stand by Harlow if the whole world were falling around them.

"Then you would've picked her no matter the circumstances." Kylie gave her a little side hug. "We've been friends for most of our lives. I know who you are, and I know what matters in here." She tapped Audrey's chest. "Harlow does too. She's just scared."

Audrey shook her head in defeat. "I don't want to lose her. I can't lose her."

Her mom wiped away the tear that had trickled down Audrey's cheek. "Oh, sweetie, just give her some space. I'm sure she'll come around. I've seen the way she looks at you."

Audrey let her forehead rest against the cool countertop. "I'm not sure any of that matters." She walked out of the kitchen before either of them had a chance to argue her point.

Audrey knew they meant well. They'd always been on her side, but it didn't matter in this situation. Their thoughtful introspection of the situation wouldn't change Harlow's mind. She wasn't sure what would, but she wanted to try.

She flopped down on her bed and pulled out her phone. She found the familiar contact and pushed the call button. After six rings, she assumed it was going to go to voice mail, but the voice she'd been craving finally came through the line.

"Hey, Audrey." Harlow sounded tired. "What's up?"

The casual words hurt more than she'd anticipated. Harlow's sultry voice and been replaced with her business voice, and Audrey's heart hurt.

"I just wanted to make sure you made it home okay." Audrey rolled her eyes. *Tell her you love her. Tell her you want to be there. Tell her she's not alone.*

"Yeah, I'm fine." There was a long pause. "You don't have to check on me anymore."

The thought of losing Harlow so abruptly, and not being able to wean herself off made her panic. "So, we can't be friends anymore?"

Harlow sighed. "I don't know that I can do that."

Audrey closed her eyes and willed herself to be brave. She dug deep in the recesses of her soul and told her to spit it out before she never had another chance. "I'm sorry I made you feel less than. That was never my intention. I care about you more than you know." *Just say it.* "I'm in love with you, Harlow. Please don't do this." The silence was deafening, and Audrey's insides screamed in pain.

Harlow finally spoke, and her tone was flat and distant. "You only feel that way because you don't really know me. My life is a mess right now. It's always been a mess. I was just able to hide it for a while. I can't be what you need, and I'm definitely not what you deserve."

"You haven't even given us a chance." Audrey knew she sounded desperate, but she didn't care. "You think you've only shown me parts of yourself, but that isn't true. I know how resilient you are. I know you're caring and compassionate and loving. I know you're scared of losing everything you've worked for while at the same time not thinking you deserve any of it." She took a deep breath and willed herself to continue. "I know you're afraid of loving me because you're scared to be happy. You're scared because you think it can all be taken away, but the only person who can ruin us is you and me, Harlow."

She couldn't be sure, but it sounded like Harlow was crying.

"You don't know what it's like to be me, Audrey. You have no idea what it's like not to know where your next meal is coming from. You don't know the fear of hearing a bottle being smashed against the wall and wondering if your father is coming for you next. You don't know the guilt of feeling both sad and relieved when that same father is finally dead. You don't know how it feels to have the only person you've ever believed loves you throw away the safety you've built together. You don't know what it's like to watch the world you've carefully built start to crack around you. You don't know how it feels for your worth to be tied up in the cheers from people who don't really know you. And you certainly don't know what it feels like to have other people's decisions threaten to take that all away." She took a long, ragged breath. "You will never get it, and I don't want you to understand. I need to help my brother through this, and I need to do it on my own. I can't worry about what it may do to you. I just can't."

Audrey covered her mouth so Harlow couldn't hear her crying. "You've already made up your mind."

"I have. Good-bye, Audrey."

Audrey turned her phone off and curled up on her bed. Her tears were hard, fast, and cooled her hot skin. She was profoundly and indisputably in love with Harlow, and there was nothing she could do to change it. It was as if someone had reached inside her chest and was squeezing her heart. She'd never felt pain like this before, and a part of her wanted desperately for it to stop. The other part of her wanted to let it continue because it helped her feel connected to Harlow.

Chapter Thirty-four

W as that Audrey Knox?"
Harlow rubbed her face. "Why are you here, Mom?"
She didn't care if her mother saw her crying. It wasn't only because her emotions felt raw and exposed, but because her mother didn't deserve any insights into her life.

"Your brother called and asked me to come." She sat on the couch, and Harlow immediately put space between them.

"Since when has our welfare mattered to you? Where have you been for the last ten years?" She didn't care how angry she sounded, and she surely didn't care if she was hurting her feelings.

"That's not fair, Harlow." She reached out to touch her, and Harlow pulled away.

"Not fair?" Harlow hadn't meant to yell, but there was no turning back now. "You don't get to tell me what's fair, Mom. Not fair is abandoning us. Not fair is letting Dad do what he did to us. Not fair is only coming around when you need money."

Her mother looked taken aback. "Harlow, I—"

Casper walked into the room and hugged her. Her body was vibrating with rage and hurt. Everything in her mind and soul was screaming. She wanted to rail against the life she'd been born into and the scars it had left. She hated how she felt, and it was easy to lay the blame at her mother's feet.

"I lied," Casper whispered against her ear. "She's never asked me for money. I was taking the money from you for my debts. She's been asking to see you for years."

Harlow stepped backward and searched his eyes. She hoped to find deceit. She wanted to look at him and see the brother who was trying to protect her from being hurt. She wanted to see *her* Casper. But all that looked back at her was betrayal. She slapped him. She hadn't realized she'd done it until it was over, and his head was bent to the side. Her hand stung from the force she'd used, and she had an overwhelming urge to do it again.

She balled her fists, trying to displace the urge to physically harm him—a reflection of how she was feeling. "How could you? Why would you?"

He had the decency to look ashamed. "There isn't an excuse I can give that would make it okay." He looked over at their mother. "I didn't trust you, and this seemed like the easiest way to keep you away from her and still get what I needed." He reached for Harlow, but she pulled away. "After spending time with her over the years, I realized how much she'd changed, but I couldn't tell you the truth without also telling you what I'd been doing."

It was like being hit in the face with a shovel. All Harlow could hear was her breathing. She was light-headed, and her limbs felt numb. She hadn't realized she'd sat on the couch until she looked down and saw her bent knees. *This can't be real. This can't be happening.* Harlow felt herself rocking, but she had no control over her body to stop it. Everything felt hot and like her body no longer belonged to her. She crossed her arms over her stomach when nausea slammed into her once again.

She needed to get out of the shrinking room. She grabbed her car keys and headed for the door.

"You shouldn't drive right now," Casper said from somewhere behind her.

She stilled her hand on the door. "You don't get to tell me what to do ever again."

The cold air slammed into her as she left the house. It was the first sense of reprieve she'd felt in the last half hour. She made it to her car and fumbled with the keys. She just wanted to get away, but her body wasn't cooperating with even the most basic movements. She finally gave up and leaned against her door, letting her body slide down the side to the cold pavement.

She sat there trying to reconcile everything she thought she knew with everything she'd just discovered. Nothing made sense. She wanted to find a reasonable explanation for it all, but she knew there was none. She wanted to cry. She wanted to scream. She wanted to run. Running was what she'd always done. She'd run from her previous life, from relationships, from hard decisions, from her own truths. Running was easy.

She got into her car, and before she could talk herself out of it, she got onto the freeway. She was going to the only place that truly belonged to her. The place where she could hide, the place where she felt safest. She headed for Monterey without looking back.

Audrey stared at her reflection as the makeup artist put the finishing touches on her perfectly created head injury. It was a long process that was rarely appreciated by anyone outside the industry. The work that went into making her beautiful, hideous, strung out, or injured was astonishing.

Jane continued to talk next to her. "You're going to Las Vegas for New Year's Eve with Sofia Linden."

Audrey sipped her water. "No, I'm not. I'm spending New Year's Eve at home. I'm not going anywhere."

Jane sighed and let her glasses slide down her nose. "I'm going to need a very good reason for that."

"Because it's what I want to do." She glanced at her. "And why exactly would I be going anywhere with Sofia Linden? I've never even met her."

"Because sulking has never been a good look on you. She's gorgeous, new on the scene, and it will up her profile. It's a win-win."

It had been three weeks since she'd spoken with Harlow, but it felt like years. She was constantly on the verge of tears, and the idea of dating anyone was not only ridiculous—it was painful. It didn't matter if Harlow didn't want her; she couldn't explain it to her heart.

"No," Audrey said. "I'm not going out with Sofia, and I don't want you setting me up on dates. I'll go when I'm ready."

Jane put her tablet in Audrey's hands. "What do you see?"

Audrey scrolled through the story, only bothering to read key bolded words. Her heart stopped when her eyes landed on the picture at the bottom. The shot wasn't a good one, taken from a good distance away, but she could make out Harlow distinctly. The photographer had only managed to get a picture of the other woman's back, so it was impossible to tell who it was. She pulled the screen closer to read the caption. *Harlow Thorne spotted cozying up to a mysterious brunette in Monterey. Is this Harlow's new leading lady? There has been no sign of Audrey Knox in weeks.*

Audrey handed the tablet back to Jane and noticed the slight tremble in her hand. "What Harlow does has no impact on my choices."

"Will you at least think about it?"

Audrey thanked the makeup artist and got out of the chair. "If I say yes, will you leave me alone?"

"Yes."

She brushed past her on the way to the set. "I'll think about it."

Audrey was lying. Jane knew she was lying. She wasn't going to consider going out with anyone. Her heart still belonged to Harlow, and realizing it wasn't reciprocal hurt more than she could handle at the moment. She'd thought, possibly foolishly, that Harlow would come back. What they'd had was special—that once-in-a-lifetime kind of relationship. She'd clearly been wrong, and the weight of losing her hit all over again.

Fortunately, this scene required her to sob over the broken body of her boyfriend after they'd been in a car accident. The tears weren't hard to muster. They flowed freely and without prompting. How had she been so wrong about Harlow, and how could she convince herself to let go?

CHAPTER THIRTY-FIVE

Emily flopped down on the couch next to the piano. "Have you eaten?"

Harlow played a few notes and then scribbled the adjustments. "Yeah."

"When?"

"Last night."

Emily handed her an apple. "That was almost twenty-four hours ago. You have to eat."

"I know," Harlow said as she continued to play. "Did you take the boat out today?"

"Don't change the subject." She smacked Harlow's arm. "I agreed to buy your groceries and bring them to you under three conditions."

Harlow took a bite of the apple. "I know, and I've followed all of them. Talk to a therapist, eat, and go outside at least once a day. I've done all those things. I even let you drag me out to the pier a few nights ago. It was freezing, by the way, which took the fun out of it."

Emily's eyes softened. "We've been friends for what, six years? I'm just worried about you."

"I know. I don't mean to make you worry."

"Have you called Audrey?"

Harlow shook her head. "And say what?"

She'd picked up the phone a hundred times to call Audrey. She'd typed out countless text messages but was never able to push the send button. It would do more harm than good. Audrey was better off being free of her, and it wasn't fair to draw her back in. She was doing the right thing by keeping her distance—even if it hurt her in the process.

Emily raised her hands in exaggeration. "I would lead with 'I'm sorry,' and then explain how miserable you've been. I'd include all the work you've been doing to heal the broken parts of you, and then close it out with 'I love you.' But hey, what do I know? I just drive boats for a living."

"She has no reason to forgive me, and I'm in no place to give her what she needs. She's better off without me."

Emily grabbed her shoulders and shook her slightly. "She would forgive you, but if she doesn't, she's a fool." Emily pulled her phone from her back pocket. "I forgot to tell you, I think the media knows where you are, and they think we're dating."

Harlow shrugged. "They don't know where I live." She took the phone and looked at the article. "You can't tell it's you."

Their conversation was cut short by the alarm system. Harlow checked the monitor. It was a car she didn't recognize, and she sighed.

"Do you want me to go tell whoever it is that they have the wrong house?" Emily stood and headed for the door.

Harlow watched the monitor, waiting for the intruder to emerge. "No. It's my mother. I'll take care of it."

Harlow walked to the front of the house as slowly as possible. She wanted to get her emotions under control and was working on the breathing techniques her therapist had been giving her. This wasn't a conversation she wanted to have, but she knew it was necessary. If she was ever going to be the type of person who didn't run from her problems, this was as good a place to start as any.

Harlow watched her for a minute before saying anything. "Can I help you?"

She'd forgotten how much she and Casper resembled their mother. She'd been in too much of a daze the last time she'd seen her to take it all in, but it was apparent now. She shared their smile, their nose, and their eyes. It was odd to think there was such a resemblance to a person with whom she shared virtually no relationship.

Her mother nervously rubbed her hands together. "I umm…I got your address from Casper. Can we talk?"

Harlow showed her inside and went to the kitchen. She pulled a bottle of whiskey from the cupboard. "Do you want anything?"

"Water would be great." She shrugged off her jacket and placed it on the chair. "This is a beautiful house."

Harlow handed her the glass of water. "What did you want to talk about, Mom?"

It wasn't that she didn't think they needed to have a conversation—she knew they did. She just didn't think she had the bandwidth to dance around it with small talk or niceties.

"After a long and difficult conversation, Casper took the deal, and I checked him into a treatment center today." She took a sip of water. "There aren't many treatment centers for gambling addiction, but this one came highly recommended." She seemed to study Harlow's reaction before she continued. "The judge was fine with it, but he'll be on house arrest when it's over."

"Who is paying for it?" Harlow knew it sounded cold, but she didn't care. "I assume it's not cheap." She took a large gulp of whiskey.

"I paid for it, and you're right, it's not."

"I'll write you a check," Harlow said, and she started to walk to her desk to find her checkbook.

"I don't want your money, Harlow. He's my son, and I don't mind helping him."

Harlow wasn't sure she'd heard correctly. "If you don't want the money, then why are you here?"

Her mom looked like she was choosing her next words carefully. "I'm here because I want a relationship with you."

Harlow tried to focus on her therapist's words. She tried to find the small space in her heart that she'd always kept reserved for her mother. Through all the turmoil, disappointment, and confusion—she still loved her. But loving someone and forgiving them were two different things, and she wasn't sure she could do the latter.

"Why now?" Harlow walked back over to the kitchen counter. She didn't want to be confined to a couch—it seemed too intimate.

Her mother let out a long sigh. "I've practiced what I'd say to you a thousand times. I've imagined your reactions, both the good and the bad. I thought I'd prepared myself for every possible outcome, but now that I'm here, it's hard to get out the words."

Harlow could've let her off the hook by filling the silence with platitudes of understanding, but she didn't.

"The truth is, I wasn't a good mother. It wasn't because I didn't want to be, but I didn't know how. I didn't know how to protect you or your brother. I should've, God knows I should've, but I just didn't."

Harlow asked the question she'd waited a lifetime to ask. "Why didn't you leave him? Why didn't you just take us and leave?"

Her mom shrugged. "I loved him."

Her words caught on the emotion in her throat, but she managed to get them out clearly. "You should've loved us more."

"You're right." Her mom reached out to touch her but changed her mind. "I can't change what I've done, Harlow. It doesn't matter how much I wish I could; I can't. I wish I had a better answer for you. I wish I could take it all back. I wish I'd been strong enough. I wish I hadn't become the person I did after he died. I wish I'd been a different person, but all that wishing changes nothing. I'd like to get to a better place with you, but it has to be what you want too."

Of all the things Harlow had imagined when she'd discussed this conversation with her therapist, she hadn't pictured the sincerity in her mother's expression. She'd expected to be met with excuses, possibly an "I'm sorry," but never the sincere guilt her mother apparently felt.

Harlow sipped her whiskey. "When Casper and I left, I never thought I'd see you again. Then when he told me you'd been coming around asking for money, it was easy to put you in a box. I had no idea what was really happening. And now…I don't know how to deal with any of it. Things are backwards. You wanted to see me, and he was fucking things up behind my back." She hadn't planned on being so honest, but she had no will to do anything but tell the truth.

Her mom nodded and let out a faint smile. "You're dealing with a lot right now. I didn't do a good job of teaching either of you how to process your emotions, and I certainly didn't teach either of you how to cope."

"I feel so betrayed." Harlow tried to fight back her tears, but she couldn't.

"Things aren't always as simple as betrayal or loyalty. People are messy and complicated and confusing. When two people are as close as you and Casper—when you've relied on each other the way you've had to, it makes sense that you feel that way."

Harlow used her palms to push the tears from her eyes. "He was supposed to love me. You were supposed to love me. I was supposed to be enough."

Her mom reached for her, and Harlow didn't pull away.

"Oh, honey, he does love you. People never talk about the painful, prickly parts of love. It's easy to get lost in the bright light it gives off, but there are so many layers. Casper didn't hurt you because he doesn't love you. He hurt you because he didn't know how to handle his sickness. You've always been enough. Our failures aren't a reflection of you; they're a reflection of us."

"I don't know how to forgive either of you." The words were cold, but they were honest.

"That's not something anyone can answer for you. But if you decide you want to, I'm here."

Harlow hadn't realized her mom was crying until her tear drops made patterns on Harlow's sweater. She pulled away and swirled the amber liquid in her glass, letting her mother's words sink in. She wasn't sure if she'd be able to let her past go, but she wanted to try. She didn't want to live like this. She didn't want to be haunted by her past, allowing it to dictate her every move. She wanted to be strong enough to move forward. She wanted to be the kind of person Audrey saw.

She studied her mother and wondered if they could have a different type of relationship. "I really fucked things up with Audrey."

"Hmm. Can you fix it?"

Harlow shook her head. "I don't know." She downed the rest of the whiskey. "I'm not sure I deserve her."

"I'm not really sure that's up to you to decide."

"You sound like her." Harlow let out a mild laugh. "I won't hold that against her, though." She looked up from her empty glass and smiled at her mom.

Her mom nodded, accepting the small jab. "Want some unsolicited advice?" She continued before Harlow could answer. "Don't leave space in your life for regrets. Make the grand gesture. Leave it all out there. Do the hard things, and let the chips fall where they will." She sighed deeply. "You can't fix regrets."

Harlow took her mom's hands. "Thank you for coming to talk to me."

Her mom stood and picked up her coat. "I'm staying in town for a few days if you'd like to talk some more?" There was trepidation in her voice.

"How about lunch tomorrow? I don't want to go out in public, but if you'd like to come here around noon, I'd like to see you."

A smile split her mother's face. "I'd like that. I'll see you then."

Harlow walked her to the door and headed back down to her recording studio. Relief and hope seemed within her grasp, and she hadn't felt it in a long time. Now all she needed to do was sort out the rest of her life.

The afternoon with her mother had gone better than she'd expected. They had lunch and walked along the beach. Harlow listened as her mother told her about her life—how she'd gone back to school, become an accountant, and married a man she described as the love of her life. Her mother answered all her questions without hesitation and didn't push into areas where Harlow was hesitant. The hours weren't like anything Harlow had imagined. Her mom was funny, kind, and different than she remembered.

"I wish Casper would've told me the truth. We lost so much time," Harlow said as they sat on the lounge chairs, staring at the ocean.

"I was sixteen when I had you two." She smiled up at the sky like she remembered something. "I had no idea what I was doing. There I was, still a kid myself, and the doctor handed me two tiny humans to take home. You two were so similar and yet so different." Her mom looked over at her with a faint smile. "Casper took to being your protector from the very beginning. As you two got older, that dedication seemed to grow. I know it doesn't feel like it right now, but I think he thought he was protecting you. He was skeptical when I first made contact several years ago, and rightfully so, but I don't believe he meant to hurt you."

"Why did you wait so long?" Harlow's chest burned with anticipation. The answer to this question felt more critical now that she'd given it life.

"You two were doing so well without me—I didn't want to ruin anything for you. I've watched you from the beginning. I've even gone to several of your shows. You are *so* talented and so courageous up on stage. I was in awe. I didn't want to risk any of that for you." She made shapes in the sand with the toe of her boot. "Can I ask you something?"

"Sure." Harlow tilted her head to listen.

"Why did you cancel your tour?"

Harlow sighed. "I've always felt like I was one misstep from falling. When all this happened with Casper and the media coverage turned sour, I couldn't bear the thought of it all being taken away. I ended it before they took it from me, before I could fuck it up even more." There it was—fear. She hadn't shared the reason with anyone, not even her therapist. Being able to say it out loud lifted a weight off her shoulders. "Music and performing were where I was able to put everything away. I felt free on stage—untouchable. I didn't feel like that anymore."

Her mother turned to face her. "And Audrey? Why did you run from her?"

Harlow's throat burned with the realization that the answer was one and the same. "I couldn't handle the thought of her leaving me first. I figured it was only a matter of time, and I couldn't stand the thought of dragging her down with me, and then her hating me in the end."

"Will you tell me about her? I mean, I know who she is. You've had a crush on her since you were a teenager. I remember that poster of her on your wall, but tell me about her."

Harlow smiled. "I still have that poster in my house." She felt the blush burning on her cheeks. "Audrey is smart and kind and caring. She has a way of making you feel like there is no one else in the room when she talks to you. She isn't like all the other celebrities I've met. She's grounded and humble. She makes me want to be a better person because of what she sees in me."

"You love her." Her mom reached out and rubbed her arm. "I'm in no place to tell you what to do, but you need to fix this."

"Just like that?" Harlow snapped her fingers. "Just fix it. I wouldn't even know where to start. Emily says to tell her I'm sorry and tell her I love her, but it won't be enough. She deserves more."

"Then give her more. Show her how you feel. Make sure there's no room for her to wonder."

Her mom was right. She wanted to give Audrey everything she deserved and more. She'd felt like half of her was missing these last few weeks, and she couldn't imagine spending a lifetime wondering what could have been if only she'd been brave enough to lay it all on the line. She wasn't sure if Audrey would forgive her, but it didn't matter. She'd never forgive herself if she didn't take the chance.

CHAPTER THIRTY-SIX

The days between Christmas and New Year's were like living in a different realm. Time seemed almost obsolete. There was no shooting schedule until after the holidays, and Audrey felt a hundred pounds heavier from the copious amounts of wine and cheese she'd been indulging in the last few days. She needed to work out. She wanted to work out. That's what she was telling herself as she stretched her legs in preparation for her run.

Kylie was bouncing around looking much too motivated for seven in the morning. "You ready? I'm pumped for this run."

Audrey begrudgingly pulled her earbuds from her pocket. "Your enthusiasm is making me tired already."

Kylie smacked her arm. "Come on. It will be good for us. Just a quick five miles."

"Can we just do three?"

Kylie started running backward. "Just think, the quicker we get back, the sooner we can open that bottle of champagne your dad brought home from France."

She had a point.

Audrey caught up with her. "I'll never forgive you for this."

"Yes, you will." Kylie matched her pace. "So, I had to put an event on your calendar, and I'm not sure you're going to be all that happy about it. Just remember that you love me."

Audrey pulled out her left earbud to hear better. "Continue."

"You're going to the GLAAD New Year's Eve Party. But don't stress, I'm going to come with you."

"I don't want to go to a New Year's party, even for GLAAD."

Kylie pointed at her. "I knew you'd say that, but we're going."

Audrey smacked Kylie's hand away. "You're not the boss of me."

Kylie shrugged. "Sometimes, I am." She smiled. "This is a favor for me, anyway. Chelsea Drake said she'd meet me to talk about the screenplay I wrote, but she doesn't do formal meetings for first introductions. She said she'd meet me there."

Audrey scrunched her nose. "Chelsea Drake? I told you that we'd produce your screenplay."

"I know, and you're going to, but you also told me to talk to as many people as possible. It helps create buzz."

Audrey sighed at her own words being used against her. "You don't *need* me there. You can manage this meeting on your own."

"True, but I want you there, and I would totally do it for you."

Audrey wanted to argue, but she couldn't. Kylie had been there for her more times than she could count. If it made her feel better to drag Audrey along, she'd let herself be dragged. "Fine."

Kylie grabbed her arm. "Thank you. You won't regret it."

Audrey went to put her earbud back in when Kylie stopped her. "There's one more thing."

Audrey braced herself. "Okay."

"I need you to look hot. Not just your normal hot, but like, hot-hot. I think Chelsea has a thing for you, and it will certainly help the conversation along if she's in a good mood before talking to me."

Audrey raised an eyebrow. "I'm not sure if I should be offended or honored."

"Let's go with honored." Kylie ran a few steps ahead. "Definitely honored."

Audrey put her earbud back in and switched on the music. Harlow's voice came on, and the familiar pang of loss thrummed through her body. She shouldn't listen to her, but she couldn't help herself. She missed her voice. Actually, she missed everything about Harlow. She missed the way her eyes lit up when she smiled. She missed the way she talked with her hands when she was excited about something. She missed the way she'd tug on her hand to pull her in for a kiss. She missed how she'd bite Audrey's lip when they kissed. *Okay. That's enough.*

It had been a month since she last spoke with her. A month of crying herself to sleep. A month of hoping she was okay. A month of feeling rejected. A month of wondering how it had gotten so out of control. She'd forced herself to go through the motions, day in and day out. But the familiar pang of loss was always there, gnawing at her insides, reminding her that she wasn't whole.

She'd focused on work as much as possible. It helped to dilute some of her pain. She managed to take several meetings and secure funding for their first film. She'd even started getting things lined up for Kylie's screenplay. Her budding production company was being taken seriously, and people were calling to work with her on it. She had every reason to be over the moon in regards to her career. But everything seemed less bright without Harlow, like the color in her world had shifted to monotone, and she didn't know how to change it back. She wasn't sure if she ever could switch it back. It was like seeing life in High-Definition for the first time and then having to go back to the reality of Standard. *You've been in the industry too long.*

Perhaps this party would be good for her. New year, with a fresh outlook. Even while she was trying to convince herself, she knew it wasn't true. Time was supposed to heal everything, but Audrey didn't believe that. Some cracks were so deep, so pronounced, nothing would fill them. The crack Harlow left, she feared, would never be whole again.

Harlow listened as the counselor laid out the ground rules for her discussion with Casper. She was trying to be fully present. She wanted to find a way to move past all the hurt with her brother, but she found herself growing more agitated by the second.

"Do you have any questions?" The therapist looked at her with his fingers steepled against his chin.

Harlow shook her head, and the therapist motioned for Casper to speak.

Casper shifted in his chair. "I know I hurt you, Low. I know you're frustrated with me, angry, and confused. I'm sorry. I'm addicted to gambling, and I'm trying to work on it."

"And how does that make you feel, Harlow?" The therapist's voice was calm, and she found it terribly irritating.

"How do I feel?" She couldn't stop the small laugh that escaped her. "I'm fucking angry. I'm mad at you for not coming to me. I'm mad at you for putting me in an impossible situation. I'm mad at you for risking your life. I'm mad at you for involving my tour and risking everything we built together. But mostly, I'm mad at you for all the lies." She put her head in her hands. "You've done nothing but lie to me for God knows how long, Casper. Not just about the addiction, but about Mom. You made me doubt myself. You made me doubt us."

"I know, and I'm sorry."

"You're sorry. Everyone is sorry. Sorry doesn't put things back together. Sorry doesn't fix our relationship."

"Casper, how does what Harlow said make you feel?" The therapist adjusted his glasses.

Casper rubbed his hands against his legs. "It makes me sad. It makes me feel guilty. I never wanted to hurt her, and I know I did."

The therapist leaned forward in his chair. "Well, as we discussed, Harlow's forgiveness is for her to give. It's not anything you can control. But what are some things you think you can do to work toward earning that from her?"

Casper looked at Harlow, and she had to keep herself from crying. His eyes were full of pain. "I know I can no longer work for you, but I'd still like to see you. I'm open to whatever schedule works for you."

"What are you going to do to keep yourself from gambling?" She tried to keep her voice level and without judgment.

"I'm going to keep going to meetings. I'm going to hire someone to handle all my finances, and I'm going to find a way to repay you no matter how long it takes. I know I've lost everything because of this."

"What about Mom? You stole so much time from us, Casper."

"I know. I can't tell you how sorry I am for that. If I could go back and change it all, I would, Low. I swear to you, I would. I know I betrayed your trust. I know the reason you quit your tour was because of me. I know I can't fix it, but I want to do better."

Harlow shook her head. "I didn't quit the tour because of you. I mean, I thought I did at first. You were an easy excuse. I quit the tour because I couldn't handle the thought of failure. I felt lost after what happened with you, and I didn't cope well. I need to take some responsibility. I've relied on you for so much, for so long, and that's not fair either." She gave him a half-smile. "We both have some work to do."

The therapist filled the silence. "I think this is great progress." He looked at Harlow. "If you're open to it, I'd like you to come back and meet with us one more time before Casper is through with treatment here."

Harlow nodded. "Sure."

Casper showed her out to a bench that sat looking at a small pond. He seemed more relaxed than she ever remembered him being. There was a peace about him that wasn't typical. The sharp shards of anger that had been pricking her skin began to fall away.

"I really appreciate you coming," he said as he took a seat next to her.

"I wasn't sure I was going to at first, but my therapist insisted."

He looked surprised. "You're seeing a therapist?"

She pulled her hood up over her head to protect herself from the winter air. "Three times a week. We all have our shit, Casper."

He chuckled. "Yeah, I guess we do."

She kicked the gravel at her feet. "I'm glad you're getting help. I don't want to lose you."

He put his arm around her and pulled her head to his shoulder. "You won't ever lose me, Low. It's always been us."

"Yeah, but now I need you to focus on yourself. I'll be okay." She was surprised that her voice didn't crack. Her emotions were a messy web—good, bad, regret, pain, anger, love. They bubbled so close to the surface, and she wasn't sure which to grab on to—so she settled on love. "I love you. I will do whatever I can to help you."

He kissed her, and she felt the soft tremble brought on by tears against her head. "Thank you."

They sat there in silence for several more minutes. It was the kind of silence that could only happen with people who shared a history. A history of loss, of love, and devotion. It was the kind of history siblings shared. She could put aside the pain because her love for him was stronger. Her mother was right. Love could be prickly. Sometimes messy. It could be imperfect because people were imperfect. What mattered more than the mistakes and regrets was the willingness to see what that person was capable of—who they could be. Loving someone meant allowing growth and change, even when it hurt. She hoped Audrey would see it the same way.

CHAPTER THIRTY-SEVEN

"Tell me again why I'm doing this." Audrey pulled at the deep vee of the Calvin Klein outfit to make sure it covered her boobs. The short red skirt and white halter top were amazing, and it would be wasted on her. It deserved to be on someone who was looking for a good time.

Kylie pulled on her shoe as she tripped out of Audrey's closet. "Okay, I told you to look hot-hot, and you've totally come through. Holy hell."

Audrey looked down. She knew she should feel beautiful, but she didn't. "Thanks. Anything for you."

"You could sound a little more convincing, but I'll take it."

Audrey took a deep breath. "I'm sorry. I'm totally here for you tonight, but I want you to remember something for me." She waited until she had Kylie's full attention. "Your worth is not tied up in what Chelsea Drake thinks of you. You wrote a brilliant screenplay, and I'm excited to produce it. I'm so proud of you. Whatever happens tonight, please don't forget that."

Kylie's eyes softened, and she rested her forearms on Audrey's shoulders. "You're the best friend I could ever have. You know that, right?" She kissed her cheek. "Thank you for always believing in me."

Audrey hugged her. "The feeling is mutual." She waved a hand in front of her face to stop herself from crying. "I can't ruin my mascara before we've walked out the door."

On the drive over, Audrey tried not to focus on all of the ways Harlow could be keeping herself busy on New Year's Eve.

Unfortunately, the possibilities were endless—images of her in bed with that woman in the photograph filled the blank spaces in her mind. Thoughts of candlelit dinners and walks along the Monterey shoreline fluttered through her thoughts. The most apparent, though, was that it wasn't that Harlow couldn't be in a relationship—it was that she couldn't be in one with her.

"You ready?" Kylie seemed like she was practically crawling out of her skin with excitement, and Audrey couldn't help but smile.

"You bet."

The event space was erupting with lights, music, and beautiful people. Servers in tuxedoes made their way around the area carrying trays of champagne and small bites of food. The word GLAAD was swirling on the floor and the walls, and there was rainbow glitter everywhere. *Cleanup is going to be a bitch.*

Audrey made her rounds with Kylie, offering dozens of obligatory face kisses and brief bouts of small talk. There was so much happiness and celebratory enthusiasm around her, she was almost able to put Harlow out of her mind. Almost. That is, of course, until she heard a few people mumbling their excitement about the guest who'd just pulled up to the party.

Audrey felt her heart catch in her chest, and she made her way to the other side of the room to see if she'd heard correctly. She weaved between people, trying to catch a glimpse of the entranceway. She was both thrilled and devastated when she finally laid eyes on her. There, walking through the front doors, looking absolutely fucking perfect, was Harlow Thorne.

Audrey hadn't realized she'd put her hand against her chest until Kylie pulled at her arm. "You okay?" Kylie gripped her wrist, looking apologetic.

"I, um—I need to go to the restroom." Audrey hurried away before Kylie could stop her.

She needed to compose herself. She needed to reel in her emotions. She needed not to be such a damn basket case. People ran into their exes all the time, especially in this industry. The bathroom was busy, so she opened one of the stall doors and sat on the toilet. She tried to calm her breathing by taking longer breaths than she'd been allowing herself. Once she didn't feel like passing out, she mentally ran through different scenarios.

You don't own Los Angeles. Harlow lives here too, and you're going to run into her from time to time. Stop being such a child. You've been broken up with before. This is no different. She didn't bring a date. Why didn't she bring a date? Oh my God, stop. She could be meeting someone here. That would be perfect. You could watch her be all over someone else for the entire night—an ideal way to spend New Year's.

There was a knock on the bathroom stall. "You okay?" Kylie's tone conveyed her concern.

Audrey ran her hands over her face. Her cheeks were hot, and her hands were clammy. "Yup. Just need a minute."

She considered hiding in the stall for the rest of the night. Then she tried to figure a way out of the party without being noticed. Perhaps she could carry the fake plant sitting in the corner of the bathroom lobby in front of her. It worked in movies.

"Honey, at least let me in." Kylie pressed her face against the small crack in the stall.

Audrey unlatched the door. "Sorry, I panicked when I saw her."

"Do you want to talk about it?" Kylie ran her hands over Audrey's shoulders. "Do you just want to get out of here?"

"We haven't gotten to talk to Chelsea Drake yet." Audrey winced at how pathetic she sounded.

"That's okay." Kylie took her hand.

Audrey closed her eyes and focused on what had brought her here. She came to support Kylie. Kylie, who would do anything for her and who had stood by her their entire lives. She was willing to give up her chance to talk to someone important, just so Audrey was comfortable. She deserved better.

"It's not okay," Audrey said. She stood and straightened her skirt. "Let's get out of here and go talk to Chelsea."

"Are you sure?" Kylie looked concerned. "It doesn't have to be tonight."

Audrey hugged her. "Yes, it does."

She followed Kylie out into the crowded room. The lights and laughter were carrying on as if she wasn't on the verge of getting sick. People danced and drank with no regard for her current emotional state. It was a good reminder that the world continued to turn whether your heart was broken or not. She did her best not to look around, but she knew where Harlow was standing. She could feel her even without being near her. She was like a beacon. Audrey wondered if there would ever be a time she didn't feel both her absence and presence to acutely.

❖

Harlow had been planning this attempt at reconciliation for several days. It was going to be her grand gesture—a way to apologize for being such a coward. But now that she was here, she was terrified. Up until now, she could only imagine Audrey's reaction. After tonight it would be a reality, and there'd be no guessing. That should bring some sense of peace. It did not.

She hadn't expected Audrey to run to her when they first made eye contact, but she also hadn't anticipated her immediate escape into the bathroom. It was as if Audrey didn't want to be in the same room with her. *Can I blame her?*

Harlow weaved in and out of people, stopping briefly for photos until she made it behind the stage. She wasn't being peppered with questions about her brother or the tour, which was a welcome surprise. People seemed genuinely excited to see her, which made her frayed nerves slightly more bearable. She found Dominic taking shots with a few very excited young women.

"Hey, gorgeous." He wrapped his arms around her and kissed her cheek. "You look fantastic." He held her at arm's length to look her over thoroughly. "I wasn't sure you'd show." He filled one of the shot glasses and handed it to her.

"Thanks for letting me crash the act tonight." She threw back the shot and covered her mouth with the back of her hand. "Jesus, what was that?"

He wrapped her arm around her shoulder and kissed her cheek. "Black Bowmore. There were only one hundred and fifty-nine bottles ever made. Fucking forty grand a bottle."

She coughed at the information. "Holy shit, Dom. Who spends that on whiskey?"

He grinned widely. "It's not every day my girl falls in love. It's a cause for celebration. When you called to tell me about your little plan, I couldn't help myself. It's for good luck."

She sucked in a deep breath. "I'm not sure if we should be celebrating just yet. I'm not sure if she'll take me back. I messed this one up pretty bad."

He poured her another shot and handed it to her. "Here's to getting everything you ever wanted." He put his forehead against hers. "You deserve to be happy, kid." He tapped the side of her cheek. "Now, go shoot your shot."

She drank the whiskey and handed the glass back, then turned toward the stage and shook her arms at her sides. The last time she was this nervous about taking a stage, she was an opening act. She had more to lose now.

She walked out onto the stage and felt the immediate and familiar heat of the spotlight, tracking her movements. She took the acoustic guitar from its stand and moved the microphone to her height level. The music that had been playing as filler while the band was on a break quieted. The void it created caused everyone to turn their attention to the stage. The sudden burst of applause and excitement was enough to make her smile.

"I thought I'd play a song for you guys tonight. Do you mind?" She strummed the guitar, needing something to keep her hands from shaking. She waited until the applause and screams of approval died down. "This song is from the album I've been working on for the last few months. I've never played it live, so I hope you all don't mind hearing it first." She sat on the stool and wiped away the bit of sweat on her forehead. "The new album is about the first and only woman I've ever loved." The crowd screamed, and she continued to strum. She looked into the crowd hoping to see Audrey, but the lighting limited her view. She thought about editing what she was going to say but changed her mind. Not only did she want Audrey to know how she felt, but she also didn't want to hide anymore. "I've had a crush on Audrey Knox since I was a teenager." Laughter and shouts of approval came from the people below. "Then I met her and found out teenage me had grossly underestimated her. Audrey is smart, funny, kind, sweet, and generous. I feel lucky to have met her, and even luckier that she gave me a chance to get to know her." She continued to play, her heart racing more furiously than it ever had on stage before. "I blew that chance, and this may not win her back, but I hope it's a start." She closed her eyes and began to sing, letting the love song fill her soul and come pouring out in her voice.

Harlow finished the song and bowed to the ecstatic crowd. The familiar rush that always accompanied a performance raced through her body, and she realized how much she needed to get back on stage. It was a crucial part of her being, and she had to feed it to keep it alive. Still, she'd give it all up if it meant she could get Audrey back.

Dominic grabbed her when she came down the stairs. "That was perfect." He kissed both her cheeks. "Now go find her and finish what you started."

Harlow thanked him and checked her phone. Her hands were shaky, and she was finding it difficult to get her breathing under control. This was it. She opened the text message from Kylie. *You nailed it. We're upstairs in the VIP area.* There was no hint as to how Audrey had received it, but that wasn't on Kylie. She'd done her a huge favor by getting Audrey here tonight, and she couldn't ask for anything more. It was up to her now.

She walked toward the stairs doing her best to remain focused. She smiled at the people offering their praise but didn't stop to talk. It was as if everything in her whole life hung in the balance. Okay, maybe that was a little dramatic, but her happiness surely did. She'd either leave here with her heart intact or completely shattered. She hoped for the former but was trying to prepare for the latter. She climbed the stairs, her mouth growing dryer by the second. A few more feet and she would know for sure.

She looked into Audrey's beautiful eyes. "Hi."

Chapter Thirty-eight

Audrey had spent over half her life acting. Some would even say she was rather good at her chosen profession. Hell, she even had a few awards to prove her worth in the field. She tried to conjure every ounce of talent when she heard Harlow's voice come through the speakers. The moment Harlow mentioned her name people turned to look at her, and she had to school her features to make sure she didn't give anything away. But she loved her voice. She loved it raspy with exhaustion, when she was excited, nervous, and when her desire flared. Harlow's voice had a way of making Audrey feel like she was being caressed.

Harlow's public declaration was sweet and honest. Audrey knew how much it would've taken her to proclaim her feelings. She'd been avoiding media attention since the incident with her brother. Seeing her walking across the crowded event was like something out of a movie. Audrey was still trying to link words together to make a coherent sentence by the time Harlow reached her.

"Can we talk?" Harlow looked down at their entwined hands.

The uncertainty in Harlow's expression tugged at her heart. She looked over at Kylie, who gave her a conspiratorial wink. "Sure. I have someone I need to speak to."

Harlow looked around and pulled her into a roped-off area in the corner. The bouncer let them through without issue, and Harlow thanked him. She sat on the couch next to Harlow and noticed she'd intentionally put space between them.

Harlow looked exceedingly nervous, so Audrey spoke first. "How have you been?"

Harlow looked like she was going to take her hand but changed her mind. "Not great. I, umm…I'm not sure where to start." She ran her hand through her hair.

"The beginning would be great." Audrey didn't mean to sound harsh, but the now-familiar sting of rejection sizzled at the surface. It had dissipated with the initial realization Harlow had come to win her back, but it didn't take away the hurt.

Harlow nodded slowly and seemed to search for the words she wanted to say. "I pushed you away. I convinced myself that I didn't deserve you, and that you'd be better off without me. I saw my old life coming back. I thought it was all going to be taken away. I thought I was going to lose you, so I made the decision before you could. I couldn't bear the thought of you realizing that I wasn't good enough for you, and I couldn't handle the guilt of messing with your career, either." She wiped a tear from her eye, but her body gave no other indication she was crying. "I didn't realize how much I had to work through until I had no other choice." She finally took her hand, running her thumb over Audrey's skin. "I love you. I should've told you before. I shouldn't have let you walk out that door. I'm so sorry."

Audrey's heart was screaming for her to grab Harlow and kiss her. She wanted to hug her and tell her everything would be okay. She wanted her to know that none of what happened mattered. But the words wouldn't come out. She couldn't let go of how easy it had been for Harlow to dismiss her when things got hard. She couldn't stop thinking about all the opportunities Harlow had to share her struggle and concern. Need and want were being rapidly replaced by fear, and no matter how badly she wanted it not to be the case—it was there.

"I need some time to think." She took Harlow's hands in her own and almost gasped at the jolt that ran through her when they touched. "I appreciate you saying everything you did. But I was devastated when you didn't want me, and you've really, really hurt me. I want to believe you now. I just need some time."

The countdown to the New Year started, and Audrey held tight to her words while trying to ignore Harlow's pained expression. She wanted desperately to kiss all the sadness from her cheeks, but she stayed rooted to her spot.

The partygoers erupted in cheers and started the New Year's ritual of hugging and kissing. But neither Audrey nor Harlow fell into celebration. Audrey leaned over and kissed Harlow's cheek. She smelled the same, and Audrey let her face rest against hers for a moment.

She finally pulled herself away. "We'll talk soon. I promise."

As she walked away to find Kylie, her heart screamed for her to stop, but her brain kept her moving forward. She wasn't sure if she was doing the right thing, but it was the safe thing. She'd never bothered to protect her heart before, and she'd always been the one left to pick up the pieces. She wasn't going to do that again. She was going to stay a little longer for the sake of appearances, but it was quickly clear all people wanted to talk about was Harlow's romantic gesture and how great it was she was coming out. Audrey found Kylie and tugged on her sleeve and didn't have to say a word. They left and although Kylie hadn't said a word the whole way home, she turned on her the moment they walked through the front door.

"Did I miss something? I thought you wanted to be with Harlow?"

Audrey dropped her purse on the kitchen table. "I did. I mean, I do. It's just not that simple."

Kylie looked frustrated as she shook her head. "You've been moping around here for a month. A full month, because you want her and didn't think you could have her. Now you can, but you're still moping. What is going on with you?"

Audrey started pacing. "I'm not sure it will make sense."

Kylie grabbed her and forced her to sit down. "Try. I've been planning that setup with Harlow for over a week because I thought it was what you wanted."

Now Kylie's persistence about going to the event made sense. "She is what I want. Of course, she's what I want. I love her."

Kylie put her hands up. "Then what's the problem?"

"Leaving came so easily the first time. It didn't even seem like she thought about it. What if I fall even more in love with her, and she does it again?" She swallowed hard against the lump in her throat. "I'm not sure I'd survive it."

Kylie's eye's softened, and she kissed her hair. "What if she doesn't?" Kylie didn't give her a chance to respond. She picked up her purse and headed for the stairs to her room, but before she disappeared, she stopped and turned toward Audrey. "Don't let fear start making decisions for you. That's not the woman I know."

The tears came like they'd been simmering under the surface, waiting for the perfect opportunity to spill in torrents. She pulled at her top, feeling suddenly suffocated. She wanted to be free, but free from what? Her hang-ups? Her fear? She'd waited a month for Harlow to come to her senses, and now that she had, Audrey had been paralyzed by fear. The fear hadn't presented itself until Harlow had publicly presented her heart to her. She'd let her doubt dictate her actions—just like Harlow had. She didn't want to be that person. It was easy to lecture Harlow about giving them a chance—taking a leap, but she needed to do the same. She had to stop focusing on what she could lose and instead think about what she could gain. She could have Harlow, and that was everything. She should've given Harlow her answer the moment she asked. But she could fix this. She would fix this.

CHAPTER THIRTY-NINE

Harlow sat on her couch and pretended to watch the Rose Bowl. It wasn't that she was a huge fan of football as much as it took very little brainpower to watch the game idly. As the players smashed into each other, she couldn't help replaying the epic crash and burn she'd suffered the night before. She knew it had been a long shot going in, but the reality of not having Audrey was far more painful than the not knowing.

Her phone buzzed with the security gate notification. She looked down at the screen to see Audrey's face. She sat up too quickly and spilled her beer down the front of her shirt.

"Hey." She rolled her eyes at her lame greeting and tapped the phone against her forehead.

"Can I come up?" Audrey's tone didn't leave a hint as to what she wanted.

"Of course." Harlow pushed the entry button and headed to the door.

This could either be very bad or very good. Audrey had said she needed time to think, but it had only been twelve hours. Was it like a jury? Did the length of deliberation give a hint to the outcome? But which was it? She couldn't remember if shorter was good or bad. *Cool. Have a random nervous breakdown in front of her.*

Harlow pulled the door open before Audrey had the chance to knock. "Hey."

Audrey's cheeks were flushed, and she looked around the room as if she were searching for someone. "Are you alone?"

Harlow looked around. "Of course, I'm alone. Why wouldn't I be?"

Audrey shrugged and took a step closer. "Someone photographed you in Monterey with a woman. I wasn't sure if she was here."

Harlow had to suppress a laugh. "You mean Emily? She's my friend. In fact, you met her. It was her boat we took out that day."

Audrey's lips formed into an o shape, and her cheeks turned a light crimson. "I feel ridiculous."

Harlow wanted to take Audrey's hand but forced herself not to move. She still wasn't sure why Audrey had come, and she didn't want to make assumptions. Audrey took another step closer, and every nerve ending in Harlow's body hummed with excitement.

Audrey touched Harlow's wrist and ran her fingers up her arm, only resting when they reached her neck. She bit her lip, and Harlow marveled at how the simple action made her stomach flutter. Audrey pulled her down so their lips were almost touching. Harlow wanted nothing more than to close the distance, but it had to be Audrey's decision. She slid her hands around Audrey's waist and was rewarded by the slight hitch in her breath.

"I should've done this last night." Audrey kissed her softly. It was almost as if she was testing something. She pulled back after a second. Her cheeks were red, and her eyes were hazy with lust. "I love you."

Harlow didn't wait any longer. She pulled her in and let her kiss convey all of the things she'd been feeling. She was consumed. Consumed by love, regret, hope, craving, and too many other things to name. It was all there, the ingredients of a song yet to be played. Audrey had made her feel things she had never imagined, and some she didn't realize could exist together. Audrey was the music of her soul.

Harlow started to pull Audrey's jacket off. "Do you want to talk?"

Audrey let the jacket fall and started pushing Harlow toward the steps. "No." She kissed her again. "Later." She raked her fingers up and down Harlow's stomach. "I need this right now."

There was nothing she wouldn't give, nothing she'd hold back—never again.

❖

Audrey had no idea what time it was. Her only reference point was the fading sun outside Harlow's window. They'd made love until they'd each gotten their fill of one another. It had started out as desperate. Both of them seemed to need the reassurance the other was there and that they wanted the other. Then it transitioned into something sweet and vulnerable. Audrey had never felt so in tune with anyone before, and the high from their connection lingered in her heart.

She stroked Harlow's stomach, loving the way it twitched under her fingertips. "I should've given you an answer last night. I didn't make you wait for dramatic effect. The idea of having you was eclipsed by the thought of losing you again."

Harlow rolled over on her side, bringing their faces closer together. "That's my fault. I shouldn't have pushed you away the first time. I think your reaction was warranted."

Audrey stroked Harlow's cheekbone with her thumb. "I wish I could've been what you needed when everything happened with Casper."

Harlow kissed her palm. "It wasn't that you weren't what I needed. I didn't know how to be what I needed. It's not up to you to fix me. Only I can do that. I'm working on it."

"I'm here and I'm not going anywhere. I want you to know that." Audrey's voice cracked when she spoke. "Do you want to tell me about your brother now?"

Audrey expected to see hesitation or discomfort, but there was none. She nodded and went on to explain everything that had transpired in their time apart. Harlow went into detail regarding the interactions with her mother—which were the most surprising. Audrey hadn't been sure what to expect when forging into this conversation, but she was pleasantly surprised. Harlow was forthcoming and honest. She explained how she was feeling and how she'd felt. This was a side of Harlow that she hadn't gotten to know yet, and she loved it.

"I appreciate you sharing that with me."

"I want to share everything with you," Harlow said as she pushed herself up in bed.

Audrey pulled at her. "Lie back down. I'm not done with you yet."

Harlow traced her finger down Audrey's face. "Kylie texted me. You're supposed to be at a family dinner in an hour."

"I completely forgot." Audrey rolled over to grab her phone. "Why was she texting you?" She looked down, and the realization hit. "Because my phone was on 'do not disturb.'" She grabbed Harlow's hand. "Do you want to come with me? I know you're going through some growing pains as a family. I don't want to make you uncomfortable. I don't want to shove my family in your face, but I'd like you to come." Audrey hoped her sincerity was clear.

"Audrey," Harlow whispered as she kissed her again. "Don't you see? I want you to be my family too."

It fell away then—the last shred of hesitation Audrey had left. She'd believed Harlow when she said she loved her. She knew she'd been sincere when she apologized, but the promise of sharing their lives had been what she wanted affirmed. She needed to know Harlow shared the devotion to a future that neither of them could see clearly.

"I need to shower. I smell like sex." Audrey hurried into the bathroom.

Harlow followed closely behind. "I'll get in with you, you know, to save time."

They both knew that wasn't true. There'd be no time saved in a shared shower, but she didn't care. Audrey turned on the spray and smiled widely as she pulled Harlow in to join her. She'd be perfectly content if she never had to shower alone again.

CHAPTER FORTY

Harlow held Audrey's hand as they weaved through the familiar streets of Beverly Hills toward Audrey's house. This day hadn't gone as planned in the best possible way. Eight hours ago, she'd thought her future with Audrey had been obliterated. She'd tried to piece together what an existence without her would look like. Now, she was like the luckiest woman on the planet. Audrey loved her. Audrey wanted her, no matter what her past had been or the baggage that remained.

Audrey kissed their joined hands when they pulled up to the house. "You sure about this? They can be a lot."

"Absolutely," Harlow said, and she meant it with every fiber of her being. She wanted to be where Audrey was, no matter who was around.

Audrey took her hand as soon as she came around the side of the car. Before she opened the door, Audrey stood on her tiptoes and kissed her. "I love you."

"I love you too," Harlow said as she took a deep breath. She didn't think she'd ever grow tired of hearing those words leaving Audrey's lips. "After you."

Kylie put a tray down when they came through the door and practically ran to greet them. She hugged Harlow first. "I can't tell you how happy I am to see you." She squeezed her biceps and then practically tackled Audrey, dragging her a few feet away.

Harlow shoved her hands in her pockets and walked toward the kitchen. Kathy Knox was swatting at a man who couldn't have been anyone but Audrey's father. She favored her mother in the looks department, but the way his eyes crinkled at the sides when he smiled was all Audrey.

Kathy noticed her first and wiped her hands on a dishtowel. "Harlow." She opened her arms for a hug, and Harlow went to her immediately. "I'm so glad you're here," she said while she rubbed her back.

"Me too." Harlow felt her eyes well up, and she blinked back the emotion. She hadn't really known how Audrey's parents would react to seeing her, and she was grateful for the warm welcome. "Nice to meet you. I'm Harlow Thorne." She stuck her hand out to her father once Kathy had finally released her.

He appraised her for several seconds until the corners of his mouth started tugging upward into a smile. "Jim Knox." He waved away her hand and pulled her into a hug. "Pleasure to meet you."

He hugged the way Audrey hugged. He hugged her like they'd known each other for years, and she was more at ease. He pulled away and went back to the oven, pulling out a delicious smelling lasagna. Harlow's mouth started watering, and it wasn't until then that she realized just how hungry she was.

Audrey's warm hand was on her back and her cheek against her shoulder. "You ready to eat?"

The evening went on the same way it had started—perfectly. The Knox family was warm, comforting, and had a lovely ease with one another. Harlow was overcome with a sense that this was how a family was supposed to be. This was what she'd been missing her whole life. It wasn't anyone's fault she hadn't experienced this before. She and Casper had done their best, but they were dealt a different set of cards than Audrey, and that was okay. She was here now, and that was enough. She finally felt like she was enough.

She helped Audrey do the dishes while the background noise of fervent laughter echoed in from the living room. Harlow smiled to herself, amazed at what a difference a day had made. Everything felt like it was exactly how it should be, and she didn't feel as if she was right on the edge of losing everything. It was wonderful.

Audrey put the last of the plates away and wrapped her hands around Harlow's waist. "What are you grinning about?"

"How lucky I feel right now. I love you." Harlow kissed the top of her head and breathed in Audrey's smell.

Audrey slid her hands under Harlow's shirt. "I love you too, and if you think you feel lucky now, just wait until we're alone."

Harlow allowed herself to be pulled into the living room to join the others. She sat on the couch next to Audrey and loved how her hand immediately went to her thigh. There were countless days and nights like this in her future, and although the road hadn't always been easy, she wouldn't change a single thing if it meant ending up here.

EPILOGUE

Two years later

Audrey paced, staring out the large windows that overlooked the valley. "I can't believe it. I appreciate you calling." Her heart was hammering, and she was slightly light-headed. "Has Kylie been notified?" Audrey hung up the phone just as Harlow walked into the room.

Harlow looked fantastic in her blue tuxedo, carrying two glasses of champagne. "Everything okay?"

Audrey took the glasses out of her hand and placed them on the side table. She ran her hands around the back of Harlow's neck, loving the way she relaxed at the practiced touch. She only hesitated for a moment before kissing her, not caring if she smudged Harlow's freshly done makeup. Audrey had yet to grow tired of the way her body reacted to the first taste of Harlow. Her lips tasted deliciously like champagne, and she ran her tongue over Harlow's bottom lip.

"Do you want to blow off the Grammys and stay home in bed?" Harlow's voice was low and husky. Audrey knew if she asked, Harlow would do exactly that.

"You're up for Album of the Year, and said album is literally named after me. We have to be there," Audrey said but kissed her again. She drew this one out—a promise for later that night.

"I just got off the phone with Jane."

"What is she wound up about this time?" Harlow's tone indicated her amusement.

Audrey let her forehead rest against Harlow's shoulder. She was still overwhelmed with the news and hadn't let it fully hit her yet. "Kylie's film—our film—has been picked up by all the major distributors. It's going to be shown worldwide."

Harlow cupped her face with both hands. "Oh my God, Audrey." She kissed her. "That's incredible. I'm so proud of you." She hugged her tightly. "Does Kylie know yet?"

Audrey's phone rang, and Harlow excitedly motioned for her to answer it. Kylie was already screaming with excitement when she answered. It all felt surreal, and she was over the moon for Kylie as well as herself. Kylie had poured her heart and soul into the script, and her effort was clearly paying off in spades. Audrey was also aware of what this type of notoriety would do for her new production company. This had been the second picture the company had produced, and they'd knocked both out of the park. She was supremely lucky and wanted to shout it from the rooftops.

She glanced over at Harlow, who held up her phone and disappeared downstairs. She continued her conversation with Kylie and only hung up because the hair and makeup people had entered the room. Her hands were still shaking with excitement as the professionals went to town, preparing her for what she knew would be an extraordinary evening.

Harlow's mom, Megan, was waiting with Harlow when she finally walked downstairs. Megan looked lovely in the gown she and Harlow had picked out together. Audrey hadn't been sure what to expect when Harlow had said she wanted them to meet. She'd been instinctively protective and wanted to be cautious. But it had been important to Harlow and part of her journey to becoming a healthier person. She'd be lying if she didn't say that Megan had become one of her favorite people. She knew Megan and Harlow still had years of distance to work out, but it was clear that they were both trying. It was also clear by the way Megan looked at her only daughter that she genuinely loved her and was proud of her. That was good enough for Audrey.

The media coverage regarding Harlow's mom's reemergence had been overwhelmingly positive. Megan and Harlow did a formal sit-down interview with one of the more prestigious media outlets and were received warmly. Megan was painfully honest about her mistakes and the circumstances that lead to Harlow and Casper's onerous childhood. It was difficult to watch Harlow cry in front of the camera but heartening to see her forgiveness and acceptance.

"My God, Audrey, you look incredible." Megan hugged her. "I also hear congratulations are in order. I'm so happy for you." She looped her arm through Harlow's and pulled her over. "I'm so happy for you both." She dabbed a tear from the corner of her eye. "Thank you for letting me come with you tonight. I can't tell you how much it means to me."

Harlow hugged her. "I'm glad you could make it."

"Honey, I wouldn't have missed it. I'm sorry Casper couldn't be here."

Harlow nodded. "Me too. He loves getting dressed up and showing off. But it's good for him to be on tour again." She stared up at the Stratocaster on the wall. Casper had lied about needing the instrument for a charity event and had sold it to a private buyer when he'd been desperate for cash. It was one of the first things he purchased and returned to her when he started to turn his life around. Harlow kept it over her fireplace.

Casper had started managing new musicians for Dominic a year before, and the hard work was finally paying off. He had a sponsor with him on tour to make sure he kept on the straight and narrow, and he and Harlow spoke weekly and had made significant strides toward repairing their relationship. He was finally finding his place in the world outside of being Harlow's brother, and Harlow was learning that she was stronger than she thought.

Megan smoothed out and adjusted her dress the whole ride over to the theater. It was clear that she was anxious, and Audrey didn't blame her. This would be her first time being at an awards show with Harlow, and Audrey knew first times like this were terrifying.

Audrey grabbed Megan's hand. "I threw up before my first red carpet. So in the scheme of things, you're doing great."

Megan covered her hand with her own. "But you were what, sixteen?" Her eyes softened. "I'll be okay, thank you."

"Just stay with Audrey and me. We'll protect you," Harlow said.

The car rolled to a stop, and the door opened. The screams of excitement were deafening, and Audrey gave Megan's hand one more reassuring squeeze. Harlow stepped out of the car first, and Audrey couldn't help but smile at the way the volume cranked up several decibels. She took Harlow's hand and allowed herself to be helped from the car. Harlow kissed her cheek and waved, then helped her mother out next, and it took everything Audrey had not to shelter her from the barrage of flashes and shouts.

To her credit, Megan only faltered momentarily. Most people wouldn't have noticed the brief, stunned expression, but Audrey knew it well. All of this would take getting used to, but Audrey had faith in Megan's capabilities and her love for her daughter.

Harlow crooked both arms and indicated for Megan and Audrey to each take one. Audrey stole glances at Harlow as they made the way down the carpet. She looked supremely happy and relaxed. It had taken her some time to figure out the subtlety of changes to Harlow's face. She hid her unease and discomfort well, especially in public. But Audrey had learned all the tells, and there were none present tonight.

By the time Album of the Year was about to be announced, Audrey thought she was far more nervous than Harlow, who looked calm as she listened to the names being called. Audrey felt like she was going to jump out of her seat. This album had been the rawest and most revealing of all her music to date, and she wanted the validation for Harlow. Audrey understood intellectually that awards didn't validate an artist's work, but she wanted it for her just the same.

"And the winner is…"

Harlow turned and looked at her when Audrey squeezed her hand. "I love you."

The album artwork flashed up on the screen. It was a picture of Audrey in Harlow's pool with her back to the camera, arms hanging over the side, looking at the valley. She'd been unaware Harlow had taken the picture, but she loved it. That had been a fantastic afternoon. They'd made love and drunk wine and passed the time talking about what the future held for them. Her skin flushed at the memory, and her stomach fluttered at the realization of what the picture on the screen meant.

"Harlow Thorne for the album, *Audrey*."

The first single from the album started blaring through the speakers, and the crowd screamed their delight and approval. Audrey jumped up and hugged her.

Harlow kissed her. "Thank you for being you." Harlow hugged her mom and walked to the stage. She took the award from the presenter and turned it around in her hands like she was making sure the inscription was correct. She placed the award on the podium and leaned closer to the microphone. "Thank you all so much." She waited for the crowd to quiet down. "First, I have to thank my fans. You're all so amazing and supportive. I couldn't do any of this without you. My recording company, thank you for always believing in my vision." She turned her line of sight to Audrey and Megan. "My mom, who taught me that second chances are possible, and my brother, Casper, who was beside me from the start and always believed in me. Family can be messy, but they're worth it." She took a deep breath. "And to Audrey Knox for showing and teaching me what love is and that I deserve it. A million lifetimes with you still wouldn't be enough. I love you."

Audrey wiped the tears away while she clapped. The words had been simple, but they were everything. Most importantly, they were the truth. A million lifetimes would never be enough. No matter how much time they had together, she'd always want more. But that's how it was supposed to be. They suffered their share of cracks, bruises, and missteps. Audrey was sure there'd be more, but none of that mattered. The love she shared with Harlow was rare and pure. The awards, the fame, the money—it all paled in comparison to how rich Harlow made her feel, and she'd spend the rest of her life making sure Harlow knew it.

About the Author

Jackie D was born and raised in the San Francisco, east bay area of California. She lives with her wife, their son, and their many furry companions. She earned a bachelor's degree in recreation administration and a dual master's degree in management and public administration. She is a Navy veteran and served in Operation Iraqi Freedom as a flight deck director onboard the USS *Abraham Lincoln*.

She spends her free time with her wife, friends, family, and their incredibly needy dogs. She enjoys playing golf but is resigned to the fact she would equally enjoy any sport where drinking beer is encouraged during gameplay. Her first book, *Infiltration*, was a finalist for a Lambda Literary Award. Her fourth book, *Lucy's Chance*, won a Goldie in 2018.

Jackie is also the co-host of the Podcast, *The Weekly Wine Down*, which can be found on iTunes, Stitcher, or Podbean.

Books Available from Bold Strokes Books

Flight SQA016 by Amanda Radley. Fastidious airline passenger Olivia Lewis is used to things being a certain way. When her routine is changed by a new, attractive member of the staff, sparks fly. (978-1-63679-045-9)

Home Is Where the Heart Is by Jenny Frame. Can Archie make the countryside her home and give Ash the fairytale romance she desires? Or will the countryside and small village life all be too much for her? (978-1-63555-922-4)

Moving Forward by PJ Trebelhorn. The last person Shelby Ryan expects to be attracted to is Iris Calhoun, the sister of the man who killed her wife four years and three thousand miles ago. (978-1-63555-953-8)

Poison Pen by Jean Copeland. Debut author Kendra Blake is finally living her best life until a nasty book review and exposed secrets threaten her promising new romance with aspiring journalist Alison Chatterley. (978-1-63555-849-4)

Seasons for Change by KC Richardson. Love, laughter, and trust develop for Shawn and Morgan throughout the changing seasons of Lake Tahoe. (978-1-63555-882-1)

Summer Lovin' by Julie Cannon. Three different women, three exotic locations, one unforgettable summer. What do you think will happen? (978-1-63555-920-0)

Unbridled by D. Jackson Leigh. A visit to a local stable turns into more than riding lessons between a novel writer and an equestrian with a taste for power play. (978-1-63555-847-0)

VIP by Jackie D. In a town where relationships are forged and shattered by perception, sometimes even love can't change who you really are. (978-1-63555-908-8)

Yearning by Gun Brooke. The sleepy town of Dennamore has an irresistible pull on those who've moved away. The mystery Darian Tennen and Samantha Pike uncover will change them forever, but the love they find along the way just might be the key to saving themselves. (978-1-63555-757-2)

A Turn of Fate by Ronica Black. Will Nev and Kinsley finally face their painful past and relent to their powerful, forbidden attraction? Or will facing their past be too much to fight through? (978-1-63555-930-9)

Desires After Dark by MJ Williamz. When her human lover falls deathly ill, Alex, a vampire, must decide which is worse, letting her go or condemning her to everlasting life. (978-1-63555-940-8)

Her Consigliere by Carsen Taite. FBI agent Royal Scott swore an oath to uphold the law, and criminal defense attorney Siobhan Collins pledged her loyalty to the only family she's ever known, but will their love be stronger than the bonds they've vowed to others, or will their competing allegiances tear them apart? (978-1-63555-924-8)

In Our Words: Queer Stories from Black, Indigenous, and People of Color Writers. Stories Selected by Anne Shade and Edited by Victoria Villaseñor. Comprising both the renowned and emerging voices of Black, Indigenous, and People of Color authors, this thoughtfully curated collection of short stories explores the intersection of racial and queer identity. (978-1-63555-936-1)

Measure of Devotion by CF Frizzell. Disguised as her late twin brother, Catherine Samson enters the Civil War to defend the Constitution as a Union soldier, never expecting her life to be altered by a Gettysburg farmer's daughter. (978-1-63555-951-4)

Not Guilty by Brit Ryder. Claire Weaver and Emery Pearson's day jobs clash, even as their desire for each other burns, and a discreet sex-only arrangement is the only option. (978-1-63555-896-8)

Opposites Attract: Butch/Femme Romances by Meghan O'Brien, Aurora Rey, Angie Williams. Sometimes opposites really do attract. Fall in love with these butch/femme romance novellas. (978-1-63555-784-8)

Swift Vengeance by Jean Copeland, Jackie D, Erin Zak. A journalist becomes the subject of her own investigation when sudden strange, violent visions summon her to a summer retreat and into the arms of a killer's possible next victim. (978-1-63555-880-7)

Under Her Influence by Amanda Radley. On their path to #truelove, will Beth and Jemma discover that reality is even better than illusion? (978-1-63555-963-7)

Wasteland by Kristin Keppler & Allisa Bahney. Danielle Clark is fighting against the National Armed Forces and finds peace as a scavenger, until the NAF general's daughter, Katelyn Turner, shows up on her doorstep and brings the fight right back to her. (978-1-63555-935-4)

When in Doubt by VK Powell. Police officer Jeri Wylder thinks she committed a crime in the line of duty but can't remember, until details emerge pointing to a cover-up by those close to her. (978-1-63555-955-2)

A Woman to Treasure by Ali Vali. An ancient scroll isn't the only treasure Levi Montbard finds as she starts her hunt for the truth—all she has to do is prove to Yasmine Hassani that there's more to her than an adventurous soul. (978-1-63555-890-6)

Before. After. Always. by Morgan Lee Miller. Still reeling from her tragic past, Eliza Walsh has sworn off taking risks, until Blake Navarro turns her world right-side up, making her question if falling in love again is worth it. (978-1-63555-845-6)

Bet the Farm by Fiona Riley. Lauren Calloway's luxury real estate sale of the century comes to a screeching halt when dairy farm heiress, and one-night stand, Thea Boudreaux calls her bluff. (978-1-63555-731-2)

Cowgirl by Nance Sparks. The last thing Aren expects is to fall for Carol. Sharing her home is one thing, but sharing her heart means sharing the demons in her past and risking everything to keep Carol safe. (978-1-63555-877-7)

Give In to Me by Elle Spencer. Gabriela Talbot never expected to sleep with her favorite author—certainly not after the scathing review she'd given Whitney Ainsworth's latest book. (978-1-63555-910-1)

Hidden Dreams by Shelley Thrasher. A lethal virus and its resulting vision send Texan Barbara Allan and her lovely guide, Dara, on a journey up Cambodia's Mekong River in search of Barbara's mother's mystifying past. (978-1-63555-856-2)

In the Spotlight by Lesley Davis. For actresses Cole Calder and Eris Whyte, their chance at love runs out fast when a fan's adoration turns to obsession. (978-1-63555-926-2)

Origins by Jen Jensen. Jamis Bachman is pulled into a dangerous mystery that becomes personal when she learns the truth of her origins as a ghost hunter. (978-1-63555-837-1)

Pursuit: A Victorian Entertainment by Felice Picano. An intelligent, handsome, ruthlessly ambitious young man who rose from the slums to become the right-hand man of the Lord Exchequer of England will stop at nothing as he pursues his Lord's vanished wife across Continental Europe. (978-1-63555-870-8)

Unrivaled by Radclyffe. Zoey Cohen will never accept second place in matters of the heart, even when her rival is a career, and Declan Black has nothing left to give of herself or her heart. (978-1-63679-013-8)

A Fae Tale by Genevieve McCluer. Dovana comes to terms with her changing feelings for her lifelong best friend and fae, Roze. (978-1-63555-918-7)

Accidental Desperados by Lee Lynch. Life is clobbering Berry, Jaudon, and their long romance. The arrival of directionless baby dyke MJ doesn't help. Can they find their passion again—and keep it? (978-1-63555-482-3)

Always Believe by Aimée. Greyson Walsden is pursuing ordination as an Anglican priest. Angela Arlingham doesn't believe in God. Do they follow their vocation or their hearts? (978-1-63555-912-5)

Best of the Wrong Reasons by Sander Santiago. For Fin Ness and Orion Starr, it takes a funeral to remind them that love is worth living for. (978-1-63555-867-8)

Courage by Jesse J. Thoma. No matter how often Natasha Parsons and Tommy Finch clash on the job, an undeniable attraction simmers just beneath the surface. Can they find the courage to change so love has room to grow? (978-1-63555-802-9)

I Am Chris by R Kent. There's one saving grace to losing everything and moving away. Nobody knows her as Chrissy Taylor. Now Chris can live who he truly is. (978-1-63555-904-0)

The Princess and the Odium by Sam Ledel. Jastyn and Princess Aurelia return to Venostes and join their families in a battle against the dark force to take back their homeland for a chance at a better tomorrow. (978-1-63555-894-4)

The Queen Has a Cold by Jane Kolven. What happens when the heir to the throne isn't a prince or a princess? (978-1-63555-878-4)

The Secret Poet by Georgia Beers. Agreeing to help her brother woo Zoe Blake seemed like a good idea to Morgan Thompson at first...until she realizes she's actually wooing Zoe for herself... (978-1-63555-858-6)

You Again by Aurora Rey. For high school sweethearts Kate Cormier and Sutton Guidry, the second chance might be the only one that matters. (978-1-63555-791-6)

Coming to Life on South High by Lee Patton. Twenty-one-year-old gay virgin Gabe Rafferty's first adult decade unfolds as an unpredictable journey into sex, love, and livelihood. (978-1-63555-906-4)

Love's Falling Star by B.D. Grayson. For country music megastar Lochlan Paige, can love conquer her fear of losing the one thing she's worked so hard to protect? (978-1-63555-873-9)

Love's Truth by C.A. Popovich. Can Lynette and Barb make love work when unhealed wounds of betrayed trust and a secret could change everything? (978-1-63555-755-8)

Next Exit Home by Dena Blake. Home may be where the heart is, but for Harper Sims and Addison Foster, is the journey back worth the pain? (978-1-63555-727-5)

Not Broken by Lyn Hemphill. Falling in love is hard enough—even more so for Rose who's carrying her ex's baby. (978-1-63555-869-2)

The Noble and the Nightingale by Barbara Ann Wright. Two women on opposite sides of empires at war risk all for a chance at love. (978-1-63555-812-8)

What a Tangled Web by Melissa Brayden. Clementine Monroe has the chance to buy the café she's managed for years, but Madison LeGrange swoops in and buys it first. Now Clementine is forced to work for the enemy and ignore her former crush. (978-1-63555-749-7)